"Funny, heartwarming, sad, and romantic . . . refreshingly original, with enough gore to satisfy any zombie fan."   —Science Fiction Book Club

"Successfully balances humor, horror, social commentary, and a page-turning narrative to great effect. A great and worthy read."
—HorrorScope

"*Breathers* will make you root for the undead. . . . For those who enjoy offbeat humor and satire, this is an excellent choice!"   —Bookopolis

"Humorous, horrific, and enthralling all at once."   —SFRevu

"*Breathers* is a zombie novel for everyone. Even people who don't like zombie novels. It's funny, weird, insightful, and endlessly entertaining."
—Jonathan Maberry, multiple Bram Stoker Award–winning author of *Patient Zero*

"Browne's black comedy debut brilliantly reinvents zombie culture for the twenty-first century . . . neatly mixes humor and extreme violence with a surprisingly tender love story, some witty social satire, and an extremely strong narrative voice."   —*Publishers Weekly* (starred review)

"A terrific comedy about the perils and joys of life beyond death . . . a zombie comedy with brains."   —*Kirkus Reviews*

"Browne confidently balances a love story with ample amounts of gore and gags that should win over fans of George Romero and *Shaun of the Dead* . . . a welcome deviation in zombie lit."   —*Booklist*

Books by S. G. Browne

Breathers

FATED

S. G. Browne

NEW AMERICAN LIBRARY

NEW AMERICAN LIBRARY
Published by New American Library, a division of
Penguin Group (USA) Inc., 375 Hudson Street,
New York, New York 10014, USA
Penguin Group (Canada), 90 Eglinton Avenue East, Suite 700, Toronto,
Ontario M4P 2Y3, Canada (a division of Pearson Penguin Canada Inc.)
Penguin Books Ltd., 80 Strand, London WC2R 0RL, England
Penguin Ireland, 25 St. Stephen's Green, Dublin 2,
Ireland (a division of Penguin Books Ltd.)
Penguin Group (Australia), 250 Camberwell Road, Camberwell, Victoria 3124,
Australia (a division of Pearson Australia Group Pty. Ltd.)
Penguin Books India Pvt. Ltd., 11 Community Centre, Panchsheel Park,
New Delhi - 110 017, India
Penguin Group (NZ), 67 Apollo Drive, Rosedale, North Shore 0632,
New Zealand (a division of Pearson New Zealand Ltd.)
Penguin Books (South Africa) (Pty.) Ltd., 24 Sturdee Avenue,
Rosebank, Johannesburg 2196, South Africa

Penguin Books Ltd., Registered Offices:
80 Strand, London WC2R 0RL, England

First published by New American Library,
a division of Penguin Group (USA) Inc.

First Printing, November 2010
10 9 8 7 6 5 4 3 2 1

REGISTERED TRADEMARK—MARCA REGISTRADA

LIBRARY OF CONGRESS CATALOGING-IN-PUBLICATION DATA:

Browne, S. G. (Scott G.)
Fated/S.G. Browne.
p. cm.
ISBN 978-0-451-23128-4
1. Mythology, Roman—Fiction.   2. Gods, Roman—Fiction.   I. Title.
PS3602.R7369F38 2010
813'.6—dc22   2010028769

Set in Simoncini Garamond
Designed by Alissa Amell

Printed in the United States of America

For my parents. Thank you for believing.

ACKNOWLEDGMENTS

The following people were put on my path for one reason or another, and I'm grateful for all that they've done to help me try to stay on it:

Michelle Brower, my agent, who constantly makes me realize how fortunate I am to have her in my corner; Wendy Sherman, who opened her doors and welcomed me in; Jessica Wade, my editor, whose questions and insights helped to improve the manuscript in ways I couldn't have accomplished without her; Kara Cesare, who believed in me and brought me on board; everyone on the team at Penguin and NAL who provided their invaluable input, support, ideas, and talents; Cliff Brooks, Ian Dudley, Heather Liston, Shannon Page, Lise Quintana, Amory Sharpe, and Keith White, who all read the first drafts and told me what worked and what needed to be fixed; Leslie Laurence, who offered her insights on Manhattan, chocolate rugelach, and relationships with mortal women; my parents, who believed in me even when I eschewed my business degree to pursue a passion that didn't promise a weekly paycheck; and my friends, who are familiar with all of my faults and aren't afraid to point them out to me. You know who you are.

FATED

CHAPTER 1

Rule #1: Don't get involved.

Such a simple rule, really. But here I am, sitting in a mall in Paramus, New Jersey, and I'm getting frustrated.

Annoyed.

Disappointed.

Eighty-three percent of humans are predictable creatures of habit who get stuck in routines and lifestyles and addictions or who go through their lives swapping one addiction for another.

My eighty-three percent. My humans. All five and a half billion of them.

The mall is one of the best places to go to see human nature at its best. Or worst, depending on how you want to look at it. Men and women, teenagers and children, shopping, eating, gossiping, filling up the vacuum of their lives with retail therapy and empty calories. My favorite malls are old-school. The ones that aren't as big as Sri Lanka and still have food courts with Orange Julius, Panda Express, and Hot Dog on a Stick.

In the United States, there are twice as many shopping centers as there are high schools, and the shopping mall has replaced the church as the temple of cultural worship. In a society that encourages its citizens to measure their worth by financial success and material possessions, American humans spend more of their income on shoes, watches, and jewelry than they do on higher education.

Sure, it keeps Greed and Envy busy, but it makes my existence a living hell.

Back when humans were still in their hunter-gatherer phase, existence was all about survival, fulfilling the basic needs of food, clothing, and shelter, so it's not like there were a lot of options for better living. Food wasn't prepared by Martha Stewart. Clothing didn't come with a Calvin Klein logo. And shelters didn't require Ralph Lauren curtains with a matching duvet.

The thing about humans is that they're addicted to products.

Habitual consumers. Indulgence abusers. Gratification automatons.

Programmed to need and want and buy.

MP3 players. Xboxes. PlayStation 3s.

TiVo. Surround sound. High-definition flat-screen TVs.

A thousand cable channels with movies and music and pay-per-view.

Distracted by their desires, overwhelmed with their needs and wants, they'll never remain on their assigned paths. Their optimal futures. Their most beneficial fates.

That's me. Capital F. Little a-t-e.

I set my humans off on their paths at birth, assigning fates that range from career criminals to CEOs of oil companies—which really aren't all that different, when you think about it. But no matter how promising a fate I assign to someone—movie studio executive, second-string NFL quarterback, governor of California—the majority of them invariably screw it up.

It's human nature to underachieve. To not live up to one's full potential. Granted, there aren't a lot of delusions of grandeur with fate. You don't get awarded a Nobel Peace Prize or become Stephen King. And when someone's future involves mental illness, drug addiction, or a career in politics, I can't really expect any pleasant surprises. Once I've assigned a fate, that's it. That's the best I can hope for. But that doesn't mean things can't go wrong.

Within each human's preassigned fate, there are significant moments of decision that will determine if and how they stay on their path. Choices that influence the way they go about living their lives.

With integrity.

With compassion.

With greed.

Every one of these choices one of my humans makes requires a reassessment of his or her future. A reassignment of his or her fate. And at every choice, I get to watch the vast majority of them make the wrong decision.

As I sit on a bench between Foot Locker and Aeropostale, eating my Hot Dog on a Stick and drinking my Orange Julius, I peruse the assortment of my mistake-prone humans and their inevitable failures.

There's a nineteen-year-old jock with a cell phone and a Game-Stop bag who could have a successful career as a utility infielder for the Philadelphia Phillies. Instead, he'll be fat, bald, unemployed, and masturbating three times a day to *Juggs* magazine when he's thirty-two.

The twenty-one-year-old Asian evangelical Christian proselytizing to shoppers outside of Bebe will find the man of her dreams when she's thirty, but will be filing for divorce and having sex with men half her age when she's forty-five.

And the eleven-year-old kid with the short hair and angelic face devouring a chocolate glazed from Dunkin' Donuts has the potential to be a wonderful father, but instead he'll be thinking about molesting his five-year-old daughter when he's twenty-nine.

It's times like this I wish Death and I had a better relationship.

Sure, the eleven-year-old is just a kid, but at least I could save his daughter the lifelong trauma and therapy if I could get Death to help me out, but that would be interfering, which is a definite no-no. Not to mention the cosmic ramifications of preventing the birth of his daughter. Plus, Death and I aren't talking, so there you go.

Instead I just sit on the bench and eat my Hot Dog on a Stick and watch the endless parade of future sexual miscreants.

Not every human being has some kind of sexual hang-up or disorder or desire waiting to be realized. But most Americans do. This probably has something to do with the fact that the United States demonizes sex and represses sexual energy. Personally, I prefer the Italian and French. To them, sex is just a part of their culture.

Speaking of sex . . .

Down the mall about halfway between me and Macy's, beyond the T-Mobile kiosk and a steady flow of future-challenged Americans, a plume of red hair is making its way toward me. I'm hoping it's not who I think it is, but then the crowd magically parts and beneath the red hair is the beatific, smiling face of Destiny.

Perfect. This is just what I need to cheer me up. The immortal personification of all that I'm not. All that I covet. All that I'm denied.

Think loathing.

Think resentment.

Think malignant tumor.

"How's your wiener?" Destiny asks, sitting down and eyeing my Hot Dog on a Stick.

The thing about Destiny is that she's a nymphomaniac.

She's wearing a red tank top, a red leather miniskirt, a pair of red go-go boots, and a perpetual smile. She's always in a good mood. Why wouldn't she be? It's not like *she* has to spend eternity dealing with child molesters and chronic consumers and more than five and a half billion other screwups, who can't seem to get their shit together.

Contrary to what most humans think, destiny and fate are not the same. Destiny can't be forced on someone. If they're forced into their circumstances, then that's their fate. And fate has a morbid association with the inevitable, with something ominous that is going to happen.

His fate was sealed.

A fatal disease.

A fate worse than death.

I mean, come on. How much worse can it get than one-upping Death on the dystopian scale?

Destiny, on the other hand, is divinatory in nature and implies a favorable outcome, which generally carries a much more positive connotation.

Destiny smiled upon him.

She was destined for greatness.

It was her destiny.

"Can I have a taste of your meat?" Destiny asks, projecting such passion and beauty that I just want to smash the rest of my unfinished corn dog in her face.

Fate predetermines and orders the course of a person's life. But even though my humans make decisions along their paths that can have an adverse impact on their futures, they don't get a say in their reassigned fates. You don't get any choice with me. I'm not into collaboration.

Think solitaire.

Think autoerotic.

Think Henry David Thoreau.

And even if I wanted to help, even if I wanted to offer some guidance or make a suggestion or give a subtle hint, I can't. The whole "free will" manifesto. Humans have to be allowed to make their choices and live with the consequences.

Think of my humans as disobedient children who don't get a say in the severity of their punishment.

But with Destiny, her humans are more involved in the process, for without a subject's willful participation, there is no destining. Her humans choose their destiny by choosing different life paths.

They can still make mistakes, but we're talking two Oscars instead of three. Maybe a Pulitzer instead of a Nobel Peace Prize.

Think of Destiny's humans as honor roll students who get to choose whatever college they want to attend.

I should have read the fine print on my job description.

"How about letting me suck on your straw?" asks Destiny.

"I'm busy," I say. "Why don't you go bother Diligence or Charity?"

"Oh, come on, Faaaaabio," she says. "I'm just having some fun."

Whenever Destiny calls me by my pseudonym, she always draws out the first syllable as if to mock me.

Not all of us have pseudonyms. Destiny prefers her given name, while Death has adopted the name Dennis. Most of the Seven Deadly Sins have noms de plume because no one really wants to be called Anger or Envy or Greed. All of the Seven Heavenly Virtues have embraced their formal names, except for Temperance, who prefers everyone just call him Tim.

"So when did you get back?" asks Destiny, twirling her hair with a coquettish flair and looking at me with big bedroom eyes. While she's not as big a slut as Lust, she definitely has her moments.

"I don't know," I say, finishing off my Hot Dog on a Stick and sucking down the last of my Orange Julius until I'm slurping the bottom of the cup. "Couple days ago."

Most of us call New York City home, though we're not there year-round. With more than six and a half billion people on the planet, we have to be fairly ubiquitous.

"Anyone else around?" I ask.

"Remorse and Hope," she says. "A few of the Deadlies, of course. And I hear Prejudice is trying to put together a poker game but he isn't having much luck."

The thing about Prejudice is that he has Tourette's syndrome.

Destiny and I sit on the bench for a few minutes in silence, watching the mall zombies stagger past, their primitive brains thinking about threesomes and iPods and Cinnabons.

"Interested in some noncontact sex?" asks Destiny.

Destiny may engender intense feelings of loathing and envy in me, but that doesn't mean I wouldn't like to watch her peel off her red miniskirt.

"Sure," I say. "Your place or mine?"

CHAPTER 2

I'm in my white boxers on my back next to a bouquet of blue hydrangeas while Destiny straddles me wearing nothing but a bright red cotton thong. The only thing that would make this more patriotic would be Jimi Hendrix playing "The Star-Spangled Banner."

The cool thing about noncontact sex between immortals is that you can be invisible on your shared rooftop garden in broad daylight and no one can see what you're doing. And right now, Destiny's red cotton thong is grinding away in the air while she looks down at me and licks her lips.

Although we can see each other when we're invisible, humans can't see us unless we choose to make our presence known. Or when one of us comes into physical contact with another immortal. Which doesn't happen in public more than a few times each century, and most of those involve Lust and at least one other Deadly Sin, though Prudence has let his guard down more than once.

Rule #5: Never materialize in front of humans.

The last time two immortals came into contact with each other in public was back in 1918 in Chicago, when Anger and Envy got into a bar fight over the Red Sox beating the Cubs in the World Series. Envy is a Cubs fan and Anger . . . Well, let's just say he knows how to push Envy's buttons.

I wasn't there, but apparently it was quite a brawl. Recorded history doesn't mention the incident, but it was pretty much the final straw that led to the 18th Amendment and fourteen years of Prohibition.

We're supposed to be facilitators, not instigators. We're to have no significant impact on the lives of humans but just play our part in their various paths and emotional arcs. Every now and then one of us screws up, either directly or indirectly, with varying degrees of catastrophic results. That's why entities get stripped of their powers. It's very embarrassing. Just ask Peace.

We're not always invisible. Just when we choose to be. One of the perks of being immortal. That and the accommodations.

I live in a two-bedroom, twentieth-floor apartment on the Upper East Side of Manhattan with parquet floors, panoramic windows with views of the East River, a full-service twenty-four-hour doorman and concierge service, a health club, and a rooftop garden.

The place runs $3,990 a month, but I get it for nothing. Not a bad perk for being Fate. Except when you compare it to Destiny's prewar SoHo loft with Hudson River views, wood floors, central air-conditioning, marble bath, and over four thousand square feet. She won't tell me how much it costs, but I did a search and found out it runs for $12,000.

I guess I shouldn't complain. Dennis lives on the Lower East

Side in a studio basement apartment with barred windows, concrete walls, and a view of the adjacent alley. But then, where else would you expect Death to live?

Destiny moves over me, her red hair pulled back in a bun, her perfect breasts and nipples barely more than an inch from my mouth. It's difficult to maintain my resolve, but I hate her so much that I don't want to give her the satisfaction of any pleasure that's not self-administered.

Plus the building superintendent is on the roof with us, showing the garden and the view to a prospective tenant. I can't see them, but I can hear them on the other side of the azaleas and rosebushes, discussing proper roof etiquette. Which I'm currently not observing.

The super's voice is nasally and high-pitched and he's going to be homeless in twenty years, picking his nose and yelling at people from a bench in Central Park.

The woman's voice is warm and mellifluous, a tenor saxophone on a deserted New Orleans night. But I can't read her. Which means she's on the Path of Destiny, born to accomplish something more significant than the majority of the human race. But even though I can't read her, there's something about her I find compelling. Something in her voice that draws me to her. Something I can't place but that is nonetheless distracting. And I'm distracted in a way that has softened my mood, so to speak. This isn't lost on Destiny.

In a flash of nimbleness and alacrity that only a female can pull off, Destiny's thong and my boxers are in the hydrangeas and her naked body is hovering tantalizingly above mine. She doesn't have a follicle of hair on her flesh.

The thing about Destiny is that she waxes.

Not surprisingly, my attention is quickly restored to its prior condition.

"That's better," she says, looking down at me, her green eyes filled with mirth.

Seconds later, her face is gone from view and I feel her warm breath caressing the most stimulated part of my anatomy.

While technically not human, we move around in fleshy shells that mimic their appearance. Man and woman suits. Makes it easier for us to exist on Earth. Humans tend to overreact when they see bright blinding lights or celestial beings with wings or supernatural entities that have more than four appendages, so it just saves a lot of work for Confusion and Panic and Hysteria if we look like the so-called intelligent life-forms on the planet. It's not as bad as you might think. Kind of like wearing an elaborate latex costume. After a couple hundred thousand years, you get used to the fit.

I can still hear the woman who is on the Path of Destiny talking to the super, telling him she'll take the apartment, but my focus is on my own particular destiny at the moment.

Destiny and I have had an on-again, off-again thing for most of the past quarter million years, though it's never been anything serious. Kind of like long-term friends with benefits.

In spite of the facts that she often sickens me with her upbeat attitude and that I can't stand how humans willfully submit to her and hate me, I have to admit Destiny is more talented at noncontact sex than Glamour, Temptation, and even Lust. Though I have to give Lust the nod when it comes to full-contact bed surfing. After all, she is Lust.

Destiny continues to arouse me, creating a pressure in the air between us that's almost palpable. That's the key to noncontact sex: to build up the arousal by simulating sex but without penetration or any form of touching. The idea is to heighten the tension to the point where release occurs without physical stimulation.

Just as I'm approaching the threshold of release, Destiny suddenly stops.

When I open my eyes, she's already halfway dressed.

"Gotta go," she says, slipping her tank top over her head.

"Now?" I ask, my hands gesturing toward my lower extremities for emphasis.

"I've got a client I have to deal with in Portugal," she says, putting on her go-go boots. "See you later."

And like that, *poof*, she's gone.

Before I can even get my boxers out of the hydrangeas, Destiny is most likely already in Portugal reassigning some would-be hero's future. One second, you're having noncontact sex on a roof in Manhattan, and the next, you're halfway around the world.

Another perk of being immortal is not having to take public transportation.

Two thousand years ago, with most of the world's two hundred million inhabitants concentrated in Europe, Asia, and Africa, we didn't have to travel much. And really, two hundred million people are pretty easy to manage, considering most of them didn't live much longer than thirty-five years, give or take. But once colonization of the Americas and Australia began in the middle of the sixteenth century, things really started to get out of hand, with the world population doubling from Columbus's screwup to the beginning of the Industrial Revolution. And it's really become un-manageable in the past two hundred years, with the global population jumping from one billion to nearly seven billion. On top of that, people live nearly twice as long as they did a hundred years ago.

I knew when humans discovered the concept of sewers that things were going to get complicated. But if I'd known human beings were going to procreate like rabbits on Viagra, I would have asked to be transferred to a different department. Like Abstinence or Chastity or SELF-CONTROL.

Or Death.

If you can't prevent humans from reproducing at the source, then you can at least control the floodgates by draining the reservoir. Though personally, I think Dennis should do his job a little better. Thin out the herd. Return a sense of normalcy to the planet so we can all take a little breather. Maybe get a chance to go to Bali or Tahiti or Disney World for a change. I've always wanted to ride Space Mountain.

Maybe I can put in a request for reassignment. Except with my luck, I'd end up getting something like Humility or Diligence. Besides, I've been Fate for so long, I probably wouldn't know what to do as anything else. Guess it's just my fate to be Fate.

By the time I put my clothes back on, the super and the new tenant are gone and I'm alone on the garden rooftop. After getting worked up by Destiny, I'm not in much of a mood to be alone, so I figure I'll see what Flattery is up to. Or maybe give Prurience a call. But before I can punch in her number on my cell phone, I get called away for a meeting with Jerry.

CHAPTER 3

Jerry's reception area is always packed, what with all the souls making the transition from earthly to ethereal, not to mention those who aren't going to be making the journey but want an audience one last time to state their case. Most of them don't get a second chance, but every now and then, Jerry shows a soft side and lets them in.

Today is no exception, though *today* is just an arbitrary term. Time and date have no real meaning here. I sat in Jerry's waiting room for what seemed like an hour one time, and when I finally got back to Earth, I'd missed the entire Third Punic War.

Of course, that was back in the late Classical Age, when the population was still manageable, so it wasn't like there was any big hurry to get back to Earth. But now, with my schedule booked, I should be in and out of here in a matter of minutes.

Problem is, while I'm waiting for the appointment ahead of me to finish up, I have to sit around with all of these human souls, most of whom were fated to end up here. And once they're free of the encumbrance of human flesh, the mysteries of the universe are revealed to them. That includes the concept of life after death, the creation of human existence, the governing of the cosmos, and recognizing me.

"So you're Fate," says the soul of what was once a forty-six-year-old woman who died of pancreatic cancer.

I ignore her and try to avoid eye contact.

"I just wanted to thank you for all of the nausea and vomiting, the loss of weight, the yellowing of my skin, the chemotherapy, and the slow, anguished, painful death I had to endure."

This is what I have to deal with whenever I come here. Angry souls taking out their frustration on me. Like most of them didn't have anything to do with it.

Chain-smoking cigarettes.

Diets rich in animal fat and low in fruits and vegetables.

A lifestyle of sitting around on their asses watching ESPN and reality television instead of adhering to a regimen of regular cardiovascular exercise.

I really hate coming here.

"Hey," she says, poking me in the arm. "I'm talking to you."

By this time, several of the other souls sitting around us have taken notice.

"What's going on?" asks a fourteen-year-old boy who got killed by a drunk driver.

The woman who died of pancreatic cancer hikes her thumb at me and says, "This guy's the reason most of us are here."

"Holy shit," says a twenty-five-year-old man who overdosed on heroin. "It's Fate."

Before I have a chance to slink away to the bathroom, the entire room notices me.

Think awkward.

Think unpleasant.

Think torch-carrying mob.

Seconds later, dozens of human souls who were condemned to their fates are in my face, telling me how much they enjoyed their agony, their deaths, their failed existences. Fingers are pointed. Spittle flies from snarled lips, hitting me in the face. Men and women and children berate me, damn me, and curse me in more languages than even I know.

My job is so rewarding.

"Fate," says the receptionist from behind her desk. "Jerry will see you now."

I get up from my chair and squeeze past the mob of angry souls as they continue to scream obscenities at me. Even for all of the anguish and misery and discomfort they had to go through during their lives, all of this venom seems a little excessive. Then I look over and see Hostility in the corner, laughing so hard he's turning red.

"Asshole," I say as I walk into Jerry's office.

"You know," says Jerry from behind his enormous oak desk, "I've ended civilizations for less than that."

"I was talking to Hostility," I say, closing the door behind me.

"Is he still out there?" says Jerry. "I thought I told him to go find some poor, oppressed people to rile up."

"Yeah, well, he's riling up everyone in your waiting room."

"Just so long as he stays out of the Middle East."

The thing about Jerry is that he's omnipotent.

Though he's pretty nondescript for an all-knowing, all-powerful deity. Average height. Average weight. Average features. No distinguishing characteristics. It kind of helps him to blend in when he makes a terrestrial trip to have a look-see.

But since he doesn't get out as much as he used to, he still likes to keep an eye on things from his office, which is made entirely of glass—including the floor and ceiling. Not exactly the most sensible way to set up shop, but it affords Jerry the chance to keep an eye on things while he's working. And it pretty much freaks everyone out. Who wouldn't feel a little awed, standing in front of the Big J with the universe expanding in a 360-degree view all around you, wondering if the floor is going to crack?

I've been here countless times before, and Jerry assures me his office is OSHA-certified, but I still take off my shoes and walk tippy-toe across the floor to his desk.

"So what did you want to see me about?" I ask, sitting down.

Jerry's known name, the one given to him in the Old Testament is, of course, Jehovah. No one around here ever calls him God or Yahweh or any of the other names ascribed to him by humans. As long as I've known him, he's always been Jerry.

"I've noticed a bit of sloppiness in your work lately," says Jerry. "Ever since the start of the Industrial Revolution."

That was more than two centuries ago. He must have a backlogged stack of paperwork in his in-box.

Back when societies were still agriculture based, humans weren't as easily distracted from their paths. Even as recently as the middle of the eighteenth century, the success rate for humans on the Path of Fate was just under sixty-two percent, which meant that six out of every ten of my humans achieved their optimal fates. Today, with the constant barrage of commercials and celebrities and pitchmen telling people whom they should aspire to be and what they need to make them happy, that number has dropped to less than three in ten.

"What's going on?" asks Jerry. "And don't give me any more of that European-colonialism crap. It was bound to happen sooner or later, so just deal with it."

It won't do any good for me to complain about my workload or the grief I have to deal with on a daily basis, considering whom I'm talking to. But lately, I've reached the point where it just doesn't seem like what I'm doing matters. Regardless of the paths I set them on when they're born, the majority of my humans end up disappointing me. So I've started assigning them random fates, missing my quotas, and overburdening various geographic regions with taxi drivers and street performers.

Quotas are very important to Jerry.

Rule #9: Meet your quotas.

So many lawyers. So many paparazzi. So many strippers. It's not as easy as it sounds. You get too many baristas, and the next thing you know, the whole cosmic wheel can get thrown out of balance.

"I don't know," I say. "I guess I'm just bored."

"Bored?" he says. "You're bored?"

I can tell from the tone of his voice that he doesn't really have time for this. But I might as well give it a shot.

"Yeah," I say. "I was kind of hoping I might get reassigned."

He lets out a laugh. And when Jerry laughs, it's not very funny. Especially when he's Earthside. Mount Vesuvius. Krakatoa. Mount Saint Helens. Good thing he doesn't have much of a sense of humor.

I glance down and wonder, not for the first time, about the integrity of the plate-glass floor.

It's not as if there's no precedent for one of us switching jobs or getting reassigned. Faith has been replaced more than once over the millennia, Fidelity was transferred to a desk job in the wake of the free-love debacle, Reason got canned after the Salem Witch Trials, and Ego lost his job after the Beatles broke up.

Just to name a few.

So it's not like I'm asking for something out of the question.

"We don't have any openings at the moment," says Jerry, once he's stopped laughing.

"What about Peace?" I say. "That opening hasn't been filled yet."

"You don't want Peace," says Jerry. "Trust me. Besides, you've been doing your job for so long that I don't have anyone on staff who could replace you."

Great. I've made myself indispensable.

"Just put a little more energy into your work," says Jerry, stamping a sheet of paper and placing it in his out-box. "Pay attention to what you're doing. Care about it more."

That's easy for him to say. People pray to him. They curse me.

I thank Jerry for his time; then I get up and tiptoe across the floor to get my shoes.

When I walk back into the reception area, the woman who accosted me earlier about her pancreatic cancer is walking toward me, apparently Jerry's next appointment. As she passes, she turns and spits in my face.

Behind me, Hostility bursts out laughing.

CHAPTER 4

I'm in Duluth, Minnesota, eating a glazed Krispy Kreme and watching a forty-four-year-old biology teacher pace back and forth on the rear porch of a house where his seventeen-year-old star biology student lives. The dilemma he's facing is that his student has told him she's interested in having him teach her private biology lessons at home. Her parents are out of town for the weekend and here he is, on her back porch at nine in the morning while his wife thinks he's off fishing. He knows if he knocks on the door, he'll be heading down a path that could possibly ruin his career and destroy his marriage.

Except his star pupil is so amazingly hot. She has perfect tits and an unbelievable ass and natural blonde hair that smells like honey and eyes that understand him and lips he just wants to suck on and she's seventeen and he's never had sex with a seventeen-year-old and she says she wants him to teach her everything he knows about sex.

Everything.

When was the last time anyone said *that* to him?

Certainly not his wife, who hasn't had sex with him in more than three weeks, and even when they do have sex, it's perfunctory and passionless. And he wants passion in his life. He needs passion. And this young woman, this nubile student, with her intelligence and her wit and her fair skin and her succulent lips and her soft, husky voice, personifies that passion.

It's so disappointing.

Searching for his bliss when the key to finding happiness resides inside himself rather than inside a seventeen-year-old girl.

At this point in his life, at this crossroads, he has multiple fates in front of him:

1) **He can turn around and walk away and go back to his dreary, passionless life with his dreary, passionless wife and masturbate every night to questionably legal teen pornography;**

2) **He can turn around and walk away and rededicate himself to his wife and to his career and continue along the reasonably happy path he was assigned at birth;**

3) **He can knock on the door, have a passionate affair with his gorgeous student, then lose his job, his marriage, and his house before drinking himself into depression and bankruptcy.**

I'd like to help. Give him a nudge in the right direction, tell him to take what's behind Door Number Two, but that would be breaking the rules.

So I just sit there, eating my Krispy Kreme, keeping my suggestions to myself, watching forty-four-year-old high school biology teacher Darren Stafford pace back and forth on the rear porch, trying to figure out what he should do. I'm rooting for him to make the right choice. I really am. But I don't have much faith in his decision making. Number one, he's horny. Number two, he's male. And number three, he's human.

He knocks on the door.

Next I'm in Compton, California, standing outside a liquor store at seven in the morning and eating another Krispy Kreme as a fifteen-year-old kid is paying a homeless guy to buy him a pint of whiskey and a couple of forties. The kid is about to embark on a path of drugs and alcohol that will lead him in and out of juvenile hall and then prison for the next dozen years for theft and robbery and drunken driving, until eventually he'll end up with a charge of vehicular manslaughter, which will put him behind bars until he's thirty-five.

Not the fate he was born with, but I can't give him a heads-up.

The homeless guy, on the other hand, is unaware that if he refuses the money from the kid, it will improve his self-esteem enough to the point that he'll stop spending his money on booze. After seeking social assistance, he'll eventually find his way back to his assigned path, land a job working for McDonald's, and in ten years he'll be managing his own franchise.

Instead, he takes the money and goes inside the liquor store.

It's so disheartening to see the life choices humans make.

A split second later I'm in Reno, Nevada, at the Silver Legacy Casino, drinking a double latte from Starbucks while I watch thirty-two-year-old Mavis Hanson turn her last five hundred dollars into chips at the blackjack table. Mavis has been playing blackjack for the past six hours and is down more than three large but she can't stop now.

Mavis owes a lot of people a lot of money. But instead of taking on a second job or working harder at her full-time job and trying to get a promotion, she decided to empty out her savings account in an attempt to win enough at the casinos so she can pay off her debts all at once. Now she's down to her last five hundred dollars. After that's gone, the only money she'll have to her name will be Monopoly money.

If she gets up now and walks away from the table, she'll realize what a big mistake she's made, but at least she won't be destitute and she'll have the courage to go back to work and try to get her affairs in order. But if she gambles the last of her savings away, she won't make it to her thirty-third birthday.

Unless, of course, Lady Luck intervenes.

"Hey, Fabio," says Lady Luck as she glides up next to me, shimmering like an Egyptian goddess in a twenty-four-karat-gold sequined dress with spaghetti straps. Her hair is in cornrows with strands of diamonds sparkling in the casino lights.

"Hey, Liza," I say, putting on my sunglasses to cut down on the glare. "You look like you just got in from Vegas."

"Monaco, sugar," she says. "I love the Mediterranean this time of year. But it's more like a vacation than work, you know?"

I nod in agreement, but I haven't had a vacation since before the French Revolution.

Lady Luck is an Intangible. A notion. A concept. Vague and

abstract. Like Serendipity, Creativity, Chance, and Fame. I think Laughter is an Intangible, while Humor is an Attribute. Not to be confused with the Emotives, who, naturally, are in charge of emotions—Love, Joy, Sadness, Fear, Compassion, Disgust, and all of the other feelings humans experience.

Emotives can get a bit theatrical and don't tend to exhibit a lot of reason, plus they can be rather single-minded, so you can't expect a lot of stimulating conversation. Intangibles are more fun to hang out with. I think it's because they don't take themselves so seriously and appreciate a wider range of subjects. But they tend to be fickle.

I seldom see Lady Luck for more than a few minutes because she can't seem to stay in one place for any length of time. She's like a honeybee, buzzing from human to human, pollinating them with luck before buzzing off.

The thing about Lady Luck is that she has ADD.

She blows a kiss at a defeated-looking elderly gentleman sitting at a dollar slot machine. Two seconds later, he wins a thousand bucks and starts laughing.

That rule about not getting involved? It applies only to Fate and Destiny and Death. After all, you can't be an Intangible or an Emotive or one of the Deadly Sins without having some kind of an impact. But it all comes down to what humans do with their luck or their fear or their jealousy that determines their eventual outcome.

That's what I am. An Eventual. Same for Destiny, Death, and Karma. There are also the Lesser Sins like Gossip and Prejudice, all of the Contrary Virtues, the Heavenly Virtues, and, of course, the Subversives—War, Hysteria, Conspiracy, and Paranoia, among others. You don't really want to plan a team-building weekend and invite any of the Subversives.

"So what brings you to the biggest little city in Nevada?" asks Lady Luck.

I nod toward Mavis Hanson, who has just busted while hitting on twelve.

"Poor thing," says Lady Luck. "She's had a run of real bad luck, hasn't she?"

"It doesn't look good," I say.

"You're telling me," she says, motioning toward the bar, where Death is sitting with his shock of white hair watching ESPN and sipping on a Shirley Temple.

I hadn't noticed Dennis before, though it wouldn't surprise me if he'd been sitting there all along and hadn't bothered to come over and say hi. We haven't spoken in more than five hundred years, ever since Dennis refused to help Columbus shuffle off this mortal coil before the Italian explorer could make a wrong turn and "discover" the New World. It would have made my job a lot easier and slowed the population growth if European colonialism into the Americas could have been delayed, but no, Dennis wouldn't bend the rules and intervene just that once. And after all I'd done for him during the Black Death.

When humans die, they need an escort to the afterlife. Someone to show them the way and explain how Bingo Night works. Sometimes, the soul or the spirit of the human doesn't want to go, so the soul has to be extracted from the body. Which can get a little messy.

The thing about Death is that he's necrophobic.

The whole image of him in the hooded black cloak, carrying around the scythe and causing people to die just by touching them with a single bony finger? Propaganda. After all, how intimidating would Death be if everyone portrayed him as wearing baby blue mortician exam gloves and a neoprene particle mask with optional air freshener?

At least he finally ditched the anticontamination suit.

We see each other now and again. It's kind of hard not to cross paths when you're Fate and Death. But we used to be inseparable.

We partied together while Rome burned, sacked and pillaged with the Vikings, learned how to make our own mead during the Crusades, and rode shotgun with Genghis Khan. Those were good times. Now it's strictly business. But at least we manage to keep it professional.

Dennis looks over at us, raises his glass to Lady Luck with a smile, then gives me the finger.

"Honestly," says Lady Luck, lightly brushing the arm of a woman at another slot machine who starts to scream when she hits the progressive jackpot. "When are you two going to stop acting like boys and put the past behind you?"

"It's not that easy," I say.

"Whatever," she says, blowing on the deck of cards at the blackjack table as the dealer shuffles them. "At least stop hanging around like vultures, waiting for these poor, innocent, hard-luck people to screw up."

On the overhead speakers in the blackjack lounge, Frank Sinatra starts to sing "Luck Be a Lady."

"They're playing my song," she says, tapping Mavis on the shoulder moments before she gets dealt a blackjack.

Then Lady Luck's off, flitting from table to table, brushing against men and women, stroking their hair, whispering in their ears, delivering her pollen, making everyone happy.

Sure, she's having fun. But at what cost? For most of the desperate gamblers, it's a temporary respite from their financial burdens. They'll walk out of here today with more money than they imagined, but it won't last. Tomorrow, the luck will be gone. Then what? Will they have learned their lesson? Or will they come back again, thinking they've learned how to beat the system, only to have their hopes and dreams crushed another day?

Sometimes, Lady Luck can do more harm than good.

But at least in the case of Mavis Hanson, it appears as though she's going to make it to her thirty-third birthday after all. When I glance up from the blackjack table, Dennis is gone, his half-finished Shirley Temple sitting on the bar.

CHAPTER 5

A few days later, I'm having lunch in the East Village at a local deli with Sloth and Gluttony, comparing field notes. Gluttony just got back from a deep-fried-Twinkie-eating contest in Memphis, while Sloth spent the weekend with a group of students at MIT who just bought a new Xbox.

"They never cracked a textbook, man," says Sloth, slouched in his chair with his feet on the table. "Just ordered pizza and drank beer and played video games for, like, thirty-six hours straight. The only time they left the dorm room was to go take a leak. It was beautiful, man."

The thing about Sloth is that he's narcoleptic.

He also watches too much television, never exercises, hasn't washed his hair since Woodstock, and always wears the same Sex Pistols T-shirt.

"What kind of pizza?" asks Gluttony around a mouthful of pastrami and rye.

"I don't know," says Sloth. "Pepperoni and sausage. Canadian bacon. What does it matter?"

"Pizza matters, dude," says Gluttony. "Pizza always matters."

The thing about Gluttony is that he's lactose intolerant.

At six feet tall and over three hundred and fifty pounds, Gluttony is never more than fifteen minutes from his next meal. His favorite wardrobe is a Hawaiian shirt and baggy sweats. His favorite food is everything.

"So what's up with you, Fabio?" asks Sloth, slouching down further in his chair.

"Same old, same old," I say. "Just watching humans make bad choices based on what you guys throw at them and reassigning them to their less-than-optimal fates."

The woman at the table next to us gives me a dubious glance, as if she thinks I might not be completely sane. Like she can talk. Nine years from now, she'll be chopping up her ex-husband and feeding him to her three cats.

"I wouldn't want your job, man," says Sloth. "Too much work."

Gluttony laughs, spraying us with food as he finishes off the last of his sandwich. "Imagine that. You not wanting to work."

"Like you're any better, fatso."

"At least I'm not a slacker."

"Eat me."

"Don't tempt me," says Gluttony. "I'm still hungry."

Two young, slender women wearing NYU sweatshirts come into the deli and glance our way. The leggy blonde whispers to the buxom redhead and they both laugh.

The blonde is going to pose for *Playboy* and spend most of the next ten years pursuing a modeling and acting career, taking walks on the beach at sunset, and getting turned off by mean people. The redhead is going to end up married with three children and wishing she'd killed her college roommate when she'd had the chance.

"Do you guys ever wish you could do something different?" I ask.

"Like what?" asks Sloth.

"I don't know," I say. "Like Pride or Justice or Honesty."

"No way," says Sloth. "Those jobs are, like, really boring. Though Pride is totally hot."

"Pride's a dude, dude," says Gluttony.

"No way," says Sloth.

Gluttony sucks down the last of his root beer, then belches. "And he's gay."

"No way," says Sloth. "Really?"

"How can you not know this?" asks Gluttony. "You've known him since the Bronze Age."

"Yeah, but I thought he was a chick with short hair who liked to wear men's clothes," says Sloth. "And he looked really good in a toga."

"How about you?" I ask Gluttony. "Ever thought about being Ambition or Courage or Valor?"

"With this body?" he says, shoveling down the last of his potato salad. "Are you kidding?"

As the two NYU students walk past us to sit down, the blonde makes a pig noise that's obviously directed at Gluttony. She and the redhead are still giggling when they reach their table.

Gluttony grabs my Coke, sucks the rest of it down, then belches and blows in the direction of the NYU students. Seconds later, they've both stopped giggling and are shoveling as much food as they can fit into their mouths.

"Beautiful, man," says Sloth. "Just beautiful."

Although their fates haven't changed, both women are going to struggle with mild cases of bulimia for the next couple of months.

"So what is all this about, anyway?" asks Gluttony. "You angling for one of our jobs?"

I shake my head. As much as I enjoy their company, Sloth and Gluttony aren't exactly inspiring.

"I don't know," I say. "I guess I'm just looking for something more."

"I know what you mean," says Gluttony, eyeing the other half of my egg-salad sandwich. "You gonna finish that?"

I leave Gluttony and Sloth at the deli—Gluttony because he's still hungry and Sloth because he's fallen asleep in his chair—then find a secluded alley to go invisible in before I head toward Union Square, my radar picking up men and women and children fated for hardships and failures and addictions.

Although I can't exactly turn off my Fate Radar, I can dial it down or tune out certain frequencies, so I dial everything down other than failures, since hardly any human ever manages to reach his or her full potential. That way, they all blend together into a kind of background static. White noise. Like an electric fan or highway traffic or the ocean surf. It can be very soothing. How else would I get to sleep at night?

Imagine trying to fall asleep or compose a letter or meditate while millions of conversations fly through the air around you. It's hard enough to concentrate, let alone have an original thought. It took me a couple of millennia just to get used to it. And that was before humans stopped dying at a reasonable age.

Of course, not every human emits a signal I can pick up.

As I head uptown through Gramercy Park, invisible to everyone yet assaulted by their endless array of fates, I occasionally come across blank areas in the fabric of my universe. It's kind of like swimming through a cold ocean or a lake and encountering a warm spot that makes you realize just how cold the water really is.

These warm places are destiny spots. The energy given off by those on the Path of Destiny.

Most of the time I ignore these pockets of nothing.

These warm embraces of air.

These reminders of my limitations.

But every now and then I stop and follow one around, trying to understand its structure, to figure out what it is about this person that makes him different. That makes him blessed. That makes him destined rather than fated.

Or, in this case, her.

A warm embrace of air in the shape of a woman is leaving an outdoor table at Pete's Tavern. She looks familiar but at first I can't place her. With over five and a half billion of my own humans to keep track of, it's not surprising I can't remember a woman who's on the Path of Destiny. You'd think I would have broken down by now and bought a BlackBerry or something, but I'm old-school.

Like to keep everything in my head. Still, every now and then I forget someone's name. Like the time I called Napoleon "Short Stack." Talk about an awkward moment.

While I'm trying to figure out where I know this woman from, she says something to the waiter as she leaves and I recognize her voice, and I realize she's the new tenant at my apartment building, who was on the roof when Destiny and I were having noncontact sex.

I follow my new neighbor, drawn to her for a reason I can't explain. It's not just my curiosity, my wanting to know what makes her different from the humans on my path. There's something else, the same something I felt on the roof when I first heard her voice, something I can't quite put my finger on.

So I trail her for several blocks, studying the way she moves, the way she walks, trying to understand what it is about her that I find so compelling. Then I notice the way everyone else on the sidewalk smiles as she passes by. She's not smiling at them and she's not saying anything to elicit a reaction; she's just talking on her cell phone. And it's not just men who smile at her because she's hot and they want to get into her pants—women notice her, too. I wonder if I'm just imagining things, if I'm just projecting the way she makes me feel onto them or if she's actually the cause of their reactions, when she catches a cab and disappears into the sea of vehicles heading uptown on Park Avenue.

From what I can tell about the new tenant in my building, there's nothing particularly unique about her that would cause strangers to smile at her on the street. But that's not indicative of anything. I used to think humans who were on the Path of Destiny would all have a particular look or a similar demeanor or some other defining characteristic that would set them apart from the humans on my path. But I've seen immaculately groomed men and saintly women fated for mediocrity, while unkempt women and arrogant men have been destined for a path beyond the scope of what I'm used to dealing with.

Inventors. Artists. Scientists.

Healers. Leaders. Teachers.

Although this last category doesn't include the likes of high school biology teacher Darren Stafford from Duluth, Minnesota. Who, at this moment, is discovering that his star pupil lied about being on the pill.

Whoops.

Throughout my existence, and more so over the past few thousand years, I've studied the humans on the Path of Destiny, looking for a glimpse into what makes them special, wanting to understand what makes them tick.

I've listened to the teachings of Plato and Aristotle.

I've stolen Albert Einstein's lunch money.

I've watched van Gogh paint and Rodin sculpt.

I've flown kites with Benjamin Franklin, sailed with Leif Eriksson, presided over the birth of Julius Caesar, and been present at the crucifixion of Christ. I've even followed Moses around to see what made him tick.

By the way, the Burning Bush? That was Destiny. She is, after all, a redhead. And fourteen hundred years before the birth of Christ, nobody had ever heard of a Brazilian wax.

But after tens of thousands of years and hundreds of millions of humans, I've come close to giving up my fruitless search for discovering the makeup of these men and women who are destined for something I cannot give them. Still, I can't help but think that if only I could grasp the essence of their unique nature, it would help me to understand my relationship with my humans and why most of them are such royal pains in the ass.

CHAPTER 6

On average, a quarter of a million humans are born into existence every day and I'm responsible for assigning fates to nearly 210,000 of them. Doing the math, that comes to 8,750 assigned fates per hour, 146 per minute, or 2.4 per second.

Like I want to spend all day sitting at my computer.

But with the Automatic Fate Generator program that Innovation wrote to help me assign fates, I can take care of all 210,000 newborn humans on my laptop while drinking a double latte at Starbucks. I should probably do this at home on a broadband connection, but I can sign into the Kingdom Come network from anywhere on Earth. Jerry claims Kingdom Come is more secure than the NSA. Still, when you're sending out fates over a wireless connection, you just hope some thirteen-year-old in Tokyo hasn't found a way to hack into the network.

The Automatic Fate Generator program doesn't do all of the work for me. I still have to enter in my quotas and set the success parameters not to exceed anything above mediocrity.

Career .250 hitters.

Single-term presidents.

One-hit wonders.

If I forget to set the parameters and end up assigning someone a future that involves an Oscar-filled career or multiple Wimbledon titles, then I'm treading dangerously close to Destiny's domain. Which is a good way to get myself suspended. Or worse. So I spend a lot of time double-checking.

I also have to factor in past lives.

When humans are born, they're set either on the Path of Fate or on the Path of Destiny. There's no opportunity for advancement. No climbing the corporate ladder. No chance of moving into a higher tax bracket. And you can't fall from the Path of Destiny. You're in a spectrum, of sorts. An invisible force field of futures.

However, the Law of Reincarnation does provide a loophole, allowing humans to transcend their fates from one lifetime to the next. Make the right choices and live up to your expectations and you get to move on. Keep screwing up and repeating the same mistakes and you get held back a grade. Theoretically, if you manage to make a good enough impression, you could end up graduating to the Path of Destiny in your next lifetime.

Of course, you don't get to take your memories with you, since past-life memories can be a bit of a burden. It's hard enough for most humans to remember appointments and anniversaries without having to deal with the knowledge that you used to be someone like Adolf Hitler.

Once I have all of the information entered into the program, I hit the "execute" button and away we go. Still, it takes some time for

210,000 fates to upload into the cosmic mainframe, providing I have a strong Wi-Fi signal. But in less than ten minutes, the fates of all my newborn humans will be uploaded, disseminated, and assigned.

Granted, it's not an exact science. Not like in the old days, when I could tailor each fate for each individual human. Kind of like making a suit that would fit just right. Or molding a future out of flesh. It was an art form, assigning fates. An acquired skill. A creative outlet for my inner Michelangelo.

Now it's all just mass production.

Cookie-cutter fates.

An assembly line of futures.

Even with a computer-generated algorithm assigning fates for me, I can't possibly keep up with the demand in a way that allows me to handcraft everyone's future and take care of all the fates I have to reassign on a daily basis.

One way or the other, I'm sacrificing quality for quantity.

One way or the other, I'm just creating product.

As the program continues with the upload to the network, I get an e-mail from Jerry. Not a personal message, but a mass mailing sent out to the Immortal staff Yahoo! group list:

Important!!!

Most of the time, when Jerry sends out something with "Important" in the subject line, it's usually one of those e-mails warning all of us about a new computer virus or asking us to forward his e-mail to help feed starving children in Africa or telling us that Applebee's is giving away free gift certificates.

Jerry's a sucker for Internet hoaxes and urban legends.

One time, he even sent out an e-mail about the U.S. Mint releasing new dollar coins that omitted the motto "In God We Trust." It took us a while to calm him down about that one.

I figure the e-mail is another one of Jerry's lame warnings or pleas, but I can't just delete it. For one, almost all of Jerry's e-mails are titled "Important" or "Urgent" or "Please Read," so I'm never sure if it's crap or something actually relevant. And two, Jerry still uses AOL and forces all of us to use it so he can check the status of his e-mails to make sure we're all reading them.

The thing about Jerry is that he's a control freak.

When I open the e-mail to read the body of the message, all it says is:

Big event coming!!!
Stay tuned!!!

This is typical Jerry. He likes to keep us in the dark about his personal projects. Build up the suspense. Make a big deal of promoting some big history-changing event and then fill us in on the details at the last moment.

Noah.

Jesus.

The 1969 Mets.

While Destiny, Death, and I play a more significant role in the paths of humans than the Intangibles, the Emotives, and the Deadly and Lesser Sins, Jerry still controls the big picture. Which is his way of reminding us who's in charge.

The thing about Jerry is that he's a megalomaniac.

When it comes to things like biblical floods, messiahs, and one of the greatest upsets in World Series history, we don't typically know Jerry's timetable. At some point, he has to fill at least one of us in on his plans, but he doesn't always give us a lot of advance warning—though Destiny had Mary on her radar from the moment of the Immaculate Conception, so she knew something was up. But even though I knew the Orioles were going to blow the Series, I had no idea they would lose to the Mets. And none of us knew about the flood until the weather forecast came out predicting that the floodgates of the sky would open for the next forty days, which pretty much screwed our spring-break trip to Tahiti.

In spite of the fact that I control the futures of more than four-fifths of the world's population, I have no idea what Jerry's got up his sleeve. And it's not like I have a lot of spare time to deal with his cryptic messages. So once today's fates have finished uploading, I save his e-mail into my "Jerry's Annoying Announcements" folder, shut down my laptop, then turn my attention to a twenty-two-year-old barista who's about to decide that the unemployed slacker ordering an iced mocha would make a good boyfriend.

CHAPTER 7

I'm in the Red Light District in Amsterdam just past dusk, mean-dering along the Oudezijds Achterburgwal canal, trying to figure out how these people actually communicate with this language. I can't even get past the first syllable. It doesn't help that I just came out of the coffee shop Extase, where I sampled something called White Widow.

Most of the time I tend to avoid alcohol or pot or psychedelic mushroom tea with honey and ginger, but I haven't been to Amsterdam since the Vietnam War, and quite a bit has changed since my last visit. And when in Rome . . .

Across the canal, there's a sign above a closed entrance that says LIVE PORNO SHOW. Next to that, a set of stairs leads past a window with a neon sign advertising CANNABIS COLLEGE. Just up the canal, you can visit the Hash Marihuana & Hemp Museum and the Sensi Seed Bank before heading over to partake in some legalized prostitution.

And I'm beginning to wonder why I'm still living in Manhattan.

On my side of the canal, open doorways with red neon lights above them and red curtains pulled to the side display women of various shapes and hair colors, all soliciting the men who walk past. Some of the doors are closed, the curtains pulled shut over the glass, the light above the doorway dark, indicating that the occupant is temporarily indisposed.

A young French couple ahead of me is arguing about whether or not they should ask if one of the prostitutes would be interested in a threesome. The woman, a nineteen-year-old student from Paris, is going to end up with an undergraduate degree in communication and a PhD in failed relationships, while her boyfriend, a twenty-one-year-old studying history, is going to be doomed to repeat it.

I can't help but laugh.

The couple glances my way and the boyfriend calls me an asshole in French.

Apparently, I forgot I wasn't invisible.

Maybe it wasn't such a good idea for me to get stoned before going to work.

I give a wide berth to the couple and continue along the canal, past the Hash Marihuana & Hemp Museum and a twenty-eight-year-old virgin from Branson, Missouri, who's going to end up falling in love with the first prostitute he sleeps with, until I reach an alley I can turn down and go invisible without drawing any unwanted attention. Kind of like Clark Kent looking for someplace discreet to morph into Superman, except I'm not exactly here to save anyone.

I've often wondered what it would be like to be a superhero, endowed with powers that I could use to help damsels in distress or thwart villains and criminals. Except I don't think my persona would exactly evoke a sense of security.

Captain Fate.

Fatal Man.

Mr. Fatalistic.

Plus I don't think I'd look good in tights and a leotard.

Halfway down the alley, I realize I'm not alone. I also realize this alley doesn't cut through to the other side.

When I turn around, I see the outline of twenty-four-year-old Nicolas Jansen in the shadows between me and the entrance to the alley. Although I can't see his face, I know he's going to be spending most of the next two decades of his life in and out of jail and drug rehab, neither of which is going to make much of a difference.

"What's up?" he says with a Dutch accent, walking toward me.

I don't tend to have many interactions with humans, especially not in this manner, and considering that I marvel at their overall ineptitude as a species, it's not surprising that my people skills are a little rusty.

"Go away," I say.

He hesitates, momentarily caught off guard by my reaction. But he mistakes it for bravado and closes the distance between us.

"I'll go when I'm ready," he says, producing a stiletto knife.

It's not like I'm worried about getting injured or killed. Sure, he can do some serious damage to my man suit, but I can just have Ingenuity make me another one. The suit I have is getting kind of worn-out anyway, which isn't surprising, considering I've had it since the Reformation.

But I don't want to have to deal with getting mugged and stabbed right now, especially since I just got stoned and it would really bum my high. Plus I still want to visit the Anne Frank House.

"Give me your wallet," he says.

"I don't have any money," I say. Which isn't true. In addition to my own cash, Sloth gave me a hundred bucks and asked me to bring him back some really good hash.

"Give me your fucking wallet," he says, brandishing the stiletto for emphasis.

I can see Nicolas Jansen's face now, young and strung out, a couple of days removed from his last shave. He hasn't been consumed by this lifestyle yet, but it's beginning to sink its teeth into him and is slowly sucking his will down to the marrow.

I could just give him my wallet and let him continue on his downward-spiraling path to desperation and failure, but I really don't want to have to deal with canceling my universal credit card or getting a new photo ID. I hate going to the DMV.

I could just do what I came in here to do in the first place and go invisible. Just blink out of existence. But that's generally frowned upon, ever since Heroism and the Joan of Arc fiasco.

Rule #6: Never dematerialize in front of humans.

On the other hand, I could try to talk him out of this, tell him it's not too late, that he can still make something out of himself, even if his best-case scenario is working for the sanitation department. But that would be interfering. Getting involved.

So instead, I opt for a different approach.

"Eat me," I say.

"What?" he says.

Diplomacy has never exactly been my strong suit.

"Eat me," I say again, taking a step toward him. He takes a step back, still holding the stiletto out in front of him.

"Don't fuck with me," Nicolas says, stopping and holding his ground. "I'll cut you. I swear to God, I'll cut you."

"Then cut me," I say, taking another step forward, calling his bluff.

While Nicolas Jansen is built for threatening people and stealing from them and using the fruits of his labors to purchase and consume mind-numbing drugs, he's not a violent person. And he most certainly is not a murderer.

"I will," he says, without much conviction.

"Here," I say, holding up my wallet and dangling it in front of him. "Take it if you've got the guts."

His eyes shift back and forth from the wallet to me. I can see the uncertainty in his expression, can almost feel the confusion rolling off of him in waves. And I know he's mere moments from turning around and discovering that life as a sanitation worker isn't so bad.

Maybe it's because I take another step forward or because I have the audacity to show him how much money I have in my wallet or because I call him a spineless pussy. Or maybe I just misjudged him.

Before I have the chance to react, Nicolas Jansen is plunging his knife into my chest and grabbing my wallet out of my hand and running away to join the growing crowds along the Oudezijds Achterburgwal, leaving me for dead in the shadows of the alley.

CHAPTER 8

It's embarrassing enough to get mugged and stabbed in an alley in Amsterdam by a mortal with a drug addiction, but once your man suit is breached, it makes it impossible to transport. Instead of making the journey as one unit, you might slip out through the opening, leaving your empty man suit behind and creating a lot of problems. Sure, it gives Hysteria and Conspiracy something to do, but the last thing we need is for the human race to figure out that something is walking around impersonating them.

It's happened once before, not long after the collapse of the Roman Empire near the end of the fifth century. It was so bad Memory had to be sent in for an emergency overhaul that had ramifications for more than five hundred years. Although the human race commonly refers to that period as the Dark Ages, it's known among the Immortals as Jerry's Big Screwup.

So, not wanting to be responsible for another five centuries of repressed written history and cultural achievements, I have to find a way to get back to New York. And without a wallet, a passport, or any fingerprints to verify my ID, I can't exactly jump on a plane or board a transatlantic cruise, even if I had any money to pay for a ticket.

So I'm forced to take desperate measures.

"Ouch!" I say, as the needle pierces my skin, pulling the stitch through after it.

Even though we can't be killed, we can still feel sensations through our suits of human flesh. Heat. Pleasure. Pain. And this feels like pain.

"Be quiet," says Secrecy. "Someone might hear you."

"It hurts," I say. "Couldn't you have given me a local?"

"You're lucky I even showed up," she says, piercing my chest again with more enthusiasm than I'd like. "You have any idea how much trouble I could get in?"

The thing about Secrecy is that she's paranoid.

We're sitting on the bed in a room on the second floor of the Victoria Hotel, a little over half a mile from where I was stabbed. The curtains are drawn and the doors are locked and I couldn't even so much as whisper until Secrecy swept the room for bugs.

"Ouch," I say again.

"You're not taping this, are you?" she asks.

She's still mad at me about Watergate.

"That was out of my hands," I tell her. "I didn't force them to reveal their secrets. They caved in to political pressure. It was their fate."

"Whatever," she says. "At least Woodward and Bernstein had some integrity."

I've known Secrecy for most of the past six thousand years. Not a lot of secrets to be kept among the human race before that, other than hiding food from one another or masturbating. More than once our paths have crossed and she's been left feeling screwed over. It took her a long time to get over the whole Judas thing, but eventually she realized it was for the best.

Secrecy finishes sewing me up, adding a couple of extra stitches either because she wants to make sure I won't leak out when I travel back to New York or because she enjoys hearing me scream.

"That should do it," she says.

"You sure?" I ask, fingering the puckered flesh on my chest.

"No," she says. "But you can call someone else if you want a second opinion."

Secrecy was the only one I could call without wondering if anyone else would ever find out. Problem is, even though her silence doesn't have to be bought, it still comes with a price.

"Thanks," I say. "What do I owe you?"

In addition to the sewing service, I couldn't pay for the room, since my credit card had vanished along with the rest of my wallet, so Secrecy took care of it. Paid in cash, of course.

But money isn't what's at stake here.

Secrecy puts an index finger to her pursed lips and says, "Hmm."

I can tell from her expression she's just doing that for effect. She knows exactly what she wants. But Secrecy isn't into material things or otherworldly goods. She's not that interested in sex, though she has had passionate love affairs with Integrity and Ambition. She doesn't care for reprisals and she's not into embarrassing anyone. The only things she's interested in are commodities of secrecy.

Humans who are fated to divulge their secrets.

Tattletales.

"I want the Roswell Incident."

"The Roswell Incident?" I say.

I thought she was going to ask for the JFK assassination or the death of Marilyn Monroe or what happened to Jimmy Hoffa. Hell, I'd be willing to give up the Freemasons, even the Holy Grail. But the Roswell Incident?

"And Area 51," she says.

"Oh, come on," I say. "That's not fair."

"Neither is expecting me to keep your little man-suit malfunction a secret," she says.

I don't have an argument. Still, giving up Roswell *and* Area 51 just kills me. If the full story of those two secrets were to finally come out, it would be so much fun to see the human race react and how it would impact their fates. Nothing like having your lifelong beliefs challenged to throw a little chaos into the equation.

And man, is Chaos going to be pissed. He's been looking forward to that moment more than I have.

"All right," I say. "You can have them both."

Secrecy smiles in triumph and gets off the bed, then gives me a look that resembles Mischief.

"There's one other thing," she says.

"What?" I ask, starting to button up my shirt.

"Close your eyes," she says, her voice soft and seductive.

I look at her and wonder if I was wrong about her wanting sex for payment. "Why?"

"Just close them," she says, starting to unbutton her own shirt.

So I close my eyes and imagine Secrecy shedding her clothes, stripping down to her underwear, then slipping out of those and standing next to me, naked. I unbutton my own shirt and slip out of my own pants in anticipation and recline back on the bed, my man suit prickling with excitement.

After what feels like too long, I finally open my eyes to discover I'm the only one in the room who thinks I'm going to have sex.

Secrecy is gone.

CHAPTER 9

"R-thirty-six, please go to window number thirteen."

I'm at the New York Department of Motor Vehicles in Upper Manhattan, just a race riot away from the East River.

I've been sitting at the DMV for nearly thirty minutes already, waiting to turn in the paperwork for my stolen ID. You can't apply for a new ID card by mail. You have to go into an office and apply in person.

If I had a New York State driver's license, I could have applied online. But Jerry doesn't want us driving after what happened to James Dean. It was kind of a knee-jerk reaction, considering none of us are as foolhardy as Reckless, but sometimes you just have to follow orders. Besides, who needs a driver's license when you can travel at the speed of light?

It's times like this when you fully appreciate the ability to go invisible.

Of course, I can't do that here. But after more than two hundred and fifty thousand years, you tend to take some things for granted.

I already put a call in to cancel my universal Visa, which has the best customer care in the universe. Literally. I can use my Visa on any planet with intelligent life and a merchant services agreement. And if my card is lost or stolen and any unauthorized charges appear on my statement, I'll get reimbursed. Even if the purchases were made on one of Jupiter's moons.

"R-thirty-seven, please go to window number five."

Window number five is off to my left, where the clerk, who'll still be working here when he's fifty and on his way to a heart attack, waits with zero expectancy for his next appointment. I'm watching him with the same level of disinterest when the new tenant who moved into my apartment building walks up to his window.

Sara Griffen is wearing a black pantsuit with a pair of sensible shoes. Her hair is pinned up and I can see the nape of her neck, pale and covered with a soft, downy coat.

The thing about Sara Griffen is that she's a mystery.

I've encountered Sara leaving our apartment building on a couple of occasions and followed her around, trying to find out why I'm compelled by her, why she's different from the future pedophile in apartment 502 or the woman in 1216 who's going to spend the rest of her life discovering that plastic surgery can't buy happiness. So far, all I can tell about Sara is that she likes to jog in Central Park, she eats a lot of take-out, and she can't stand the sound of screaming babies.

I've also discovered that she definitely has an effect on people.

I watch the DMV agent at the window, watch him watching Sara, and I notice that rather than the surly countenance he displayed moments earlier, he's more engaged. There's a spark in his eyes that wasn't there before. An animation in his manner that is spirited. A smile that isn't forced.

Maybe it's because he's desperate to get laid and he hopes Sara will find him attractive. Maybe it's because he just enjoys flirting with women. Or maybe it's because there's something about Sara that just makes him happier.

What would make *me* happier is if I didn't have to spend half my morning at the DMV.

"D-fifty-one, please go to window number two."

As I watch her, I wonder again why Sara Griffen is on the Path of Destiny, what it is she has that makes her different from the soon-to-be-unemployed video game addict on my left and the seventeen-year-old future adulteress sitting to my right.

I also wonder how I ended up with a lineup of underachievers and mediocre talents and marginal leaders while Destiny gets the Michael Jordans and the John Lennons and the Winston Churchills of the world. You'd think I'd remember something like that, but it's kind of hard to recall the moments immediately after your creation. That's when Jerry christened us with our job titles. Didn't really give us a choice, which I think was by design. When you've just emerged out of the cosmic goo, blinking your eyes and wondering what the hell happened, the last thing you're concerned about is how you're going to earn a living. Still, it would have been nice to at least fill out an application.

In spite of the fact that I can't stand Destiny and I covet her client list, I also realize we need each other. And humans need us. Without Fate and Destiny, there would be no purpose for humans. No path to follow. No reason to exist.

Think unnecessary.

Think pointless.

Think any *Matrix* sequel.

So in essence, Destiny and I maintain the cosmic balance of human life on the planet.

But I still can't get a table on a Friday night at Elaine's. And when it comes to speedy customer service at the DMV, they're not exactly showering me with any perks.

"R-thirty-eight, please go to window number eleven."

Ten minutes later, I'm still waiting for them to call my number when Sara Griffen walks out the door.

I see her again a few days later in Central Park.

I'm watching a four-year-old kid screaming at his mother to get him a strawberry-shortcake Good Humor ice-cream bar from an ice-cream cart when Sara comes jogging past in running shorts, a T-shirt, and a New York Mets baseball cap.

For a moment I completely forget about the mother and her brat and watch Sara run past, singing silently along to whatever song is playing on the headphones of her iPod. And I'm not the only one who notices.

The ice-cream-cart vendor looks up and follows Sara's progress. A seventy-two-year-old man who'll be dead before he's seventy-five perks up as she passes. An eleven-year-old boy who has "college dropout" written all over him walks into a garbage can.

Sure. It could just be that she has a really nice ass and a pair of legs that you'd beg to shave. Except women notice her as well. Young women. Old women. Married and single women. Future flight attendants and strippers and surgeons who'll get sued for malpractice. They all notice Sara as she momentarily disturbs the air around them. And then, when she's gone, whatever it was they felt is gone, too, and they resume whatever they were doing.

I continue to watch Sara until she disappears around a bend; then I turn back to the screaming monster who'll be raped in prison when he's twenty-four.

Less than a week later, I encounter Sara again on the subway.

I'm heading uptown from Houston Street when she walks into my car and sits down directly across from me.

The subway is one of the few places where I don't go invisible. Just because no one can see me doesn't mean they can't sit on me or bump into me or notice when I experience uncontrollable flatulence.

It happens.

Sure, I could just transport back to my apartment and avoid the whole scene, but the point of observing humans is to observe. I can't very well do that by avoiding them. Besides, the subway is a great place to reassign fates.

So I just stay visible and hope some crack addict doesn't pass out on the seat next to me and drool on my man suit.

It's a little awkward sitting across from Sara like this. I can't watch her the way I have before or watch the way others react to her without coming across as a little creepy. But unlike the other humans sharing the subway car with us, she's the only one I can't read.

The thing about Sara Griffen is that she's pretty, but not drop-dead gorgeous.

I look away, trying to appear nonchalant, but I feel like I'm acting too casual. When I look back, she's looking at me. I cross my legs, then uncross them. I clear my throat. I pretend to look at something very interesting on the floor between my feet. Then I look up and she's still looking at me.

I wonder if I should introduce myself. Or get off at the next stop. Or tell her she's sitting next to a woman who's going to contract genital herpes.

Instead, I just smile.

She smiles back.

I'm not exactly sure what it is about Sara Griffen that fascinates me. Maybe it's the way she seems so at peace whenever I see her. Maybe it's the effect she seems to have on others. Or maybe it's because when she smiles, it makes me smile.

We ride this way in silence, watching each other across the three feet of space between us, smiling as if sharing some secret joke. When the train reaches Times Square, Sara gets off, but not without a final glance cast my way. Then the doors shut and I'm left with a bunch of fetishists, philanderers, and telemarketers on their way to the Upper West Side.

The rest of the train ride, I keep thinking about destiny and fate and the number of people on this subway train who need some serious counseling. But mostly I keep thinking about Sara and the places in Manhattan our paths have crossed lately.

The DMV.

Central Park.

The subway.

In a city with more than eight million human inhabitants, I randomly run into the same woman three different times in three different locations in barely more than a week.

I'd say fate was trying to tell me something if I didn't know better.

CHAPTER 10

During the next couple of weeks, I see Sara again at the Guggenheim, the Central Park Zoo, Le Figaro Café in Greenwich Village, at a Yankees game, and sunbathing on the roof of our building.

Okay, maybe the last one was more like stalking than a chance encounter.

I know she's really none of my concern and that I should be spending my time taking care of the humans on my own path, but after running into her so many times, I can't help but be intrigued.

So over the next few weeks, I follow her.

To her job at Halstead Property on Third Avenue, where she brokers condominiums and homes that typically run in the seven figures.

To Central Park, where she eats her lunch at the Bethesda Fountain, then buys a couple of sandwiches from a New York Picnic Company cart and gives them to a homeless couple.

To a pet-friendly, two-bedroom condo in Gramercy Park that she sells to a young stockbroker for $1.995 million.

To the Downtown Athletic Club, where she swims twenty laps in the seventy-five-foot heated pool and then gets a forty-five-minute massage.

To the Metropolitan Art Museum, where she spends three hours, most of it viewing a special exhibit of Cézanne.

To the farmer's market in Union Square.

To a two-bedroom loft in SoHo.

To the Blue Note Jazz Club in Greenwich Village.

To a memorial for victims of the World Trade Center.

To a three-bedroom condo in Midtown.

To a bar called Bongo in Chelsea, where a hotshot twenty-eight-year-old financial planner buys her a drink.

Sure, it's technically stalking, but I have a license. And it's not like I'm going to chop her up and store her in my freezer. Still, she could do so much better than this loser. In less than ten years, he's going to be in drug rehab to try to kick the cocaine habit that ate up most of his paychecks.

You'd think people on the Path of Destiny would manage to hook up with other people on the same path. Kind of like kindred souls who found each other through the chaotic journey of life. But I guess unless the people are destined for each other, they're as likely to make bad relationship choices as the humans I have to deal with.

So I'm standing outside Bongo, watching Sara and the hotshot drug addict through the window, wondering if I should go inside to make sure this loser doesn't slip some GHB into her drink. Sure, it's a lame excuse. But I've been following Sara around for nearly a month and I've grown accustomed to her presence. I follow her almost everywhere.

To the park.

To the movie theater.

To the women's locker room at her health club.

To the grocery store.

To the dry cleaner's.

To her gynecologist appointment.

I've watched her overtip a cabdriver and compliment a kid with a mohawk and cry at a Kodak commercial. I've watched her walk into a sliding glass door and eat a Polish sausage and buy tampons. I've even watched her pick her nose. Only once, but it was a definite pick.

I've watched her day after day, night after night, and still I know nothing about what makes her special. All I've learned is that she sometimes laughs when she brushes her teeth. That her voice seems to resonate from deep within her throat. That the smell of her shampoo trails after her when she walks unknowingly past me. That she looks so content and beautiful when she's sleeping or when she's reading or when she's sitting in Central Park watching the turtles.

And then it hits me.

I've fallen in love.

CHAPTER 11

Rule #7: Don't fall in love.

Having sex with humans, while not encouraged, is tolerated more often than not. We have the Greek gods to thank for setting the precedent on that one. Even Jerry dipped his nib in the mortal ink once, so to speak. Which, of course, resulted in the birth of Josh and led to grumblings of nepotism among the rest of the immortals, but eventually we all got over it. Except for Resentment. Go figure.

But where the Greek gods often fathered progeny with their mortal conquests, other than Jerry the rest of us don't have the ability to procreate. Wouldn't do to have us flitting around the globe, creating half-Immortals and altering the gene pool. So while our DNA prevents us from breeding, even with one another, we can still get our groove on without creating any cosmic repercussions. But developing feelings for humans and contemplating or pursuing a relationship with them is a definite no-no.

"What should I do?" I ask.

"Why don't you try talking to her?" says Honesty.

"Talk to her?" I say.

"It's called communication," she says, stubbing out her ciga-rette. "Women like that sort of thing."

In cases like this, it helps to get some good advice, and I know Honesty will always be candid and confidential. She's kind of like a therapist for immortal entities.

Honesty lives on the Upper West Side in a three-thousand-square-foot, two-bedroom flat on the top floor of a six-story build-ing with a view of Central Park. From the couch in her living room, I can see the North Meadow through the picture window.

"But if I talk to her," I say, "won't that encourage a relationship?"

"Is that a problem?" she says.

"Well, isn't fraternizing with human women against the rules?" I ask.

"Whose rules?" says Honesty. "Your rules? Jerry's rules? The rules of emotionally unavailable men?"

"Is that a multiple-choice question?" I ask.

Honesty lights up another cigarette, then takes a drag, leans back in her chair, crosses her legs, and says, "Are you afraid of intimacy?"

The thing about Honesty is that she's passive-aggressive.

Being an Attribute, Honesty doesn't so much have an impact on the decisions humans make but instead provides them with one of the tools they need to overcome the challenges thrown at them by Temptation and Shame and Anger.

Oh, by the way, while Anger pulls double duty as an Emotive, payroll has him officially listed as a Deadly Sin.

"So you think I should talk to her," I say. "Maybe ask her if she wants to have some coffee or invite her out to a nice dinner?"

"That's generally what humans do," says Honesty. "And I know you've interacted with human women before."

It's true that I've had a few dalliances with human women over the past five thousand years or so. Up until about twelve thousand years ago, man was still evolving from his apelike ancestors. You really didn't want to get involved with Paleolithic women. Trust me. They didn't call it the Stone Age for nothing. Even early Neolithic women weren't much to look at. Sometimes you still couldn't tell the difference between the males and the females. And none of them looked as good in a mammoth-skin bikini as Raquel Welch in *One Million Years B.C.*

You pretty much stayed away from hominid women until the Greek civilization began to rise around 3000 B.C. After that, human women started to look pretty good.

Nefertiti.

Helen of Troy.

Marie Antoinette.

And who *didn't* want to sleep with Cleopatra? Show of hands? I didn't think so.

My countless affairs with human women were nothing more than fanciful larks, one-night stands that resulted in pure sexual gratification. But this . . . these feelings I have for a mortal female . . . it's unprecedented.

It's a bad enough idea to develop a romantic relationship with someone who lives in the same apartment building, because if things don't work out, it could make your living situation uncomfortable. It's even worse to develop a romantic relationship with someone who lives in the same building when you're Fate and you know ahead of time when you're going to have an argument and what it's going to be about, how many pets you're going to have, the vacations you'll take, the sex you'll have, and when your human partner is going to die.

Except since Sara's not on my path, I can't see how her life is going to develop, so I can't see how a potential relationship between us would turn out. Still, it's against the rules. It's interaction. Interference. Influence. All of which are bad.

Bad. Bad. Bad.

Problem is, everything about Sara makes me feel good.

Good. Good. Good.

I want to watch her and be near her and touch her and kiss her. I want to shower her with affection and adoration. I want to run out and buy her flowers and candy and other things that will wilt and die or rot her teeth.

"Is there any way I can just make this go away?" I ask.

Honesty takes a drag on her cigarette and blows the smoke in my face. "Make what go away?"

"This," I say, gesturing toward my body with my hands but not knowing where to point. "This warm, tingly sensation I get just thinking about her."

Honesty looks at me and smiles, the way she does when I know she's going to say something brutally honest.

Something truthful that can't be denied.

Something I don't want to hear.

"No."

CHAPTER 12

Instead of taking Honesty's advice and talking to Sara, asking her out or making small talk to get to know her, I decide to take a different approach, one successfully taken over the course of history by so many human men.

I go to a strip club.

"Hey, honey," says a brown-haired cutie in a black G-string and a black mesh bra who sits on my knee and tells me her name is Bambi.

Bambi is nineteen and says she's earning money so she can go to college. Which is a load of crap. She never intends to go to college but will instead use the money she earns here to buy a BMW and then end up working as a cocktail waitress at a martini bar in Jersey.

I'm at a place called Scandals in Queens, just on the other side of the East River in Long Island City. More like the Jersey warehouse-style strip clubs than their uptight New York City counterparts, Scandals is a little more hands-on than the clubs in Manhattan, which is why I like to come here.

Not that I go to strip clubs all the time. Just whenever I get the chance. It's kind of like homework for me, a place where I can go to find humans in their most primal element. Some of the places are a little seedy and can occasionally get rowdy, like this one, but I understand why human men enjoy going to strip clubs.

Beautiful women dressed in not much, walking up to you and sitting on your lap, smelling like yummy. Not to mention the private rooms and pole dancing and naked flesh in Technicolor abundance. True, the strippers are being paid to be nice and flirtatious and desirous, but technically, when you go out on a date with a woman, you're paying for it, too. And unless you're Greed or Frugality or a tightfisted bastard who insists on going Dutch, you're going to spend about as much money on a date as you are at a strip club.

Of course, if you and your date don't connect for whatever reason, you're stuck on the date for at least a couple of hours until it ends. You can't just walk out after paying the cover charge and say, "Thanks a lot." And when the evening finally does come to an end, chances are your date won't rub up against you, give you a lap dance, and brush her breasts against your face and say, "Oops."

"Oops," says Bambi, as I slip another twenty into her G-string.

I'm sitting in the lounge area, back in the shadows in one of the booths that ring the outer edge of the club. In the center of the club, a circular bar surrounds the dance floor, which provides for maximum intoxication while you watch the endless parade of women removing their clothing as they dance around the pole.

From my vantage point, I can view the entire bar. That is, when Bambi's breasts aren't in my face. In the middle of the afternoon, there aren't a lot of customers, just a dozen middle-aged men who are all looking at a lonely future full of ESPN, pepperoni pizza, and Internet porn. But then I spot a familiar figure sitting at the far side of the bar, someone who wasn't there when I came in an hour ago.

Once Bambi is done with my lap dance, she asks me if I want to adjourn to one of the VIP rooms. It's very tempting. And it's not like I can't afford the treatment. But I'm not so desperate I need to pay for a hand job. So I tell her I'll pass, slip another twenty into her G-string, then grab my Jack and Coke and head over to the bar.

The figure sitting at the end of the bar nursing a bottle of Budweiser looks more pathetic than all of the other doomed men in the club. He glances up from his beer, looks over and sees me with his baggy, bloodshot eyes, and offers a wan smile.

The thing about Failure is that he's manic-depressive.

He also has a perpetual half-grown beard, his unwashed hair is limp and greasy beneath his faded Chicago Cubs hat, and his chinos are so wrinkled it looks like a fashion statement.

I pull up a stool next to him.

"Fabio," he says, without much enthusiasm. "How's business?"

"Predictable," I say. "And you?"

"A rousing success," he says, taking a swig of beer. I can't tell if he's being serious or facetious. Either way works, I suppose.

I run into Failure now and then, which isn't surprising, considering most of my humans don't earn a passing grade on life. Once in a while I find him hanging out with Addiction or Guilt or one of the other Lesser Sins. You don't tend to find the Lesser Sins socializing with any of the Deadlies, who look down at the more venial vices as second-class sins.

We sit in silence while a bleached blonde with breast implants climbs up the dance pole, wraps her thighs around it, then slides down inverted until her hands are touching the stage. I'm not that impressed, but I throw a couple of dollar bills out for the effort. Besides, she's going to need the money for liposuction treatment when she's forty-five.

"So I hear you had a meeting with Jerry," says Failure.

"That so?" I say. "Where did you hear that?"

Failure looks at me with an expression that says: *Where else?*

Gossip. That little whore. Can't she ever mind her own business?

"So how's Jerry?" he asks.

"Omnipotent as always," I say. "Cracking the whip. Making sure I'm doing my job."

"Really?" says Failure. "I always thought he was kind of a pussy."

Somehow, Failure always seems to find a way of making conversation awkward.

"So what are you doing to keep yourself busy?" I ask.

"Oh, the usual," says Failure. "High schools, racetracks, movie studios. Every now and then I take a trip down to D.C. to fuck with democracy, but that's pretty much taking care of itself, so I don't bother."

Another stripper—this one a slender Korean who'll be leaving her job as a flight attendant to pursue a career in pornography—joins the counterfeit blonde onstage and starts caressing her thighs.

"I hang out in places like this a lot," says Failure, taking another pull from his Budweiser. "Not so much for the women. Most of them are just here to make some easy money. But most of the men come here because they're failures at something. Work. Life. Sports. A lot of them are here because they're failures at relationships."

I glance around the club and can't help but agree.

"They don't know how to communicate with real women," he says. "So they come here and feel like they're successful because they can have a real conversation with a beautiful woman without taking the risk of rejection."

I nod, though I suddenly don't like where this conversation is going.

"It's the ultimate in failure," he says, wiping his nose with the sleeve of his shirt. "Even if they're wealthy or physically fit, intelligent or fluent in three languages, they're incapable of speaking the language of love. Of sharing themselves honestly with a woman."

I signal to the bartender for another Jack and Coke. "Make it a double," I say.

On the stage, a petite brunette with nipple rings and an undiagnosed case of cervical cancer crawls toward us on her hands and knees.

"They're afraid of honesty," says Failure. "They're afraid of commitment. Of communication. Of intimacy. Of opening themselves up to something that requires more than just physical prowess or financial acumen or insightful witticisms."

I'm wondering where the bartender is with my drink. And if Bambi is still available in the VIP room.

Failure turns to look at me. "Pretty pathetic, don't you think?"

CHAPTER 13

I'm on the rooftop garden of my apartment building, sunbathing nude and thinking about Sara. Not in a sexual or French-maid-fantasy kind of way. I'm thinking about her smile and her walk and the way she crinkles her nose sometimes when she's talking. I'm thinking about her scent and her voice and the way she laughs out loud at movies when she's alone in her apartment. I'm thinking about the way I lose track of time watching her and how I feel excited when I'm around her and why I can't get up the nerve to talk to her.

Here I am, an immortal entity, existing since the dawn of man, and I'm afraid to talk to one harmless human female.

My parents would be so proud.

Though, technically, I don't really have parents. I suppose Necessity could be considered my mother, but that's stretching it. Jerry's the closest thing I have to a father, and I can't tell you how much *that* embarrasses me.

I did have three stepsisters for a while—Clotho, Lachesis, and

Atropos, who were born during the heyday of Greek culture and mythology. They never cared for me. Considered me old-school, washed up, a relic of the Stone Age. Thought they were the next big thing, what with their trendy white robes and their "thread of life" image. They even went so far as to compose a collection of hymns.

Meet the Moirae.

It included songs like "I Cut Your Thread," "Your Fate Is Mine," and the holiday classic, "You Won't Be Home for Hanukkah."

Didn't sell very well. Humans back then just weren't interested in shelling out their hard-earned drachmas for a self-absorbed musical composition created by a trio of cold, remorseless harpies.

And when the Golden Age of Greece came to an end fifteen hundred years ago, those three little shrews found out that banking your future on a doomed mythology is a bad career move.

Think Ramses ignoring the warnings of Moses.

Think Custer's Battle at Little Bighorn.

Think *Gigli*.

But then, I'm not exactly qualified to critique vocational choices. I've fallen in love with a mortal woman who's on the Path of Destiny, which is a good way to get yourself reassigned to something like Disease or Incest.

Not where I see myself in a thousand years.

Problem is, I'm too smitten with Sara to just forget about her. I considered moving to another apartment building so I wouldn't have the temptation so close at hand, but I've grown fond of the rooftop garden. Reminds me of Eden. Which doesn't really help with the whole temptation scenario.

But even if I moved to Brooklyn or Queens or Long Island, I'd still know where Sara lived and where she worked and when she'd most likely be taking a steam bath at her health club. Besides, I hate packing. And having to set up DSL again is such a hassle. So I crossed "moving" off my list.

I could see if Memory would do her thing on me, wipe Sara from my data banks. But Memory can be kind of selective sometimes and really screw things up. The last thing I want is to end up wandering around for the next few hundred years trying to figure out where I left my keys.

So I'm stuck with my Upper East Side apartment and my feelings for Sara and the general realization that I have no idea what I should do.

At times like this, I like to meditate. And nothing beats invisible nude sunbathing in my rooftop garden for relaxing the mind and finding some clarity.

My eyes are closed, my body simmering in a Coppertone glaze, the warm sun slowly cooking my brand-new man suit to a nice, even bronze.

When I got back from Amsterdam, I had Ingenuity repair the stitches from my stab wound, buying his silence with a quarter ounce of the White Widow I brought back from one of the hash bars. Ingenuity does his best work on mind-altering substances. So when he mentioned that my man suit looked a little dated and showed me the latest model, I threw in three grams of magic mushrooms for an updated version that reflects the current perception of the perfect male body: sculpted chest, toned arms and legs, six-pack abs, and unblemished, hairless flesh. I also upgraded the most masculine part of my anatomy.

Although I can't prove it, I'd swear Vanity had a hand in my decision making.

Naturally, my outer physical appearance had to remain the same—face, hair, skin color, height—so I had to wait a couple of weeks for my custom man suit to arrive. After all, you can't just buy a man suit off the rack and walk out the door. Not unless you want to make *Style*'s annual "Top Ten Immortal Fashion Faux Pas" issue.

I'm hoping my new man suit gives me the confidence I need to approach Sara. Still, physical appearance alone isn't going to solve my dilemma. I need to find my center.

My breath is slow and rhythmic, the only image behind my eyelids that of darkness as my mind floats along, calm and focused, all the sounds of New York City and the fates of its more than eight million inhabitants nothing but muffled static in the background, like the ocean's roar, soothing and monotonous.

Naturally, it would be easier to maintain my focus if the object of my dilemma didn't appear on the rooftop singing "Hot Stuff" by Donna Summer and wearing a brand-new black French-cut bikini.

When I open my eyes and glance over at her, Sara stops singing and removes her iPod headphones, then opens up her folding beach chair and begins to set up camp. I figure even though I'm invisible I should put on some clothes, just to be proper, when Sara looks my way and says, "Mind if I join you?"

I forgot to turn on my cloaking again. Not exactly the way I envisioned our official introduction.

I move to cover up, but she stops me.

"It's okay," she says. "I don't mind."

You think you know everything about a mortal woman and then she doesn't bat an eye at your naked man suit. Which, by the way, is custom-designed to never lose muscle tone or develop a spare tire. And Ingenuity didn't skimp on the accessories.

"I didn't know they allowed nude sunbathing up here," she says from about ten feet away.

"They don't," I say, throwing my shirt over my nakedness in spite of her protests. It's the gentlemanly thing to do. That and she looks really hot in her bathing suit, which is about to cause me to sport some wood.

She's looking at me with a quizzical expression. "You look familiar."

I still remember our encounter on the subway nearly two months ago like it was yesterday. But then, when you've been around for more than two hundred and fifty millennia, seven weeks *is* kind of like yesterday.

"I live in apartment twenty fourteen," I say, hoping that settles it.

She shakes her head. "No. I haven't seen you around here. I'm pretty sure of that."

"I travel a lot," I say. Whatever that means. I have no idea what I'm saying.

Sara's looking at me the way she did on the subway, her eyes stripping me naked, which doesn't take much at the moment.

"No," she says. "It was someplace else. Someplace around town. Do you work in real estate?"

I shake my head. "I'm in futures and options."

"So you're a stockbroker?"

"Sort of."

She nods as if that explains everything, then walks toward me. "Sara Griffen," she says, extending her right hand.

I take it.

If watching Sara wash her hands and handle other objects with them was tantalizing, physically touching them is absolutely exhilarating.

"Fabio," I say, nearly choking out my name.

"Really," she says. She tilts her head and studies me. "You don't look like a Fabio."

"What do I look like?" I say, still holding her hand.

She stares into my eyes, then shifts her gaze to my perfectly sculpted, hairless torso, then to the rather sizable pup tent rising below my waist. When her attention returns to my face, she's wearing a playful smile.

"You look like you could use a hand."

CHAPTER 14

The last time I had sex with a mortal woman was on the RMS *Titanic*, just before it hit the iceberg. Her name was Dorothy Wilde and was she ever. Barely twenty years old and traveling in second class, fated to get hit by a falling safe in Brooklyn less than a week after surviving the disaster, Dorothy taught me things about early-twentieth-century women that most mortal men had to pay top dollar for. It didn't hurt my cause that she believed I was the heir apparent to the estate of millionaire John Jacob Astor IV, who wasn't going to make it off the *Titanic* alive.

Even before the cruise liner hit the iceberg, I knew what was going to happen, but Dorothy Wilde didn't seem to notice anything was wrong until the stern started to rise out of the water. Wallace Hartley and the rest of the ship's band weren't the only ones who kept on playing after the waterline continued to climb. I won't go into details, but let's just say that as the *Titanic* was going down, so was Dorothy Wilde.

But Dorothy had nothing on Sara Griffen.

"Oh, my Jerry," I say as Sara rolls off and onto the bed beside me, laughing and gasping for breath at the same time.

"Jerry?" she says, grabbing a half-smoked joint off my bedside table and lighting it up. "Who's Jerry?"

I'm not aware I mentioned him until she says something. "Oh. Just this guy I know who reminds me of God."

"God?" she says, letting out a puff of smoke as she hands the joint to me. "Do you believe in God?"

This is not the kind of postcoital conversation I want to have. Problem is, after good sex, I tend to open up like a penitent pilgrim in front of the pope.

I really need to learn to keep my mouth shut after I have an orgasm.

Fortunately, I can take a moment to gather my thoughts before answering while I take a hit on the joint. I hold it in as long as I can, hoping that maybe while waiting for me to respond Sara will change the topic of conversation.

"Well, do you?" she asks again, turning her head on her pillow to look at me.

I empty my lungs and look over at Sara—her lips moist, her skin slick with perspiration, her soft brown hair draped across her shoulders.

"When I look at you, I do."

Funny thing is, that's not what I planned to say. But it seems to do the trick, because she smiles and drops the conversation and sticks her tongue down my throat.

An hour later, when we're both gasping for breath again, Sara asks me if I remember meeting her on the subway.

I stare at my mirrored ceiling and try to pretend I don't know what she's talking about.

"A few weeks ago," she says. "I got on at Houston Street and sat down across from you. You were wearing a Boston Red Sox cap and a T-shirt that said, 'Fuck New York.'"

Sometimes I like to wear something incendiary just to see how humans will react. True, it's technically interfering, but I haven't drastically changed anyone's fate by doing it. Except this one time when I swung by the Tower of London during Henry VIII's reign wearing a tunic that read, *Your Wife Is a Treasonous Whore*.

Oops.

"At first I couldn't believe you could get away with wearing something like that on a subway in Manhattan," says Sara. "But no one had the courage to confront you. You had this aura about you that no one wanted to mess with. Except instead of intimidating or combative, you had this expression of absolute boredom. Like you didn't care what anyone thought."

Pretty much.

"That's what intrigued me so much about you," she says. "I couldn't take my eyes off you. Do you remember?"

I nod. Damn afterglow honesty.

"I knew it," she says, rolling over on to one elbow and staring at me with her captivating eyes. "I could tell by the way you looked at me on the rooftop. You recognized me, too. But your recognition was deeper. As if you'd known me for much longer than a chance encounter."

I don't want to do this. I don't want to have to answer her, to tell her the truth. But I can't lie to her. I can't pretend I haven't been following her around off and on since she moved in, trying to get up the courage to talk to her.

"I've been stalking you," I say.

Probably not the best way to put it, but there you have it.

She looks at me, not laughing because she thinks I'm making a joke, but just staring, studying me, making me feel like I should get up and leave.

"Really?" she asks.

I nod.

"Since the subway?"

I nod again. I only started stalking her afterward. Which should be good for something.

She stares at me in silence long enough for me to think that I might have to ask Memory for a favor so I don't end up with a police record. Then Sara smiles and says, "I've never been stalked before."

"Is that good or bad?" I ask.

"Good," she says, the word coming out so soft and sultry it almost sounds like she's purring. "Definitely good."

The next few moments pass by in a combination of relief and sexual tension, as it's all I can do to keep from showing her my appreciation for not slapping me with a restraining order.

"What are you thinking?" she asks.

I look at her, at this woman who helps the homeless and who doesn't raise her voice in anger and who listens to people with genuine interest. This woman who smokes pot and who likes to be stalked and who has sex with an immortal entity she just met. This woman who has screwed Fate and who is on the Path of Destiny.

"You're a conundrum," I say.

She studies me, still leaning on one elbow, her head propped on her hand. "You're one of the most unusual men I've ever met," she says, her other hand sliding along my chest and past my stomach, where her fingers wrap around my aroused accessory. "And the most potent."

Thank you, Ingenuity.

CHAPTER 15

One of the biggest problems with dating a mortal woman, since I'm technically breaking the rules about falling in love and getting involved, is that it's not a good idea for me to be seen with Sara in public. Which kind of limits our options.

No theaters.

No restaurants.

No strip clubs.

So for our first official date, rather than taking Sara out for a nice dinner at the Blue Water Grill or for some his-and-her lap dances at Scandals, I've invited her over to my place for Chinese take-out. Not the most romantic of gestures, but my culinary skills leave a lot to be desired. Plus I haven't cooked for anyone since I had Instigation and Destruction and a few of the Deadly Sins over for a barbecue during the Peloponnesian War. And that was more of a potluck.

Of course, having Sara over to my place presents its own challenges.

I have to hide any physical evidence of my identity, which includes my predestination dry-erase calendar, several memos from Jerry about upcoming droughts and famines and other natural disasters, and a framed photo of me with the Donner Party.

And I have to remember to keep the toilet seat down.

I know I shouldn't have anything to worry about. But I'm anxious and nervous, wanting to make a good impression. So I clean and I prepare and I buy scented candles and I put on some Velvet Underground, trying to make everything perfect. It's as if I've forgotten I'm immortal.

As soon as Sara shows up, we sit down at the kitchen table to eat mango prawns and General Tso's chicken. Just for the record, General Tso didn't care for sweet-and-spicy deep-fried chicken. Spicy food irritated his bowels. But he was a sucker for custard pie.

The whole time we're eating, I'm trying to figure out what to talk about, stumbling through the conversation. For obvious reasons, I can't be too forthcoming about my existence, but for the most part, I figure it shouldn't be a problem. Just so long as she doesn't ask me what I do for a living.

"So tell me more about what you do," says Sara.

I'm trying to think of a way we can just have sex and avoid this whole honesty thing, but I'm not getting the sex vibe from Sara. Plus all of this anxiety is causing my man suit to malfunction, so to speak, which doesn't leave me with a whole lot of options.

"I travel a lot," I say, hoping that satisfies her.

"Where do you travel?" she asks.

"Lots of places," I say. Which is true. So I'm not technically lying.

She laughs. "Can you be any more vague?"

"I can try," I say.

Sara laughs again and I think I've managed to avoid any further discussion about my existence until she says, "What exactly does someone do who is in futures and options?"

I can sense Persistence having a hand in this, the relentless bastard.

"Mostly customer service and problem solving," I say.

There, that should do it. So long as she doesn't ask me what kind of problems.

"What kind of problems?" she asks.

"The usual kind."

Sara stares at me with an amused smile.

"You're not much for small talk, are you?" she asks.

I shrug my shoulders.

"Would you rather just fool around?"

"Is that an option?" I say. "I thought we had to finish dinner first."

Sara laughs. "Do all men just think about sex?"

The short answer is: yes. All men just think about sex. At least, the men I have to deal with. It's one of the reasons they get so distracted from their original paths.

Singles bars.

Strip clubs.

Online pornography.

I've lost more productive human hours to the pursuit of sexual pleasure than I have to plagues, genocide, and all of the wars combined.

Sara gets out of her chair, walks over to me, and sits down on my lap, straddling me, then gives me a long, lingering kiss. When she pulls back, her eyes regard me with so much warmth and sincerity that I realize all of my anxiety has drained away.

"How do you do that?" I ask.

"Do what?" she says.

"That thing you do," I say, studying her face just inches from mine. "The way you manage to make me feel better with just a kiss."

"I don't know," she says. "But I'm glad I make you feel that way."

We sit and stare at each other, her straddling me and me getting lost in her face, the sexual tension building until I wonder which one of us is going to crack first.

Or maybe it's just me.

"I want you to know, I don't normally have sex with someone I've just met," says Sara.

"Me either," I say, hoping the fact that I'm not technically a person cancels out the fact that I've had sex with more than a hundred thousand mortal women.

"I didn't even lose my virginity until I was twenty-five."

The thing about Sara is that she's unabashedly honest.

"How old are you now?" I ask.

"Twenty-nine."

I look at her, wanting to ask, more out of curiosity than jealousy or any sense of competition. But before I can get up the nerve, she holds up three fingers.

"Three?" I say.

She nods. "The first one was just to get it over with. The second one was a mistake. And the third one . . ." she says, tracing her finger along my face.

I start to offer up an amusing reply, but there's something about the look on her face that makes me reconsider. Instead, what comes out of my mouth is:

"Maybe the third time's the charm."

Sara looks at me and smiles. "There's something about you. Something different. Something that makes me feel connected to you. Something I can't quite put my finger on."

"I can give you some suggestions."

"I'm serious," she says. "It's as though something has clicked into place inside of me and everything just feels right. Does that freak you out?"

"No," I say.

"It would probably freak most guys out."

"I'm not most guys."

"I know," she says. "That's what I like about you."

Sara kisses me again, softly, then smiles and brushes the hair away from my temple, and I realize that in all of my existence, no one has ever touched me like this. No one has ever looked at me like this. No one has ever made me feel this way.

Powerless and invincible.

Frightened and courageous.

Filled with hope and doubt.

All at the same time.

I have to admit that while I've had my share of unusual experiences, this whole being-in-love thing is a little disconcerting.

No wonder it's against the rules.

CHAPTER 16

"Sex is the new black."

I'm having a drink at Marion's Marquee Lounge in the Bow-ery during happy hour, listening to Infatuation wax philosophical about the current state of love.

"Love is out of style," he continues. "It's old-fashioned. Like homemade ice cream or petticoats or horse-drawn carriages. Quaint but impractical. Men and women don't have time for love anymore. Instead, they share a few laughs, down a few drinks, have sex, and figure they've found love. Just look around this place."

I glance around the lounge, filled with small round tables and vintage lamps and men and women gathered together in the sub-dued lighting, sharing drinks and conversation and sexual tension. I came here looking for some answers about human relationships, hoping to get some insight from the likes of Love or Romance or Affection, but Infatuation offered to buy me a drink, so I couldn't exactly turn him down.

The thing about Infatuation is that he's narcissistic.

"Every one of these humans sees someone they imagine could be their perfect partner," says Infatuation, smiling at himself in the base of a nearby lamp. "But their perception is skewed by their infatuation for the person sitting across from them, their eyes and thoughts filled with passion and desire. See what I mean?"

He motions toward the corner of the lounge, where Passion and Desire are wearing cocktail dresses and drinking margaritas.

The thing about Passion is that she's bulimic.

The thing about Desire is that she's obsessive-compulsive.

"Now, Love will try to tell you nothing clouds good judgment like pure, unadulterated *amore*," he says, examining both of his profiles in his half-empty highball glass. "But humans fall in love with one another *in spite* of their faults and deficiencies. When it comes to Infatuation, Desire, Passion, and Lust, those shortcomings disappear. Hell, we're the original beer goggles."

The twenty-nine-year-old man at the table next to us is as good-looking as Vanity and about as sharp as Incompetence, but that doesn't matter to the thirty-four-year-old woman he's with who can't stop thinking about how beautiful he is. She won't be thinking that in another eighteen years, when her husband is unemployed and their two teenage children are taking remedial courses.

"Most humans today get married because of passion and desire," says Infatuation, leaning over to check himself out in the polished surface of our table. "Especially those who meet over a few gin and tonics. You just don't tend to find love in bars. Not in Lower Manhattan, anyway."

Before I can respond, Infatuation leans over and says, "Speak of the devil."

When one of us says, *Speak of the devil*, it's not uncommon to actually see Satan come strolling through the door. And when that happens, it's a good idea to just mind your own business. You don't want to get on Satan's bad side, especially now that he's trying to quit smoking.

In this instance, however, Infatuation was speaking in the figurative sense.

Contrary to popular mythology, Love is not a naked, winged being shooting arrows at mortals and causing them to fall in love. Instead, she wears a black sequined pantsuit with a black velvet cape and looks more like Judy Garland in *A Star Is Born*.

"Between you and me," says Infatuation, leaning over to whisper, "I think she could use a good makeover."

The thing about Love is that she's codependent.

I don't run into Love very often, since most of the people on my path don't tend to find her with any regularity, and I notice beneath the confident stride and inviting smile she appears to be fighting back tears. Even though there are more than a dozen couples in the lounge and many of them are physically attracted to one another, no one in here is looking for love.

Moments after entering the lounge, Love walks back toward the bar, escorted by laughter and catcalls from Passion and Desire, who are both drunk and starting to bloat.

"You know . . ." says Infatuation, pulling out a compact and flipping it open.

"Hold that thought," I say, getting up and following Love toward the bar, where I find her sitting at the end next to a drunk thirty-two-year-old man who'll be developing cirrhosis of the liver when he's forty-five.

"You're really cute," he slurs to Love, who is trying unsuccessfully to ignore him. "Can I buy you a drink?"

"Why don't you buy your wife a drink?" she says, indicating the woman sitting on the other side of him.

"Harry, can we go now?" says the woman, obviously not happy with the situation.

Maybe it's just me, but there doesn't seem to be any love between them.

"Just one more drink," says Harry. "One for me and one for this beautiful little lady who's stolen my heart."

"That's it," the wife says, getting up. "We're leaving."

"Scotch on the rocks," Love says to the bartender.

"But I love her," Harry says as his wife drags him out of the bar. "I love her!"

Love just ignores him and lights up a Winston, blowing the smoke at another man who has started to approach her with amorous intentions.

I pull up a stool next to her. "Tough day?"

"Why is it that every mortal man seems to think he's in love with the idea of me," she says, "rather than the person he's supposed to be in love with?"

"Is every human supposed to be in love with another?" I ask.

"In theory," she says. "But for some reason, it's just not working out that way. Lust and Desire and Infatuation seem to be the flavors of the day. Winston?" she asks, offering me the pack of cigarettes.

"No, thanks," I say. "Never developed a taste for them and don't want to start now."

"Not a good idea to tempt Fate—is that it?"

"Something like that," I say.

We make small talk for a while, long enough for Love to empty most of the Scotch from her rocks, until I finally get around to broaching the subject that's on my mind.

"Why do humans fall in love?" I ask.

"You say that as if it's some kind of choice."

"Point taken," I say. "Okay, so *how* do humans fall in love? How do you create the awareness that makes them realize they were meant for each other?"

"First of all, they don't so much fall in love as they discover it," she says. "Falling implies you're out of control, which is what Passion and Lust and Desire want you to feel. The problem is, they've done such a good job of marketing themselves that most humans who aren't ready for love get confused between me and their physical yearning."

I have to admit, I've seen my share of humans who screwed up their fates in the pursuit of love when all they really wanted was to get laid.

"The truth is, Fabio," she says, downing the rest of her Scotch, "love is a like a good book you can't put down and you wish would never end. But with Infatuation and Lust, rather than enjoying how the story unfolds, you just skip to the last chapter."

While I'm absorbing all of this, Love orders another Scotch on the rocks. In the back of the lounge, I hear Passion and Desire cackling.

"And second," says Love, pointing toward the lounge, "not everyone's ready to embrace me. Those couples back there, all caught up in their passion and their desire, they're not ready for love. They wouldn't know what to do with it. So I'm not going to waste my time on some man or woman who won't appreciate what I've given them."

"Okay," I say. "So if you're ready for love, then how do you know it's you and not Infatuation or Desire?"

Love smiles and looks down into her drink. "You just know."

Jerry used to say that all the time during his class on practical omniscience. Drove me nuts. I hated that class. Got a C-minus, and that's only because he graded on a bell curve.

"So what's all this interest in love, Fabio?" she asks.

"Just curious," I say, feigning indifference.

"Just curious, huh?" she says. "Well, if you ask me, there's a reason you've found each other."

"Found who?" I ask.

"Whoever it is you've fallen in love with."

"I don't know what you're talking about," I say.

"Come on, Fabio," she says. "Contrary to what they say about me, I'm not blind."

"Shakespeare said that, didn't he?" I say, trying to change the subject. "I think it was in *The Merchant of Venice*."

"Look," she says. "It's none of my business, but if you want my advice, don't go around sharing this with any of the others. If it gets back to Jerry, that'll be the end of it, and I don't want to see that happen because I have the feeling whoever she is, she's very special."

"Thanks," I say.

"And don't worry," Love says with a wink. "You're secret's safe with me."

We spend the rest of her second Scotch on the rocks talking about Romance and Affection and the good old days; then I leave just as a fifty-five-year-old man with an adolescent case of Alzheimer's approaches Love and asks her to marry him.

CHAPTER 17

I'm stalking Sara a few days later while she shows a three-bedroom condo in Harlem to a married couple who will divorce and re-marry each other three times over the next sixteen years, when I learn that Nicolas Jansen, the fine young man I goaded into stabbing me in an Amsterdam alley, has joined a monastery.

Uh-oh.

This most definitely wasn't in his future, immediate or other-wise, when I met him in that alley. He was supposed to bounce from drugs to prison and back again. Maybe even spend a little time eating leftover food out of garbage cans. Developing lesions. Breeding head lice.

Turns out after stabbing and presumably killing me, Nicolas felt so guilty about what he'd done and so afraid of being caught and sent off to prison that he sobered up waiting for the police to find him. But when the authorities failed to show up to haul him off and when news of the murder never showed up in the media, Nicolas saw that as a sign from Jerry and realized he'd been given a chance to start a new life, which he commenced by joining the Orthodox Monastery of Saint-Nicolas, located in the mountains in the South of France.

His fate more than likely changed the moment he stabbed me, but I was too preoccupied with getting my man suit repaired and falling in love with Sara to notice.

I probably should have kept tabs on Nicolas Jansen to see how things were going to play out for him, but I just figured he was going to spend more time in jail than in rehab. Plus it's not like I'm in constant, conscious awareness of what every one of my humans is doing. I suppose that's part of what Jerry was talking about when he told me to do my job better, but I just get so sick and tired of the same old story over and over and over that I tend to tune them out. Kind of like I do with Redundancy.

Then today, I do a quick scan and discover that my would-be murderer has improved his fate. Or rather, I improved his fate.

Rule #2: Don't improve anyone's assigned future.

This isn't exactly going to help my chances of getting employee of the month.

It's not like I did it on purpose. It was an accident. A reaction. A mistake. Still, I hope my role in Nicolas Jansen's improved fate manages to slip through the cracks without Jerry figuring out what happened. After all, we're talking about joining a monastery. It's not like Nicolas Jansen is going to be canonized. So there's really no reason for Jerry to notice, not unless he happens to do a random quality-control check on this month's predetermination balances. But Jerry's so behind in his paperwork I shouldn't have to worry.

Then why do I get the feeling there's something wrong?

"Hey, Faaaaabio."

A moment later, Destiny appears at my side, her mane of red hair flowing halfway down her bare back.

She's wearing a red satin, ankle-length, backless dress with a plunging neckline and red Italian pumps. From the glimpse of her cleavage and the absence of a panty line, she doesn't appear to be wearing any undergarments.

I'm not sure if it's the sexual heat radiating from Destiny, or the fact that I'm in love with a mortal woman who is on the path of an immortal sex maniac and both of them are in the same room, but my man suit is beginning to perspire.

"What brings you to Harlem?" I ask, trying to sound casual.

She nods toward Sara, who is showing the doomed-to-repeat-the-same-mistake-thrice married couple the features of the condo's gourmet kitchen. "Just checking up on one of my clients. You?"

"The same," I say, gesturing toward George and Carla Baer, who are already arguing with each other over whether or not they can afford the $1.973 million the condo will cost them.

"Are you sure you're not here for her?" says Destiny.

"Why would I be here for her?" I ask.

If red is the color of guilt, then color me scarlet.

"Oh, I don't know," says Destiny, crawling up on to the kitchen counter and lying down on her side. "Maybe because you're in love with her."

Honesty. That veracious bitch. I should have known better than to trust her.

"I don't know what you're talking about," I say.

"Really?" she says, kicking off her pumps and stretching out on her back like a cat, her breasts and nipples outlined in red satin. "Then how about we play some noncontact doctor?"

I look at her stretched out on the kitchen counter, looking hot and mouthwatering in her trappings of sexuality. The last thing I want is to admit how I feel about Sara to Destiny. But I can't risk accepting Destiny's invitation and inadvertently making contact with her and suddenly appearing in front of Sara.

And by "inadvertently making contact," I mean having sex.

Destiny slides off the counter, her dress hiking up to reveal that, indeed, she's not wearing any underwear. "Take off your clothes."

"No," I say.

"Come on, Fabio," she says, moving toward me, her perfect breasts unencumbered inside her satin dress.

I back away toward the living room, trying to think about gladiators.

"You know you want me," she says, cornering me against an arm of the black leather couch, the dress slipping off her shoulders and falling to the ground around her feet in a puddle of red.

I don't have to be Honesty to admit I want her. But at the moment I'm trying to channel Chastity.

"It's your fate," she whispers maddeningly, her naked body inches away, her lips almost brushing against my ear.

Gladiators and Chastity are no match for the sexual allure of Destiny, so instead of standing up to her, I fall back over the arm of the couch, roll on to my feet, then run around to the other side.

"Coward," she says, crawling on to the couch on her hands and knees. "Come over here and teach me to be a good girl."

"You're a slut," I say.

"Oh, Faaaaabio," she says, rolling over and tossing her head back, cupping her breasts. "I love it when you talk dirty. I wish I'd worn my collar."

"I'm not interested," I say.

"Are you sure?" she asks, rolling onto her side. "I'll even let you wear my dress."

"I don't look good in red," I say.

"Suit yourself," says Destiny, vacating the couch just before the married couple sits down on it to discuss whether or not they should buy the condo. "I'll just have to find someone else who can fit into a size six."

As the couple and Sara go about their business, completely unaware of the sexual battle that just transpired, Destiny slips back into her dress.

"I think it's kind of cute," says Destiny.

"What's kind of cute?"

"The fact that you have a crush on her," she says. "Weird, but cute."

"What's weird about it?" I ask, realizing I've just admitted to my feelings.

Destiny just smiles as she slides her feet back into her pumps. "By the way," she says, looking me up and down, "is that a new man suit?"

First Honesty and now Secrecy? Doesn't anyone adhere to any standards anymore?

Destiny circles around me, licking her lips. "Looks good, Fabio. What happened to the one Secrecy stitched up for you?"

"What did she tell you?" I ask.

"Oh, a little of this and a little of that," says Destiny. "She's pretty talkative, that Secrecy, once she's had a few drinks."

Great. Not only does Destiny know I've fallen in love with a mortal, but she knows about Amsterdam. But how much does she know? I guess it doesn't matter. All Jerry needs is a reason to investigate one of my humans and discover I've altered his fate and before you know it, I'm shoveling brimstone dog shit at one of Satan's dogfighting farms during Mardi Gras.

"So what do you want from me?" I ask, as if I didn't know.

"Don't worry, Fabio," she says, sliding up close to me, her lips a breath away from my ear. "Your secret is safe with me."

And with that, she's gone. Off to Las Vegas or Bangkok or wherever it is that omnipresent, immortal sluts go.

When I return my attention to the mortals in the condo with me, Sara has excused herself to the balcony, where she's enjoying the breathtaking view of Central Park, while the soon-to-be-divorced couple argues about the condo.

The wife wants to buy it while the husband thinks it's a bad idea. They can't afford it. He's lobbying for something smaller, maybe in Chelsea. But she's not having any of that. She wants the floor-to-ceiling windows and the marble bathroom and the gourmet kitchen and the uptown prestige. She's going to get her way, as usual, and he's going to resent her for it. As usual.

This is the death knell for their first go-round. They'll buy the condo, live in it for less than two years, and then he'll file for divorce. Five years later, after they've remarried, they'll do it all again, only without the $2 million condo, but with the same results.

Sometimes I feel like I'm a babysitter for a bunch of undisciplined, uncontrollable brats.

It would make my job a lot easier if they didn't buy this place, if he would just stand up to her and say, "No, we can't afford it."

That's all she wants, really. A strong, forceful man who stands his ground and takes control of situations. Someone who will make all of the decisions for her. Someone the complete opposite of her father, who fell apart when their mother died, so she, the oldest child, had to take care of the family until her younger siblings had graduated from high school.

But he's not that man. He wants to placate her, to make her happy, to give her the things she wants because he doesn't realize he's doing just the opposite. And so he sits there and surrenders to her arguments and acquiesces to her demands and submits to her every wish because he loves her and he just wants her to be happy rather than standing up for himself. Rather than taking charge of the situation and telling his controlling, baggage-carrying wife to just shut the hell up.

That's what I wish he would do. Right now. Take control of the situation. Show her he's in charge. Be the man she wants him to be.

Irritated and frustrated, both by this maddening couple and my encounter with Destiny, I walk over behind the couch, lean down close enough to George Baer that I can smell his sweat and cologne, and shout, "Just tell her to shut the hell up!"

"Will you just shut the hell up?" he says.

His wife and I stare at him, our lower jaws unhinged.

"What?" she says.

What? I think.

"We're not buying this place," he says. "We can't afford it. So we're just going to have to find another place that's more reasonably priced."

I don't know who's more surprised—her, the husband, or me. But just like that, I can see it unfolding before me. A shifting of reality. A new future.

Uh-oh. I think I did it again.

They're not going to get divorced in a year. Or at all, for that matter. Instead, the wife is finally going to get to give in to her desire to be taken care of, to have all of her decisions made for her, to be relieved of the burden of responsibility. Eventually, their new dynamic will lead to a dominant/submissive relationship that will develop into a full-blown journey into the world of BDSM. This time next year, she'll be wearing a ball gag and a leather mono-glove while confined to a custom-built cage complete with tethers and restraints.

Maybe not as noble as joining a monastery, but it's still an improvement on their assigned fates.

Although Carla Baer is unhappy about not getting the condo, she's so shocked by her husband's sudden decisiveness and authority that she barely musters a cursory rebuttal. By the time they leave, the husband's new take-charge demeanor has given him the confidence to make dinner reservations at his favorite restaurant and to tell his wife they'll be vacationing in Mexico this year. And I'm wondering if I've inadvertently made things better or worse.

Maybe it wasn't my subliminally shouted suggestion.

Maybe it was just a coincidence.

Maybe he changed their fate all on his own.

Right. And maybe Destiny will become a nun.

CHAPTER 18

I've never been a big fan of change. I like my routines and the way my furniture is arranged and how my pillows are fluffed. I'm a Taurus, after all. But this is a little more significant than what side of the bed I sleep on.

Changing the fates of humans isn't like changing a lightbulb. It can create serious repercussions, not only for the human whose fate you changed but for every other human that person comes into contact with. It's the whole six-degrees-of-separation concept, only instead of just being a number of steps away from knowing someone, each human is a number of steps away from impacting the fate of every other human on the planet.

A kind word from one person to another can lead to another kind word, paying the kindness forward in a series of beneficent words or deeds that can change the paths of everyone involved. Similarly, disparaging words or acts of violence can end up affecting more than just the initial recipient. Just look at Ed Gein or Ted Bundy or any number of abusers or molesters or serial killers throughout history. The number of lives they impacted is immeasurable.

Not that I'm expecting Nicolas Jansen to hack up his newfound monastic brothers or George and Carla Baer to start stocking their refrigerator with human body parts, but I have to consider the consequences of my actions.

All the people who would have fallen victim to Nicolas Jansen's life of crime and drugs will no longer have that experience as a factor in their lives. All of his would-be cell mates and dealers and street family won't know his negative influence. And all of those who would have tried to help Nicolas will not have to face the disappointment of his failures.

His parents finally have hope for his future. The other monks at the Orthodox Monastery of Saint-Nicolas will be affected by their new brother. And the humans Nicolas comes into contact with will be inspired by his words and deeds.

Similarly, George and Carla Baer won't inflict their insecurities or neuroses upon anyone else. They'll be happier people and will spread that happiness to the other people in their lives, and those people will in turn be affected in a positive manner and will pass those vibes along to the people they know and meet. And so on, and so on, and so on.

So without meaning to, I've affected several million humans. Some more than others. But they're all better off to some extent today than they were yesterday. And most of them don't even know it. They're oblivious to their fate. To me. To the changing circumstances of their lives.

And I'm wondering if I'm going to get away with this.

"Get away with what?" asks Sara.

Apparently, I was wondering in my out-loud voice again.

Sara and I are snuggling on her couch, watching *No Reservations with Anthony Bourdain* on the Travel Channel, and eating popcorn. This is not something I've ever done. Any of it. I've never snuggled, I've never watched the Travel Channel, and I hate popcorn. If Styrofoam had a flavor, it would taste like popcorn. But I'm sharing it with Sara and pretending to like it because I enjoy any activity that involves being with her.

"Nothing," I say. "It's just work stuff."

"What kind of work stuff?" asks Sara, grabbing a handful of popcorn as Anthony Bourdain eats his way around Naples, Italy.

That's another one of the problems I've discovered about dating a mortal woman. She likes to talk about everything.

Problems.

Feelings.

Sex.

Typically, any mortal sex I've had has been a one-night stand. Even my trysts with other immortals can't be described as relationships. And while Destiny and I have had an off-and-on thing for most of our existence, we haven't exactly been exclusive.

So deep, meaningful, let's-get-to-know-each-other conversation has never been something I've practiced. Not to mention the fact that any significant conversation is going to involve revealing details about me, about who I am and what I do.

Rule #3: Never reveal that you're immortal.

Naturally that means I have to lie. Which I'm beginning to discover bothers me more than I realized it would.

"I made a mistake," I say.

"Everyone makes mistakes," says Sara. "That's just part of being human."

I almost laugh, until I realize she's being serious.

When you make a mistake at Round Table Pizza, you're affecting somebody's meal. When you make a mistake at the Gap, you're affecting somebody's wardrobe. When you make a mistake at Charles Schwab, you're affecting somebody's financial security. But when you make a mistake in my line of work, you kind of have to factor in how it will affect the fate of all mankind.

To an extent, human beings are kind of like pizzas and relaxed-fit jeans and retirement accounts—some of them are of more consequence than others. Though to be fair, there are a lot more pizzas in the world than IRAs. Still, that doesn't mean a pizza can't have an impact on someone's financial future.

On the television, Anthony Bourdain is eating pizza.

"So what did you do?" asks Sara.

"I gave someone the wrong information," I say.

Sara is under the impression I'm a stockbroker, working in international commodities. Which isn't entirely false. After all, I broker stock in human beings and I trade in the commodity of fate.

"What kind of wrong information?" she asks.

"The kind that could get me in trouble," I say.

The thing about Sara is that she has infinite patience.

"Okay," she says, putting down the popcorn. "This mistake you made. Is it going to kill anyone?"

"No."

"Is it going to cause the end of the world?"

I have to think about that one before I shake my head. "I don't think so."

"Is it going to get you fired?"

Chances are that with everything else he has to contend with, Jerry isn't going to notice the artificially adjusted fates of three inconsequential pizzas. It's not as though they did anything remarkable or memorable or groundbreaking, like lay the foundation for Western philosophy or refuse to give up their seat on a bus or shoot a fifty-nine at the Masters. They made choices that thousands of humans make every day.

"Probably not," I say.

"Then let it go," says Sara, curling up next to me. "Whatever mistake you made, it's probably not as big a deal as you think. And even if it ends up being a problem, you have everything you need inside of you to fix it."

Sara has one knee across my thigh, one hand across my chest, and her head against my shoulder. I smell her hair, the scent of her shampoo. I hear the soft exhalations of her breath. I feel her pulse vibrating through my man suit. And I suddenly feel better about everything.

This is a strange sensation, this affection and familiarity, this intimacy without sex. This having someone care about me, about my concerns, and making me feel better. That warm and tingly sensation I get whenever I think about Sara is suddenly a full-blown fever. And I'm filled with an exhilaration I've never experienced.

So I do something I've never done before. I squeeze Sara and hold her close; then I kiss her on the crown of her head, enjoying the feel of her without wanting sex. When she looks up at me, I kiss both of her eyes and her forehead, then smile at her. She smiles back before returning her attention to the television, snuggling in closer.

And just like that, I feel better about everything.

When I first realized what I'd done, that I'd interfered in the fates of several humans, I wondered how I could fix it, how I could put them back on the paths they'd been on before I got in the way. But the more I think about it, the more I realize that putting everything back the way it was isn't possible. And I wouldn't want to put it back even if I could.

For my entire existence I've known what was coming next. For myself and for my humans. Now, all of a sudden, my world is filled with uncertainty. With the unknown. With excitement. There's something about the not knowing what's going to happen that I find thrilling. With me. With Sara. With the three humans I've helped to choose a better path.

And I'm thinking, Could I get away with it if I did it again?

I mean, Jerry didn't exactly become an omniscient being by taking shop classes and falling asleep during physics. So there's a good chance he'll catch on eventually. Unless he's so distracted that I could fly under the radar. Which is possible. Jerry's very busy these days and has a tendency to let things slide. Except when the things involve Destiny or Fate or one of the Revelations. So I have to be careful if I'm going to meddle in the lives of my simpleton charges.

I realize I'll be breaking the first rule, but if I just give them suggestions, subtle hints, a gentle nudge in the right direction, then it's not like I'm exceeding the parameters of their preassigned fates. I'm just helping to set them back on their original paths. I'm just helping them to optimize their futures. And if I can help some of them by pointing them in the right direction, by crafting their fates in spite of the messes they've made of their lives, maybe I can help myself. Maybe I can rediscover why I used to enjoy this job in the first place.

For the first time in five hundred years, I feel like I'm relevant again.

CHAPTER 19

The last time I felt like I mattered was during the waning decades of the Renaissance. True, Destiny had the lion's share of those responsible for the rebirth of human achievement—Cervantes, da Vinci, Shakespeare. But instead of being fed to the lions like so many of my clients during Rome's prosperity, those on my list during the Renaissance—Dante, Botticelli, Raphael—at least played a part in changing human existence for the better.

Ever since then, things have gone gradually downhill.

Sure, great thinkers and scientists and painters like Nietzsche and Edison and van Gogh came along after that, but they weren't on my path. No. I got stuck with missionaries and dictators and presidents who spread religion and waged war and dropped nuclear bombs. Not to mention I had to endure the fates of the tens of millions of humans who were directly or indirectly killed by their actions.

So when I discover that I've made a difference in the fates of twenty-first-century humans, even if it's just sending a drug addict to a French monastery or a dysfunctional married couple to a future of bondage and discipline, I almost feel like I've found a new lease on the inevitable. As if I have the opportunity to reinvent myself.

A new and improved Fate.

Benefactor of mankind.

Or at least of human train wrecks.

My first official attempt at altering the fate of a human is Amanda Drake, a forty-five-year-old crystal meth addict who lives in London's East End. She's been on crank off and on for most of her adult life and done prison time for shoplifting, forgery, petty theft, and impersonating a member of the royal family. She's also spent an accumulated three years in drug rehab.

I picked Amanda Drake for several reasons.

One, she's on today's schedule.

Two, she needs help.

And three, I closed my eyes and pointed to her name on my list.

The last thing I want to do is create any kind of a pattern, help too many humans in any one demographic or geographic category. So I figure randomly choosing someone is the smartest thing for me to do. Though I don't know if intelligence is much of a factor in my decision-making process.

Amanda's original assigned path had her working as a waitress and never getting married and dying alone in a convalescent hospital at the age of sixty-eight. Not the most fulfilling of fates, but better than the one she's managed to create for herself.

When I pop in on her unannounced, Amanda is consuming a

breakfast of pseudoephedrine, muriatic acid, brake cleaner, acetone, lye, and denatured alcohol. Personally, I would have ordered the waffles and bacon.

Amanda lives in a two-bedroom apartment on top of a dry cleaner's and shares the space with a young, drug-free, unmarried couple who told her last night she has to move out. She also recently lost her job at the dry cleaner's downstairs when the owner caught her huffing dry-cleaning solvents.

Without a job or a place to live, Amanda will end up on the streets begging for money and eventually turning to prostitution in order to support her drug habit. She'll lose weight, develop kidney problems, get raped more than once, and discover that no matter how low she gets, there's always another ladder leading down.

In less than five years, Amanda Drake will be dead.

Why couldn't I have picked someone a little easier to start out with? Like a cat fetishist or a compulsive eater or a submissive coprophilliac? Some human with just one major issue instead of a woman with enough problems to fill an entire week's worth of *Jerry Springer*?

Honestly, I don't understand how human beings ended up like this. They're the only creatures on the planet who think they're supposed to be happy. They worry about money and their future and their legacy. They worry about war and disease and death. They worry about sex and love and relationships. But mostly they worry about why they're not happy.

After more than five thousand years of advanced civilization, it still boggles my mind.

So here sits Amanda Drake, borderline anorexic with scabs on her face, a victim of her own misery, a woman who could have chosen to make her life better but instead chose to allow it to fall apart, year by year, until she finally reached the point where Dennis is waiting just around the proverbial corner.

As I sit and watch her pack up what few possessions she still owns into a worn and dirty canvas knapsack, its shoulder strap held together with safety pins, I begin to wonder what I'm doing here. This woman can't be helped. And even if she could, does she deserve to be? She's had every opportunity to fix her life on her own, without my help. What she needs, instead, is to be put out of her misery.

But as much as I'd like to help her, I'm not the one for that job. She'll have to wait until Dennis comes calling in five years. In the meantime, I have a plethora of other disheartened, disenchanted, and discontented humans to practice my newfound benevolence on. So I pull out my list and close my eyes and wave my index finger in the air to select another human.

Before I can make my selection and dematerialize out of there, Amanda lets out a sound that makes me stop. I hesitate a moment, my back turned to her, hoping what I thought I heard wasn't what I thought I heard. But then Amanda lets out another sob.

I turn around and find Amanda on her knees, doubled over the half-packed knapsack, her hands covering her face, her body shaking with the force of her sobs.

Damn it. And I was so close to making a clean getaway.

I've never been much of a comforting presence and I've never known what to say to a crying woman, so I start thinking positive thoughts to try to get Amanda to stop. But she just keeps sobbing, reaching the point where sound is no longer escaping her lips and saliva has started to drip from her mouth.

Sometimes humans really gross me out.

So I start speaking out loud.

"Hey, it's okay. You don't have to cry.

"Come on, Amanda. Things will get better.

"Jesus, will you put a cork in it, already?"

I keep thinking maybe something will get through to her like it did to George Baer back in the condo. Instead, I seem to be making things worse.

Finally, faced with no other options and getting frustrated, I look around to make sure we're alone; then I materialize and say the two words that always seem to get the desired result.

"Shut up!"

It works. Amanda shuts up. The crying stops. The drooling continues, but you can't expect miracles.

"What . . . ?" she says, looking at me, her eyes filled first with confusion, then terror. "What . . . ?"

"I said, shut up."

She closes her mouth, her lips still trembling, tears glistening on her cheeks and spittle running down her chin.

"That's better," I say.

I'm sure she thinks I'm here to hurt her or rape her or commit some atrocity, so I need to proceed with caution. Make sure I don't say anything that might alarm her. Just give her a subtle nudge in the right direction.

"Now listen to me, you pathetic waste of Jerry's talents," I say.

"If you don't get your shit together, you're going to be dead inside of five years."

Okay. Maybe not so subtle, but at least I made my point.

"Dead?" she says.

"Yes, that's right. Dead. D-E-A-D. Dead. Is that what you want?"

She shakes her head vigorously from side to side.

While I'm sure she's telling the truth, that she doesn't want to die, I still don't see her making it to her fiftieth birthday. Instead, because of my sudden appearance and announcement of her impending death, she's going to end up snorting so much crystal meth that her pipes will get permanently cleaned inside of a year.

Apparently, this helping people is trickier than I thought.

"Look," I say. "I know you're probably sincere about not wanting to die, but I'm just not buying it. So let's try this again. Do you want to die?"

She suddenly starts crying again.

"What?" I ask.

She lets out a couple of sobs, then wipes her runny nose with the sleeve of one arm. "Are y-y-you . . . g-gonna . . . k-k-kill m-m-me?"

"Do I look like Death?" I say. "Is my hair white? Do I have colored contacts? Am I wearing mortician's gloves?"

She shakes her head, even though she's not sure about the colored contacts.

"So no, I'm not here to kill you," I say. "I'm here to save your sorry ass."

Her sobs taper off, turning into sniffles. When she looks up, there's something like bewilderment in her eyes. "You're here to save me?"

"That's what I've been trying to tell you."

Honestly, humans can be so difficult to deal with sometimes. They're worse than baboons. Harder to toilet train, too.

"Are you from the clinic?" she asks.

Clinic? What clinic?

"No, I'm not from the clinic."

"Did Mrs. Devon send you?"

Again with the questions. "Look," I say, "will you just shut up? You're making this a lot more work than it needs to be."

"But I don't understand," she says.

"What's there to understand?" I say. "You need to stop doing drugs. You need to get a job. And you need to put your life back together. It's pretty simple, really."

"But I don't know how," she says, the tears starting to flow again. "I've made so many mistakes. . . ."

I wonder if Jerry had this much trouble trying to convince Noah to build his ark.

So I stand there and I think, trying to figure out what I can do to convince Amanda that things aren't as hopeless as she thinks they are, that she can fix her life.

And then it comes to me.

"Everyone makes mistakes," I say, walking over and crouching down in front of her. "That's just part of being human. But you have everything you need inside of you to fix it."

Sara's words coming out of my mouth.

"Really?" she says, staring up at me. For the first time since I showed up, her face actually expresses something that looks like hope.

"Really," I say. "You've just forgotten how to find it. But it's there."

Before I know it, I'm reaching over and brushing away her tears with my thumb.

And then it happens. Her fate changes. I see her clean and sober, working part-time at a clothing store near Piccadilly Circus and volunteering at a women's shelter. I even see the potential for romance. A slight improvement over her assigned fate, but nothing I'm worried about. After all, she's still going to die before she turns seventy.

"Who are you?" she asks.

"I'm your guardian angel," I say, standing up. "So don't piss me off."

And with that, I vanish into thin air.

CHAPTER 20

I'm at a bar in Duluth, Minnesota. Not exactly my first choice for a great place to hang out, but this is where Darren Stafford spends most of his time since he lost his job teaching high school biology—not to mention his home, his wife, his self-respect, and the paternity suit brought against him by his star seventeen-year-old biology student. So even though his two teenage sons are nearly out of high school, he'll still be paying child support for the next eighteen years.

Fortunately for Darren, the age of consent in Minnesota is sixteen, which means he didn't lose his freedom for banging one of his students. However, had she been an American woodcock, a snowy owl, a boreal chickadee, or a common loon, Darren would have been looking at six months' probation and over a hundred hours of community service, since Minnesota's law prohibits sex between humans and birds.

I'm not making this up.

As sexually deviant as human beings are, I'm always amazed

at the lengths they'll go to in order to satisfy their urges. Still, it's mind-boggling to think that someone can look at a crow or a hummingbird or a red-breasted wren and say, "Mmm, I'd like to get me some of that."

As far as I know, Darren Stafford isn't a beak-and-feathers man, but he is a Jim Beam man. Straight up. And right now, he's almost through his second round of the day, which isn't even twelve hours old yet.

"What'll you have?" asks the bartender, a forty-nine-year-old career mixologist who'll be doing this until he dies of lung cancer before he turns sixty.

"Jim Beam," I say, sitting down a few stools away from Darren. "Straight up."

I hate drinking alcohol unchilled or without ice, but I've learned I can't expect humans to flat-out believe me when I tell them I know what's going to happen to them, so I figure developing a little trust is the best way to get my message across.

Darren Stafford glances down the bar, raises his nearly empty glass to me, then downs the rest of his Jim Beam in a single gulp.

"And whatever he's drinking," I say to the bartender.

"Make it a double," says Darren, as he moves down the bar a couple of stools closer.

I admit, picking Darren Stafford wasn't a random choice like Amanda. But the next person on my List of Stupid Humans to Help lives in North Dakota, so I popped over to the Land of 10,000 Lakes to see how my favorite disgraced high school biology teacher was doing.

"Tough week," I say.

"You have no idea," says Darren.

There's nothing like buying a drink for a lonely drunk to make him your best friend. Unless, of course, you buy him two or three. The drinks come and Darren spills his story to his new bestest buddy, which is far more skewed a tale in his defense than I could have thought possible. It's almost like a fairy tale of love and innocence and betrayal, rather than a really stupid decision on his part.

This, coupled with his taking advantage of my generosity by ordering a double and the fact that I can barely choke down my drink without vomiting into my glass, makes me question just how dedicated I am to saving him from his path of drunken despair. Until he suddenly breaks down and starts crying.

"Listen," I say, putting one arm on his shoulder to offer comfort.

Other than the mortal women I've had sex with over the millennia, I avoid touching humans. My humans, anyway. It's not so much the texture of their bodies as it is the qualities they emanate. It's like touching flesh glistening with sweat and emitting a foul body odor.

"Listen," I say, withdrawing my hand and trying to breathe through my mouth. "You don't have to stay here and do this to yourself. You have a choice."

I want to add *moron*, but I don't think that would be constructive criticism.

"Choice?" he says, wiping his nose on his sleeve. "What choice? I'm fucked."

"No," I say. "You got fucked and you fucked someone you

shouldn't have, and because you did A you got B, but that doesn't mean you have to stay fucked."

He doesn't believe me. Not until I start to tell him the details of his affair, filling in the blanks he purposely left out and correcting the tale of fantasy he spun.

"How do you know all of this?" he asks, his eyes suddenly filled with suspicion. "You a cop or a lawyer or something?"

"Just a friend," I say, nearly gagging on the word. "Someone who knows you better than you know yourself."

"Well, if you know me so well," he says, slurring his words and sloshing half of his newly refreshed drink over the sides of his glass, "then maybe you can tell me why I slept with that little bitch in the first place."

I tell him why. Then I tell him what was going through his head the morning he stood on his prize pupil's back porch. I tell him what he wanted to be when he grew up and all of the bad choices he made along the way that prevented him from realizing his dreams. Then I tell him what's going to become of him if he doesn't get out of this bar right now.

"I'm going to be having sex with birds?" he says.

No. But I thought it sounded better than homelessness and crabs. Besides, you can never be too careful. That and I belong to the National Audubon Society.

But I don't have to worry about Darren Stafford having sex with any loons. And I don't have to worry about him wallowing in a drunken depression for the next dozen years. After our little chat here today, he's going to discover he can start over and that there's life after a massive screwup. Though he will fall in love with a nineteen-year-old science student at the community college where he'll be teaching.

Some things never change.

"But why would I be having sex with birds?" asks Darren.

I tell him I don't know. Maybe it has something to do with self-flagellation for the mistakes he's made and the lives he's ruined.

"Having sex with birds is against the law in Minnesota," says the bartender, tapping the ashes from his Camel into an ashtray.

"It's against the law where I come from, too," I say.

"And where's that?" asks the bartender, well on his way to developing lung cancer.

"Heaven," I say, then blink out of existence.

I always loved *It's a Wonderful Life*.

A few seconds later, before the bartender or Darren has a chance to react, I rematerialize at the bar.

"By the way," I say to the bartender, "you might want to give up smoking if you want to keep both of your lungs and live to see your grandson play college football at Michigan."

Then I'm gone again.

I know it's not a good idea to show off like that, but sometimes I just can't help myself. Besides, neither one of them is going to mention a thing about me to anyone else. Not even to each other. After today, Darren Stafford is never going to step foot in that bar, or any other bar, for the rest of his life. And the bartender, though still fated to die of lung cancer, will at least make it to see his grandson play starting weak side linebacker for the University of Michigan.

There's not much I can do once a disease has taken hold of

someone. It's not like I can reverse the damage that's done or prevent it from evolving. But I can tell them they can fight it. That they don't have to believe all of the statistics and the percentages and the odds against them surviving longer than what the specialists tell them. I can give them hope. Which, admittedly, isn't exactly my strong suit.

Hopelessness. Failure. Despair. These are the instruments of my trade, have been for longer than I care to remember. I've grown used to them. Comfortable with them. They've become as much a part of my daily existence as eating and breathing and noncontact sex. They're part of my routine. They're part of my lifestyle. They're part of my nature.

I realize I've been a lot like my humans—stuck in a rut and used to doing things in such a way that I couldn't see any other way of doing them. And that really bothers me, on a level that goes beyond disgust and self-loathing.

I'm like my humans. We're the same. They're a reflection of me. I'm a reflection of them. And that's a bigger dose of reality than I'm prepared to handle right now.

CHAPTER 21

Over the next couple of weeks I traverse the globe, from Bogotá to Budapest to Bali, helping men and women and children fated to futures of mediocrity and oppression and bad haircuts. Go ahead—scoff if you want. But you have no idea the impact a bad haircut can have on a person's future.

I don't have to appear in the flesh to help most of them, and I don't pull a repeat of materializing out of thin air like I did with Amanda Drake or Darren Stafford. Not a good idea to have too many humans talking about a guardian angel appearing before them. Before you know it, my picture's all over the papers and airwaves and I'm being booked for interviews on *Larry King* and *Oprah*, which would really piss off Jerry. Oprah has *never* invited him on her show.

On a couple of occasions, however, I'm forced to interact with my humans as one of their own, offering words of encouragement or friendly suggestions or sometimes a smack on the back of the head. That one didn't go over real well with the abusive husband in Munich. Which would explain why I had to call up Ingenuity again to repair my face.

I'm still getting the hang of this.

When you've spent the better part of the last few hundred years growing jaded and bitter toward inferior creatures who excel at making asses of themselves on a regular basis, changing your attitude toward them isn't something that happens overnight. But I'm trying to work with my humans, teach them how to get their lives back on track so that they're happier, which in turn makes me happier. I feel like I'm beginning to understand them a little better, though I'm still behind the learning curve when it comes to Sara. I'm not any closer to understanding her destiny than I was before. If anything, I feel like I'm farther from finding the answers. It's as if by getting closer to her, I've lost the ability to see clearly.

"Good morning," says Sara, lying on her side, staring at me from her pillow.

It's Sunday morning and we're in Sara's bedroom, which, while laid out exactly like mine, is much warmer and more inviting.

Deep red walls.

Earth-tone bedding.

No mirrored ceiling.

"Do you know that you never wake up with a shadow?" she says.

"What?" I ask, thinking this is the beginning of some kind of philosophical discussion about archetypes and Jungian psychology.

"A shadow," she says. "Facial hair continues to grow overnight on men, so even if they shave at night they wake up with a shadow."

Sara brushes her fingers against my face. "Your skin's as smooth as when you went to sleep."

That's another problem with dating a mortal woman. She notices things about me that no one's ever supposed to notice. Like the fact that I don't have any body odor.

Or that I never have to clip my fingernails.

Or that I don't need to shave.

"I had laser hair removal," I say, because it's the only answer I can come up with.

"That's too bad," she says. "I like an occasional scruffy look."

Note to self: Have Ingenuity install some facial hair follicles.

"So what did you want to be when you were a little boy?" asks Sara, tracing a finger across my chest.

"Me?" I say.

"No," says Sara. "The other guy I'm sleeping with."

"Why do you want to know what I was like when I was a little boy?" I ask.

"Just curious," she says, her long, delicate finger working its way toward my navel. If I had ever been a little boy, what she's doing would make me forget all about climbing trees and playing stickball. Then her finger starts tracing another part of my anatomy.

"I wanted to determine the fates of all human beings on the planet," I blurt out.

"Really?" she says, her hand sliding back up past my waist as she places her chin on my chest and looks at me. "Isn't that kind of ambitious for a little boy?"

I just shrug. There's no need to tell her that Ambition is a woman.

"Well, then," she says, throwing one leg across my hips and climbing on top of me, her lips against my ear. "If you're so interested in people's fates, why don't you start with mine?"

Half an hour later, we're at the kitchen table wearing bathrobes, drinking coffee, and eating cold leftover pasta from Nick's. Sara eats like this all the time. Never cooks. Doesn't even bother to heat leftovers in the oven but eats them right out of the box or container—Chinese food, pasta, omelettes. Even soup. As it turns out, she doesn't own any dishes, which explains why I'm eating spaghetti marinara with meatballs out of a travel coffee mug from Starbucks.

"So what did *you* want to be when you grew up?" I ask.

I'm still trying to understand Sara, hoping she'll reveal something that will shed some light on her destiny. Give me a glimpse into her future.

"When I was a little girl, I wanted to be a Gypsy."

"A Gypsy?" I say, not really sure how that helps me.

"I wanted to roam the countryside performing for people," she says. "I wanted to entertain them and make them laugh and sell them bottles of water they thought were magic potion."

"So you wanted to make fools of people," I say.

"Then I wanted to be a nun," she says.

"Why a nun?"

"I think it was to make up for wanting to be a Gypsy."

Makes sense.

"After that, I wanted to be a cowgirl, a rock star, a dentist, a madam, a barista, a human pincushion, a lounge singer, a dog walker, a cheerleader, a trapeze artist, a cabdriver, a paleontologist, and a bounty hunter."

So much for learning about Sara's future from her past.

"Why did you get into real estate?" I ask.

"I just sort of fell into it," she says. "But there's something rewarding about helping someone find someplace they can call home. It's like helping people find their dreams."

Okay, now we're getting somewhere.

Of course, just because Sara possesses some noble qualities doesn't explain why people react to her the way they do. Her effect on people isn't necessarily a reflection of who she is but of who she's destined to become.

It's both exciting and disconcerting to be this close to her and yet have really no idea who she is or where she's headed. When you're used to reading the futures of eighty-three percent of the world's population and knowing how things turn out, being unable to read the person you're in love with takes some getting used to. She's like a blank television screen. All I can see is an opaque reflection of the present.

I suppose I should be concerned with Destiny's knowledge about my interest in Sara, considering I'm now guilty of multiple counts of interfering. So far, I've purposely altered the fates of more than two hundred mortals. Not exactly a significant number in the grand cosmic scheme, and most of them were just set back on their original paths, but when you take into consideration the impact those two hundred or so humans will have on the other humans they come in contact with, the numbers could conceivably increase exponentially.

Kind of like a plague, only I'm spreading hope instead of disease.

But I'm on a high from helping people. I feel invigorated. Inviolate. Invincible. Which isn't much of a stretch, considering I'm immortal. Besides, I haven't seen Destiny in a more than a month. Maybe she's forgotten about me and decided to let me have my fun.

"Do you believe in destiny?" asks Sara.

Having spaghetti and meatballs come shooting out of your nose isn't nearly as much fun as it sounds.

"Destiny?" I say, coughing.

"You know," she says. "The inevitable path that determines your life."

"That's fate," I say, removing a chunk of meatball from my left nostril.

"Really?" she asks. "Are you sure about that?"

"I'm pretty sure."

"Then what's destiny?"

I explain the difference to her without getting too technical or portraying Destiny as a whore, which isn't easy.

"Mostly it comes down to a matter of choice," I say. "With fate, there is none. Your outcome is determined by a force outside of your choosing. With destiny, you're more involved in the decision-making process."

"So destiny is better," she says.

"Well, I wouldn't go so far as to say—"

"And fate pretty much sucks."

This conversation isn't going in a direction that works for me.

"Fate's just misunderstood," I say. Which isn't entirely accurate. I do suck. But I'm working on it.

"Why do you want to know if I believe in destiny?" I ask, trying to steer the conversation away from my shortcomings.

"I don't know," she says, taking a bite of pizza and talking with her mouth full. "I just have this feeling you and I were destined to meet."

While that's an endearing thought, it's not likely. Immortals can't show up on one another's radar. And we most definitely can't show up on the paths of mortals.

"And I've become friends with this woman I met in Central Park and we just started talking about fate and destiny," says Sara. "I guess it kind of stuck with me."

"Woman?" I ask, suspicious. "What woman?"

"Her name's Delilah," says Sara. "Gorgeous redhead. Fantastic body. Monochromatic wardrobe. Lives in SoHo. We're getting together for lunch next week."

No wonder I haven't seen much of Destiny lately. She's been hanging out with my girlfriend while I'm off fixing the fates of drug addicts, fallen teachers, and career politicians.

Destiny's breaking Rule #1. Not that I have any room to talk . . .

"What else did she say?" I ask.

Apparently, Destiny's been extolling the virtues of feminism, the empowerment of celibacy, and the benefits of self-gratification. I can almost hear Destiny's throaty laughter and I suddenly wonder if she's watching us right now.

Most of the time, when Destiny's around, I can sense her. We're kind of like identical twins that way, except we don't look anything alike and we occasionally have sex. But Sara is so distracting I suppose it's possible I never noticed Destiny watching us.

I shiver once in disgust and glance around Sara's apartment, checking to see if I can spot anything red situated conspicuously out of place, but all I see is earth tones. Sara's bedroom, on the other hand, has more red in it than Addiction's eyes.

"How do you know so much about fate and destiny, anyway?" asks Sara.

"Just a hobby," I say, getting up and walking toward the bedroom.

"Strange hobby," she says.

I stand at the entrance to the bedroom, looking around, knowing that Destiny isn't in there but unable to shake the feeling that she's somewhere nearby, keeping tabs on me. Or maybe I'm paranoid. Just in case, I extend both of my middle fingers, raise my arms and gesture emphatically, then stick my tongue out and let loose a solid raspberry.

"What are you doing?" Sara asks from the kitchen.

"Nothing," I say, walking back to her. "Just looking for Destiny."

"Well, you're looking in the wrong place," she says, leaning against the kitchen table, her bathrobe falling partially open, revealing a glimpse of her left breast. "Destiny is waiting for you right over here."

I have to say, Sara looks rather fetching partially disrobed among an assortment of take-out containers and plastic mugs. But Destiny poses a larger obstacle than I realized in my continued pursuit of happiness with Sara, which means I'm going to need some help. I know Sloth and Gluttony would be more than willing to offer their services, but a lactose-intolerant glutton and a pot-smoking narcoleptic aren't exactly what I have in mind.

I can't believe I'm about to say this, but . . .

"I can't," I say. "I have to go to work."

"But it's Sunday," says Sara, disappointment clouding her face and making me feel like Guilt. "I thought we were going to spend the day together."

"I know," I say. "But I have to meet with a client regarding international futures."

While not the truth, it's not entirely a prevarication, either. But I can't tell Sara I'm leaving the country to track down Death.

She moves away from the table, not bothering to close up her robe, and glides over to me.

"You sure you can't call in sick?" she asks, pressing against me.

I try to think about baseball or roadkill or Attila the Hun in a thong. Anything to keep my mind off Sara's warm, naked body.

"I wish I could," I say. "But I have to go."

"When will you be back?" she asks, putting her arms around me and holding tight, her breath tickling my ear.

"As soon as possible," I say. And that's no lie.

She pulls back and looks at me, her face an exquisite work of art I can picture in perfect detail when I close my eyes.

"Promise to stalk me later?" she asks.

Like I have to promise.

CHAPTER 22

You have to understand about Dennis.

First of all, even when he's not holding a five-hundred-year-old grudge against someone who used to be his best friend, he can come across as a little surly. After all, he is Death. Which wreaks havoc on his social life. In spite of his occasional attempts to throw dinner parties and host potlucks, it's kind of hard to escape the stigma associated with ending the lives of all humans. Most of the other Immortals think the job carries with it a burden of guilt. But when you've spent countless aeons dishing out plague and genocide and terrorism, you tend to develop a knack for dispassionate disposal.

Dennis once told me being Death was like conducting an orchestra that had been playing the same symphony forever and that he'd become so familiar with every meter and measure and movement he no longer gave any thought to his actions. The orchestration of death just came to him naturally.

Really, in spite of our falling-out, Dennis isn't a bad guy. He's just misunderstood.

It's not like he forces humans to consume diets rich in heart-clogging fats or to climb onto the rear of motorboats while the engine is running. Other than old age, airplane crashes, and the occasional natural disaster, most people nowadays die because they make bad choices.

Smoking tobacco.

Binge drinking.

Eating blowfish.

Other humans are just inherently stupid.

Drinking and driving.

Setting themselves on fire.

Trying to stop a chain saw with their femoral artery.

And they blame Dennis? Honestly, no one wants to take responsibility for their own death anymore.

Even before Destiny became aware of my affection for Sara, I'd been thinking about Death a lot lately. Maybe it's because I've been feeling good about helping my humans discover a less bleak future. Or maybe it's because I've fallen in love with a mortal. Or maybe it's because I don't want Sara to end up as collateral damage in a dispute between two immortal entities. But I've decided it's finally time to put an end to this whole Columbus rift.

So here I am, in Vienna, Austria, outside a UPS distribution center, eating a sausage with mustard and drinking a Pfiff of Märzen, watching forty-eight-year-old Guenther Zivick load a bunch of empty cardboard boxes into a trash compactor in the back of the facility. Guenther has worked for UPS for the past fifteen years and has used the hydraulic press multiple times. But today, it's his turn to display the full extent of his human stupidity.

Once Guenther has finished filling the hydraulic press with empty boxes, he's going to turn on the compactor, climb up onto the edge of the press, then smash the boxes down into the compactor with his foot, which will get caught by the press. No one will realize what's happened until his coworkers discover Guenther's crushed corpse tomorrow morning.

There's no sign of Dennis yet, which doesn't surprise me. With over 150,000 worldwide deaths per day to contend with, he can't exactly attend each and every one, so he tends to pick and choose, letting Devastation and Despair handle most of the infant mortalities and people who die from natural causes. He prefers to take care of the rest himself—martyrs, heroes, murder victims. And in cases like this, Dennis tends to show up at the last minute. Plus he was never a big fan of Austrian cuisine.

I take another bite of my sausage as Guenther starts up the hydraulic press before he climbs over to the edge of the charging hole and uses his right foot to press the boxes further into the trash compactor. Honestly, I'm surprised he's managed to draw his life out nearly five decades.

I watch him shoving his foot into the operating trash compactor and shake my head. The old me would have just finished off my sausage and downed the rest of my beer while Guenther got dragged into the trash compactor and met his fate, which, while unpleasant, would at least remove him from the gene pool.

Maybe it's because I've lived with them for so long, but in spite of their limited imaginations and their gratuitous conflicts and the ridiculous faces they make during sex, I've begun to develop a quaint fondness for my bumbling, self-destructive, misguided humans. I know I can't help them all, but I can't just stand by and watch one of them get compacted when I can do something about it.

Just before the press seizes his foot and drags Guenther into the chamber to turn him into a human pancake, I grab him by the back of his brown uniform and yank him away from the trash compactor. I think about remaining invisible, but then Guenther wouldn't realize what had almost happened to him. So I materialize before I grab him.

"Hey," he shouts out in German upon seeing me. "What the hell are you doing?"

"Saving your life," I respond, also in German, before I take another bite of my sausage. "Do you have any idea how dangerous it is to put your foot into a working trash compactor?"

For emphasis, I drain the rest of my beer, then toss it into the compactor, which eats up the can in a brief series of crunches and pops.

"Imagine that's happening to you," I say. "Only all over."

He looks at the trash compactor, then at me, then back at the compactor like he's trying to figure out which one of us is telling the truth. I'm beginning to wonder if saving Guenther Zivick was such a good idea.

"Do you work here?" he asks.

With my hands, I motion to my attire, which consists of flip-flops, a pair of teal diamond mosaic board shorts, and a canary yellow T-shirt that says *Prostitutes Suck*. "Do I look like I work here?"

He studies me as if considering the question.

"Then who are you?" he asks.

"I'm the safety inspector," I say. "And if you don't get out of my sight in five seconds, you're going in my report."

"But I was just—"

"One. Two . . ."

Before I can say, "Three," Guenther is running away toward the rear entrance of the building. I watch him go while finishing off the last of my sausage, bemoaning the fact that I don't have any more beer to wash it down with. I'm wondering if I can make a quick trip to the nearest pub, but when I turn around, Dennis is standing there wearing a neoprene particle mask, industrial-strength mortician's gloves, and an annoyed expression.

"What the hell is this?"

"Surprise," I say, with a smile I hope doesn't look as forced as it feels.

Dennis studies me with those ice blue eyes of his beneath his shock of white hair and above his particle mask. "I don't like surprises."

It's true. I tried to throw him a surprise victory party after the destruction of Pompeii and he killed the caterer.

"What are you doing here?" he asks, pulling the particle mask down.

I open my mouth to explain why I'm here, but it's not easy to apologize to Death. I forgot how intimidating he can be.

"You saved that human's life," says Dennis.

Talk about your awkward moments. I'm here to make amends with Death and ask him for help with Destiny and I end up rescuing one of his would-be clients.

"Yeah, well, it looked like it was going to be pretty painful," I say. "And it's not like he's going to be around that much longer."

It turns out that although I saved his life today, Guenther Zivick will, in fact, last two more years before he gets fired, wanders home in a drunken stupor, loses his apartment keys and climbs in through his kitchen window, then passes out halfway through the window with his head in the sink, but not before inadvertently turning on the hot water and drowning himself.

Dennis stares at me, not blinking. I hate it when he does that. It creeps me out.

"How've you been?" I ask.

"How've I been?" he says, as if asking if that's the best I can come up with. "Let's see . . . a handful of revolutions, a dozen civil wars, innumerable riots, some ethnic cleansing, a couple world wars, Iraq, Vietnam, the Middle East, countless acts of terrorism, the Holocaust, a bunch of serial killers, a few nuclear bombs, rebellions, uprisings, assassinations, murders, plane crashes, earthquakes, tsunamis, hurricanes, and HIV."

Okay. A little repressed hostility. I expected that. I probably even deserve it. But still . . .

"Well, if you would have just sunk the *Santa Maria*," I say. "Or started a mutiny. Or infected the ship with the plague . . ."

"Do you want to start in on that again?" he says. "Because I can go all day."

"Look," I say. "All I meant was—"

"I'm not the one who asked his best friend to break the rules," says Dennis. "I'm not the one who wanted his best friend to change the fate of mankind. And I'm not the one who just saved a human from a trash compactor."

The way he says it makes it sound so unsavory.

This isn't how I saw this going. I didn't come here to rehash old arguments. I came here to patch things up. To apologize. To forge a new partnership. But that's the problem with being Fate. Sometimes I just can't accept myself.

"I'm sorry," I say, blurting it out. "For Columbus. For the five centuries of fighting. For the trash compactor. For everything. It's my fault. I'm sorry."

Dennis studies me, as if he's not sure he heard right. "You're sorry?"

I nod.

"Really?"

I nod again. "Really."

"Cross your heart and hope to die?"

"Well, if I actually had a heart, I'd cross it," I say. "And if I could die, I guess that's what I'd hope for."

Dennis stares at me a moment before finally nodding as if to indicate he believes me. Then, for the first time in centuries, he smiles. It's just a small one, but a smile nonetheless. And hard as it may be to believe, there's no one in the universe with a smile as dazzling or as radiant as Death.

This time, my own smile doesn't feel forced.

We stand again in an awkward silence, neither one of us knowing how to proceed. I notice Dennis's eyes are glassy. While I can't say it's the first time I've seen him get choked up, it's always a little disconcerting when Death starts to cry.

"You look good," I say, trying to break the ice.

"You, too," he says. "That a new man suit?"

"Latest model," I say, flexing my biceps. "Popular with the ladies."

He nods and smiles and I wonder when he last got laid.

We spend a few minutes catching up on our latest exploits and trying to ignore the fact that we've allowed five hundred years to pass before doing this. But we can't spend more than a few minutes chatting, since both our schedules are pretty booked. So we make plans to get together once we're back in Manhattan.

"Hey, Fabio," says Dennis.

"What is it?"

I can see from the expression on his face he has something serious he wants to share.

"You know you're not supposed to get involved with humans."

I nod, though I wonder if he's talking about Guenther Zivick or if he somehow knows about Sara, but I guess it doesn't really matter.

"You going to report me to Jerry?" I ask.

He shakes his head. "Just be careful. Humans can be more trouble than they're worth." And then he's gone, leaving me to ponder the wisdom of my actions. But I don't get to ponder them for long, as Guenther Zivick comes back with security to kick me off the property.

This is the thanks I get for saving his life.

CHAPTER 23

The Buddhist counterpart to the concepts of fate and destiny is karma—the sum of all that a human has done, is doing, and will do. The effects of all actions and deeds create past, present, and future experiences. But karma is not destiny, since humans, to some degree, act of their own free will to create their destiny. And a particular action now doesn't condemn you to some predetermined fate. It simply leads to a karmic consequence.

Like that of the Hindu Indian sitting at the table near the front door.

"This guy didn't stop to help a woman who dropped her bag of groceries on her way home," says Karma, soaking up some of his lamb curry with a piece of naan and washing it down with the last of his beer. "Couldn't be bothered, the prick. Now watch this."

The Hindu, who is going to be unhappily married and cheating on his wife in nine years, reaches for his glass of water and drags the sleeve of his white shirt through his yellow daal. When he realizes what he's done, he jerks his arm away so fast, he hits the elbow of the waiter passing by, causing the waiter to dump his tray full of chai into the Indian man's lap.

"Bull's-eye," says Karma.

I've known Karma pretty much since I came into existence. We met in Primordial Soup 101 and became instant friends, even roomed together during Path Orientation and signed up as lab partners for Fundamentals of Human Existence. Jerry taught that course, which Karma and I ditched on more than one occasion to smoke some buds and catch some waves off the shores of South Africa. In spite of our attempts to convince Jerry we were doing field research on Homo erectus, we had to make up our classes during the decline of Neanderthal man.

I haven't seen Karma in a while, not since the Great Depression, as he tends to spend most of his time in India. It's not easy trying to find anyone among the more than one billion humans squished into one subcontinent. But in addition to Death, it's good to have Karma on your side, so I tracked him down at a bar in New Delhi and invited him to lunch.

The thing about Karma is that he's an alcoholic.

Beer, wine, whiskey. Anything that brews, ferments, or distills. His favorite activities are attending Oktoberfest in Munich, going bar hopping on St. Patrick's Day in Dublin, and drinking shots during Cinco de Mayo in Tijuana. And when Karma drinks, he's not a happy drunk.

Think loud.

Think obnoxious.

Think American tourist.

"Yo, Apu," says Karma, waving his empty bottle at the waiter. "How about another beer?"

The waiter, who is taking an order at another table, gives Karma a dirty look, which probably isn't a good idea. As soon as the waiter turns around, he trips and falls into a table of Russian tourists.

"So what's your take on this big event Jerry keeps talking about?" asks Karma.

"I don't know," I say, watching as the waiter apologizes to the tourists. "I haven't really given it much thought."

Over the past couple of months, Jerry's sent out several more e-mails about his Big Event, each one as cryptic as the first. Though he did mention something about significant global implications.

"Well, Chance is running a pool if you want to get in on it," says Karma. "The smart money's on a worldwide pandemic, though there's a lot of action on another ice age and a nuclear holocaust. And last I heard, the return of the Messiah is getting twelve-to-one odds."

The return of the Messiah always gets twelve-to-one odds. Go figure.

"So what do you say?" asks Karma, trying to flag down another waiter by waving his empty beer bottle.

"What type of pandemic?" I say. "Are we talking influenza or plague?"

"Doesn't matter," says Karma. "A pandemic is a pandemic. Chance isn't splitting hairs."

Although I hadn't given it much thought lately, a worldwide

plague could do wonders for freeing up more of my personal days.

I'm thinking about putting my money on a pandemic, or maybe a nuclear holocaust, but both of those options strike me as bad karma, so I decide to go with ice age. It's not as flashy, but I figure it's the safe bet. We haven't had one of those in a while.

"Hey!" Karma shouts to anyone who'll listen. "I'm getting thirsty over here!"

All the patrons at the other tables look our way. In the back of the restaurant, I can see the manager talking to several members of the service staff.

"You might want to keep your voice down," I say, leaning forward. "The humans are starting to notice you."

"It's about time they noticed," he says, shoving a forkful of vegetable masala into his mouth. "Most of the time they go through their pointless lives wearing blinders, completely unaware of how their actions affect their pathetic existence."

You can see why we always got along so well.

A waiter finally brings Karma another beer, shutting him up for the time being, which gives me a chance to ask him the question that's been on my mind ever since Sara said she thought we were destined to meet. Sure, it's highly improbable. But so was human evolution.

"Is it possible for me to be on the Path of Destiny?" I ask.

Karma drains half of his beer. "Have you been hanging out with Insanity again?"

The thing about Insanity is that, well, you know . . .

"No," I say. "I was just wondering—"

"Predestination Law clearly states that Destiny, Fate, and Karma can never cross paths, share the same path, or appear on one another's path," he says. "It's a cosmic impossibility."

Karma always was a better student than me.

"So it's not possible for a mortal to be destined to meet an immortal?" I ask. "Not just to take my order or serve me drinks, but with a definite design or purpose?"

Karma looks at me the way Pope Urban VIII looked at Galileo when he argued that the sun was the center of the universe.

"Look around this place," says Karma, pointing with his half-empty beer bottle at the patrons and employees. "You think any of these humans, these mortal subcreatures, are destined to meet either one of us with a design or a purpose? To meet Karma or Fate?" He takes another pull on his beer. "Maybe Embarrassment or Mediocrity . . ."

The future inhibited ejaculator sitting at the adjacent table is staring at us.

"What are you looking at?" asks Karma.

The man looks away and takes a drink of his tea.

"That's right," says Karma. "Ignore us. Pretend we're not here. Pretend your actions won't have any cosmic consequences."

The man continues to ignore us, asking a passing waiter for his bill.

"Maybe you should take it easy," I say.

"Take it easy?" says Karma, finishing off the rest of his beer. "How am I supposed to take it easy when all around me these creatures are in a perpetual state of ignorance?"

Sounds familiar.

"They're just human," I say. "They can't help it."

"Sure they can," says Karma, his voice rising. "But instead, all they focus on is how much money they make or what kind of car they drive or whose name is on the label of their underwear."

Half of the patrons in the restaurant are looking our way.

"Go back to your pathetic little human thoughts about money and personal possessions," he shouts.

"Maybe you should tone it down," I say.

Karma stands up on his chair, still holding on to his empty beer bottle, and shouts, "How about a little less focus on material goods and a little more emphasis on personal reflection?"

Not exactly what I meant by "toning it down."

I glance over at the manager, who is headed our way.

"Maybe we should leave," I say.

"Good idea," says Karma, then blinks out of existence, leaving me to deal with the aftermath and stiffing me with the bill.

CHAPTER 24

When I get home, Sara is waiting for me in my apartment.

It probably wasn't the smartest idea for me to give her a key. Not that I don't trust her or enjoy being greeted with a kiss and a warm embrace. The problem is, I'm used to just transporting in and out of the comfort of my apartment, which is tough to do when your mortal girlfriend has prepared a romantic evening.

I completely forgot about date night.

I walk through the front door, worn out from my latest attempts to help my humans rediscover their optimal paths. Sure, when you have the ability to transport at the speed of light, transcontinental travel is a piece of cake. But when you hit four continents and thirty-two countries in three days while trying to improve the fates of humans and reconcile with Death, you just want to take a hot shower, wring out your man suit, and call it a day.

Date night was Sara's idea. Not that we don't spend a lot of time together. Probably more than we should, since I'm behind on my quotas and our relationship isn't exactly sanctioned by Jerry. But considering my odd working hours and the fact that I keep making excuses about why we never go out together in public, Sara wanted to set aside one evening for the two of us to do something special.

So before I even have a chance to take a shower or change my clothes, Sara leads me over to the couch for a game of strip Scrabble.

The rules of strip Scrabble are pretty simple:

1) **A player who cannot score higher than the other player in any given round must remove an article of clothing;**

2) **A player who spells a sexual word gets to make the other player remove an article of clothing and is also exempt from removing any clothing during that same round, even if he has the lowest score of the round;**

3) **If a player challenges a word and wins, he can put an article of clothing back on, but if he loses, he must remove an article of clothing;**

4) **The winner of the game can make one request of the losing player.**

It's a fun and informative way to get naked. Since I'm the host, I let Sara go first, which turns out to be a mistake. Not only does she get the automatic double word score, but she spells the word *fated*.

For some reason, this doesn't strike me as amusing.

"So how was your trip?" asks Sara.

"Fine," I say.

"Did you do anything fun?"

"Not really."

I spell the word *tits*. It's worth only six points to Sara's twenty-two, but, invoking the second rule, I make her lose her sweater.

"What did you do?"

"Just work stuff," I say, shuffling my letters around. When I look up from my tile rack, I can tell from the expression on her face that Sara's upset about something.

"Is everything okay?" I ask.

"Yes," she says. "It's just that you never want to share anything about your work."

Sara spells the word *aloof*.

"It's not that interesting," I say.

"It's interesting to me," says Sara.

"Why?" I ask. Honestly, who would want to hear about what someone does who allegedly works in international commodities?

"Because it's part of what you do," says Sara. "It's part of who you are."

I spell the word *crap* and take off one of my socks.

So being as vague as possible, I tell her how I handle millions of clients and how most of them tend to lack good judgment and make bad decisions.

"Aren't you supposed to advise them?" she asks, spelling the word *semen* for a double word score. "Give them some guidance?"

"It's not that simple," I say.

"Why not?" she asks.

"Because."

All I have are vowels and one-point consonants, so the best I can do is *stall*. Since Sara won the round and spelled a sexual word, that counts for two articles of clothing. So I lose the other sock and my shirt.

"Because why?" asks Sara.

"It's complicated."

"Give me an example," she says.

"Can't we talk about something else?"

Sara spells the word *whine*, then folds her arms and stares across the table at me, a slight smirk on her face.

"Okay," I say. "It's like this. My clients seldom do what they're supposed to do. So even with my advice and guidance, there's no guarantee they'll follow it. And even if they do, chances are they'll screw it up somewhere down the road."

Sara looks at me, then cocks her head to one side. "Are you sure you should be in customer service?"

"The problem is, most people never realize their potential," I say. "Instead, they allow it to get buried beneath all of the societal expectations and the constant routine of an existence that condemns them to their fate."

I spell the word *loser* and remove my pants.

"You know what I believe?" says Sara, shuffling the tiles on her rack. "I believe people try to do their best. That even when they're struggling or making bad decisions, they're still working toward a greater purpose."

I try to keep a straight face, but her naïveté is just so cute.

Sara spells the word *hope*.

The thing about Sara is that she's sincere.

"Yeah, well, most of the people I do business with have a history of making bad decisions," I say.

"Then do something else," says Sara. "Something where you can work with other people who won't disappoint you."

"That job's already taken," I say.

I spell the word *whore*.

With my double victory, Sara removes her jeans and her bra, leaving both of us in just our underwear, though she's still wearing her socks.

"Besides, some of my clients are actually starting to listen to me," I say. "So I think I'll stick with them and see what happens."

Sara looks across the table at me and smiles. "Thank you."

"For what?" I ask.

"For sharing," she says, then spells the word *fellatio*.

From the look on Sara's face and the fact that I can't possibly outscore her, I slip out of my underwear and wait for her to claim the spoils of her victory. Hopefully by performing her winning word.

With a seductive smile and a playful glance, Sara gets up from the table, takes me by the hand, and leads me over to the couch.

"You want to try something new?" she asks.

"You won," I say, lying down. "Whatever you want."

Sara straddles me, one hand on either side of my head, her face inches from mine. She leans down to kiss me, her lips parting, her tongue provocatively moist; then she slides away at the last moment and heads down toward my waist. I watch her move past my perfect, hairless, sculpted chest, past my flat, six-pack stomach; then I lean back and close my eyes, feeling her breath caress me, the anticipation almost too much for me to bear.

I'm not sure how much time passes, but at some point I realize I'm still waiting for physical contact. When I open my eyes, I look down to find Sara performing a simulation of oral sex.

"What are you doing?" I ask.

"What do you mean?" she says, looking up at me.

"Why are you pretending to give me a blow job?"

"It's called noncontact sex," she says, crawling toward me until her hips are above mine, moving back and forth without touching me. "Delilah told me about it. Said it was better than actual intercourse."

Great. I leave for two days and Destiny convinces my girlfriend to stop having sex with me.

"What do you think?" asks Sara.

I think Destiny's been spending too much time with my girlfriend—that's what I think.

I imagine her watching us, hiding in the corner, wearing red stockings and garters and hip-hugger panties and a red push-up bra, smirking while eating a red candied apple.

Used to be just thinking about Destiny in an outfit like that would turn me on. And I always did get a thrill watching a woman eat an apple. I'm a sucker for religious symbolism. But with Sara floating above me, her gorgeous face as sublime as anything Michelangelo ever sculpted, I find the allure of Destiny a distraction. I don't want to think about her. I just want to think about Sara. About how I feel when I'm with her. About how I treasure every moment we spend together. About how I feel more complete. Like I've been missing something my entire existence and I didn't even realize what I was missing until I found her.

She's honest and compassionate.

She's generous and sincere.

She's patient and understanding.

In short, she's all the things I'm not.

It's as though in Sara, I've found my perfect complement. She's the eraser to my pencil. The Camembert to my baguette. The yin to my yang.

I look up at Sara and find her looking down at me, a soft smile touching her lips, her eyes focused on mine, and I realize I don't care that Destiny has befriended my girlfriend. I don't care that she's trying to disrupt our sex life by teaching Sara about non-contact sex. The joke's on her. I feel closer to Sara now than ever before.

CHAPTER 25

It never ceases to amaze me how human beings constantly seek happiness in instant gratification.

Cell phones. E-mail. Overnight delivery.

Fast food. Microwaves. Prepackaged meals.

Credit cards. ATMs. Lottery tickets.

No one wants to delay their gratification. To wait for a reply or a package. To work to achieve or obtain financial success. They want the house and the car and the marriage and the family and the condo in Hawaii and they want it *now*.

Take the twenty-six-year-old disillusioned ex–high school star quarterback and his twenty-two-year-old superficial wife, for example.

They're walking down the Champs-Élysées, decked out in Versace and Fendi and Gucci, their hands filled with bags filled with packages filled with Lacoste and Cartier and Louis Vuitton. They can't afford what they're wearing, let alone what they've purchased. They can't even afford the trip to Paris, but they feel entitled to the luxury and to the lifestyle because of their good looks and their untapped potential for greatness.

If only they knew that in less than ten years they'll both be divorced, remarried, and divorced again, working in cubicles without any natural lighting, and still paying off the credit card bills from this vacation.

Of course, they're not the only ones indulging in excess on the most famous avenue in Paris. Thousands of other consumers from all over the world are here to patronize the specialty shops and dine in the chic bistros and cafés and be seen in one of the hip clubs.

Realtors and artists and financial consultants.

Writers and dog trainers and CEOs.

Architects and editors and interior decorators.

All of them looking for something to make them feel special. To make them feel desirable. To make them feel like they belong.

All of them looking for instant gratification.

Well, maybe not all of them, but most of them. Enough to keep me busy for a few hours trying to convince as many of these misguided humans as I can that the key to divining a more beneficial fate lies not in filling up the emptiness of their lives with material goods but with personal reflection.

I'm beginning to sound like Karma.

I talk to a forty-two-year-old pathological shopper and explain to her how owning six major credit cards, four of which are maxed out, isn't the best way to plan for her financial future.

I stop a twenty-nine-year-old dog walker who has just blown two days' pay on a single pair of jeans and tell him that Darwin would probably put him in the gene pool of humans unfit for natural selection.

I ask a married couple with more money than integrity if their wealth wouldn't be better spent feeding homeless children rather than feeding their insatiable appetite for designer furniture and imported caviar.

I'm not making a lot of friends.

Convincing humans to give up their self-destructive consumer lifestyles is harder than I thought. Of course, it would be easier if Common Sense were still around, but she disappeared during the Vietnam War and hasn't been heard from since.

And it doesn't help that I have to compete with Flamboyance and Vanity.

They're walking along the promenade on the other side of the Champs-Élysées, working the tourists and the locals like politicians collecting votes. Vanity is wearing a flattering skintight black Donna Karan dress with a plunging neckline and a knee-high hem while she convinces a trio of college girls that they need an entire wardrobe makeover. Flamboyance, on the other hand, wins over his converts as he preens and parades around like Mick Jagger in his leather pants and satin shirt.

The thing about Vanity is that she's a hypochondriac.

The thing about Flamboyance is that he's a misogynist.

As I watch the two of them move through the crowds, convincing humans of their needs and desires and the importance of style over substance, a husky voice behind me says, "Not as easy as it looks, is it?"

I turn around, knowing who I'll find sitting on the bench before I see Destiny in a red leather V-neck zippered jumpsuit by Guess and a pair of matching thigh-high patent-leather boots.

"What's not as easy?" I ask, trying to pretend I don't know what she's talking about.

"Oh, come on, Faaaaabio," she says. "I've been watching you for the past half an hour, trying to convince your humans to change their ways. It's admirable. Pointless, but admirable."

I'm not sure what bothers me more: the fact that Destiny has been watching me for the past half an hour without my knowing it or that she thinks what I'm doing is pointless.

"What are you doing here?" I ask.

"Slumming," she says. "Seeing how the other eighty-three percent lives. I don't know how you put up with them, Fabio. They're all just so . . . ordinary."

That may be true, but they're still my humans and I don't appreciate having them judged by an immortal entity who's had sex with every Deadly Sin.

"They're not so bad," I say. "You just have to get to know them."

Destiny brays laughter.

While part of me can't believe I'm defending my humans, a larger part of me can't stand Destiny's contempt for them.

"They may not be destined to save someone's life or to win a Pulitzer Prize or to discover a cure for AIDS, but they all have some redeeming value," I say. "Once you get past all of the failures and the hangups and the self-destructive behaviors."

"This isn't like you, Fabio," she says. "You used to be so objective. So unemotional. Why do you suddenly have such an interest in your humans?"

"Maybe I'm tired of watching them screw up their lives," I say. "Maybe I want to help them find their dreams."

Again, Sara's words coming out of my mouth.

"You know you're asking for trouble, Fabio," she says. "Interfering is a big no-no."

"Yeah, well, you haven't exactly been following company policy with Sara," I say, before I can help myself.

"If you realized how special she is," says Destiny, "you'd understand."

"I know how special she is," I say.

"You have no idea," says Destiny. "You're in over your head, Fabio. You need to get out before you end up getting hurt."

"I'm fine," I say.

"You know it can't work," says Destiny. "You can't have a relationship with her. It's not only against company policy; it's impossible."

"I'm fine," I say again.

For a few moments we say nothing, just stare at each other— me standing there wishing she'd go away and her standing there like a giant red exclamation point.

Destiny cocks her head at me and smiles.

"What?" I say.

"I miss you, Fabio," she says. "I miss all the good times we had."

"It was just sex," I say.

"Maybe," she says. "But it was good sex."

I can't really argue with her on that one.

She continues to stare at me, her head cocked, that Cheshire-cat grin plastered on her face.

"What?" I ask again.

As if I didn't know.

She slides up to me, her long, firm, leather-clad legs less than an inch from my man suit, one hand pulling down her zipper, exposing a mountain range of cleavage.

"I can't," I say, closing my eyes. I'd swear it's my imagination, but she smells like cinnamon.

"Come on, Faaaaabio," she purrs, her breath brushing tantalizingly past my ear. "For old times' sake?"

I just shake my head and hold my breath and think about Gluttony. When I open my eyes, I expect to see her standing naked in front of me, that seductive smirk on her face. Instead, I turn and see her red, leather-clad body sauntering away up the Champs-Élysées toward the Arc de Triomphe.

CHAPTER 26

After I finish up in Paris, I spend a few hours in England dealing with an assortment of losers and has-beens and members of Parliament, then take a tour of the Tower of London. The tour guide, a wannabe Beefeater, gets so many facts about the Tower's history wrong that I have to start correcting him. By the end of the tour, I'm asked to never come back. Just as well. The place was much livelier when people were actually getting beheaded.

From England, I head to Belgium and Germany, then make a pass through Austria, Hungary, and Greece on my way to Southeast Asia before swinging through Australia and then doubling back to China and Russia. A quick jump over the Bering Strait and a whirlwind jaunt across Canada and before you can say, "Destiny is a redheaded bitch," I'm back in New York in time for my dinner date with Sara.

Santa Claus doesn't get around this fast.

Of course, he's leaving all the good little boys and girls the material possessions they're expecting to receive for their impeccable behavior, while I'm filling the stockings of my charges with suggestions for how to hold down a job, why it's inappropriate to have sex with your mother-in-law, and when to stop investing your retirement account at the roulette table.

Not every human is open to my suggestions. Some of them are so set in their ways and so convinced of their own infinite wisdom that they brush me off or call the cops or attack me with pepper spray. Still, in spite of the dismissals and the near arrests and the feeling of having my face drenched in gasoline and set on fire, I've discovered just how hungry most humans are for someone to actually take an interest in their lives. To give them some direction. To provide a sense of purpose. To offer help and comfort—even if it is sprinkled with phrases like "embarrassment to intelligent life" and "worthless waste of carbon."

Sometimes it's hard to hear the truth.

But at least I feel like I'm beginning to make a difference rather than just standing back and watching my humans ruin their lives. I know the circumstances of their fates aren't supposed to be participatory, that their paths are supposed to be determined by their uninfluenced choices, but why should Destiny's humans get to have a say in their futures while mine are stuck with their crappy fates?

"You're mumbling again," says Sara.

I look up from my sixteen-spice chicken and realize I've been voicing my private thoughts out loud again.

"What did I say?" I ask.

"Something about fate and destiny," she says, taking a bite of her grilled lamb porterhouse chops.

We're at Mesa Grill—a loud, popular Southwestern dining establishment named the best American regional restaurant in New York for five years running. Personally, I don't see what all the fuss is about. As far as I can tell, my sixteen-spice chicken is at least three spices short of its advertised seasoning. At $27 for the entree, that comes to $1.69 per spice, which means I should get a refund of $5.07.

It's not the smartest thing for me to be seen out in public with Sara. You never know when you'll run into Integrity or Gossip. But Sara started to complain that after nearly three months together, we haven't had a date that's taken place outside of our apartment building.

So because I want her to be happy, I booked us a table at the Mesa Grill for dinner. Not exactly a hole-in-the-wall, but I figured if I'm going to go out in public, I might as well get it over with. Besides, it's not as if I'm trying to hide my relationship with Sara from Destiny. And realistically, I can't expect Sara to be content with sex, cable television, and take-out Chinese forever. Plus Sara's refrigerator was empty and she needed some leftovers.

"So what were you mumbling?" asks Sara, taking another bite of her porterhouse chops with garlic mashed potatoes.

"It's nothing," I say.

"It's not nothing," says Sara. "You talk about it all the time."

"Talk about what all the time?"

"Fate and destiny," she says. "It's almost like an obsession with you. You even talk about it in your sleep."

I hadn't realized I talked about it that much. And I had no idea I talked in my sleep.

"I'm not obsessed," I say. "I'm just . . . preoccupied."

"Why is that?" she asks.

Another thing about mortal women: They ask a lot of questions. Which can prove to be a challenge when you're trying to avoid telling the truth.

"I don't know," I say. "You're the one who started it."

There. I've deflected blame. That should solve the problem.

"Me?" she says. "How did I start it?"

"When you asked me if I believed in destiny," I say.

"Yes, but when I asked you how come you knew so much about fate and destiny, you told me it was a hobby of yours."

I don't know why I let myself get painted into a corner like this. I mean, it's not like I couldn't see it coming.

Suddenly I'm not interested in the rest of my thirteen-spice chicken.

"Listen," says Sara, reaching across the table and taking my hand. "I'm just trying to understand you. To get to know you. To discover the person inside. And I can't do that if you keep me at a distance."

She's right. But I don't know how to discuss this with Sara without explaining who I am and what I do. Of course, I haven't exactly been adhering to company guidelines lately, but being the kind of honest she needs is asking for trouble.

So I have to improvise.

"You remember how you said you thought we were destined to meet?" I ask.

Sara nods.

"What made you think that?" I ask.

"I don't know," she says. "Just a feeling. Like there was some greater purpose for our meeting. Something unique. Something . . ."

"Special?"

Sara nods and smiles.

I reach across the table and take Sara's hands in mine. "If you ask me, what's special about us is you."

Which isn't me improvising or trying to change the subject or angling for a blow job. It's just the honest-to-Jerry truth.

"And what you said about thinking you and I were destined to be together," I say. "I think it, too."

And the thing is, I realize I really do.

Sara smiles again, then leans across my thirteen-spice chicken and kisses me before returning to her porterhouse chops.

The remainder of the meal passes without further conversation about fate and destiny, though Sara does make a comment about how she'd much rather be destined than fated any day of the week, which does wonders for my ego. It also reminds me that it's time for us to get out of here. It's almost impossible to go out to a restaurant or a bar in Manhattan and not run into Inebriation or Anxiety or one of the Deadlies. So far, I haven't seen anyone else, but I don't want to push my luck by complaining about my spice-challenged chicken or ordering dessert.

On our way out, Sara stops and gives her leftovers to a homeless woman on Fifth Avenue, which means we're going to have to get some pizza or Chinese delivered so Sara has something to eat for breakfast. While Sara's fishing a twenty out of her wallet to give to the woman, I turn around to find Destiny staring at me from inside the Mesa Grill.

Destiny is on the other side of the window wearing a formfitting red silk sweater, skintight red jeans, red leather tennis shoes, and a red beret. If she weren't invisible, every single human male in the restaurant would either be asking Destiny for her number or getting slapped by his date.

She continues to stare at me, licking the window and pressing herself up against the glass, so I turn around and watch Sara with the homeless woman, talking to her, comforting her, getting her to laugh, casting the same spell over her that she seems to cast over everyone she meets. The same spell she has cast over me.

I think about what my existence was like before Sara—mundane and fruitless, filled with frustration and disappointment and with empty, meaningless, noncontact sex. Now my existence is exciting and hopeful, filled with purpose and satisfaction and with emotional, intimate, full-contact bed surfing.

I've never experienced anything remotely similar to what I feel for Sara. This wanting to be with her. To see her and taste her and touch her. To inhale her aroma and listen to the symphony of her voice. To engulf my senses in everything Sara.

As I stand and watch her offer the homeless woman more comfort with her words and a warm touch than with the twenty-dollar bill, I think about how I enjoy the simple pleasures being with Sara provides, like the weight of her hand in mine or the way her scent lingers on her pillow or the warmth of her body curled up next to mine. But most of all, I think about how she's changed my attitude.

Made me look forward to my job for the first time in centuries. Influenced me in positive ways I never would have imagined.

I think about how I'm so much happier when I'm with her.

Before I can stop myself, I walk over to Sara, turn her around, and kiss her as if I haven't seen her in weeks.

Maybe it's because she can't stand to see us together. Or maybe she had another emergency. Or maybe she just got tired of being ignored.

When I turn back around, Destiny's gone.

CHAPTER 27

I used to think I knew who I was. What I wanted. How I was going to spend the rest of eternity.

Doesn't everyone?

When you're human, you only *think* you know how things are going to turn out. But when you're Fate, you have a pretty good idea of what your own future holds. I get to see my own fate laid out before me in one long Cecil B. DeMille epic. Only without Charlton Heston, who looks nothing like Moses, by the way. Moses was short and pale and balding and had bad teeth. Sharp dresser, though. And he made a mean matzo-ball soup.

Like *The Ten Commandments*, my own epic story was pretty predictable. That is, until Sara came along. Ever since I fell in love, I've suddenly lost the last reel of my movie and I have no idea how it's going to end. Plot points that seemed inevitable have taken an indefinite turn and I find myself wandering along without any idea of where I'm going or what's going to be waiting for me when I arrive.

I guess that's to be expected when an upstanding immortal entity decides to start breaking the laws of the universe.

For hundreds of millennia I've been a voyeur, watching humans live their lives and make bad decisions and behave in a generally stupid manner. Now here I am getting involved, altering futures, saving people from trash compactors and excessive consumption and hallucinogenic drugs.

I'm on the Oregon coast, watching several college students from the University of Oregon who are hunting for psychedelic mushrooms. It's strange, but I never imagined I would enjoy spending time with inferior creatures who believe they can find enlightenment in a fungus that grows in cow excrement.

"Dude!" says Brian Tompkins, a twenty-year-old communications major, as he discovers a cache of liberty caps that he holds up to display for his buddies. "Score!"

Brian was a sensible teenager until he arrived in college. Never did drugs and drank only an occasional beer when he knew he wasn't going to be driving. But the college experience and the new friends he's made have led him to discover the wonders of hallucinogenic drugs.

While the psychedelic mushrooms aren't going to kill Brian, and all the pot he's going to smoke isn't going to have a negative impact on his 3.75 GPA, the three hits of acid he's going to take on his personal journey to enlightenment will convince him he has the ability to dematerialize, which he will put to the test by standing in front of an Amtrak train bound for Des Moines.

So I nudge Brian from his path, from his approaching death, by whispering in his ear that eating mushrooms and dropping acid instill in male humans an intense desire to have oral sex with venomous snakes.

That seems to do the trick. He drops the mushrooms and runs off screaming and will eschew drugs as a means of enlightenment, instead choosing to take the path of spiritual transcendence by studying Buddhism, Taoism, and Zen philosophies. Maybe not as adventurous as his prior path, but entirely less fatal.

I pick up the mushrooms abandoned by Brian Tompkins and pocket them to prevent his friend from tempting him. As Oscar Wilde said, the only sure way to get rid of temptation is to give in to it. And humans are nothing if not easily tempted, even when there exists the possibility they might end up getting a blow job from a viper.

Speaking of snakes . . .

"That's not fair," says Temptation, appearing moments after I pocket the mushrooms, a sultry pout on her lips. "He might change his mind."

"I wouldn't doubt it," I say.

While not inclined to wear fuck-me pumps like Destiny or parade around in lingerie like Lust, Temptation manages to exude more sexuality by revealing less. Just enough cleavage and a glimpse of an undergarment beneath the virgin white sundress that hides her figure, while at the same time hinting at the curves and wonders beneath the cotton fabric. But unlike the in-your-face sexuality of Lust and Destiny, Temptation never actually lets you get past first base. She's more of a cock tease.

Temptation is the one responsible for the "original sin" fiasco involving Adam and Eve, who have been depicted throughout history as the ones responsible for the seed of future evil choices and the effects of those choices for the entire human race. Talk about a guilt trip. No wonder they stopped doing interviews and took their kids out of public school. As far as I'm concerned, they were set up, though Eve did have a thing for apples and serpents.

"I wasn't going to make him do anything he didn't want to do," she says.

"I bet."

"Really," she says. "All I wanted to do was show him how to recognize which mushrooms are poisonous."

The thing about Temptation is that she's a pathological liar.

"So why don't you put them back?" she says, moving in closer, her fingers nearly brushing my hand, her hips sliding past mine, the scent of cinnamon rolls wafting off her. "For me?"

The aroma of cinnamon rolls is almost overwhelming, but I know it's just a ruse. She doesn't really smell like a freshly heated Cinnabon. That's just my favorite scent. And she knows it. For someone else, she might smell like jasmine. For another person, lavender. For another person, bacon. It's amazing what she can get someone to do just by enticing them with aromas.

But as much as I would really love a cinnamon roll right now, I can't give in to her.

"I can't," I say.

"Please?" says Temptation, whispering in my ear, her scent engulfing my nostrils, enticing both my culinary and sexual appetites. I try to think about baseball, but it just doesn't work for me ever since Fraud ruined the game with steroids and human growth hormones.

Before I realize what I'm doing, I'm reaching into my front pocket for the mushrooms.

"You won't be sorry," says Temptation.

She's right. I won't. But Brian Tompkins will.

Before I can give in to the intoxicating aroma of cinnamon rolls, I get called away for another meeting with Jerry.

CHAPTER 28

"Jerry will see you now."

I get up from my chair and take the long walk down the hall to Jerry's office door. While I keep trying to tell myself this is a routine meeting and that the timing is just coincidental, I can smell Destiny all over this. Her odor. Her sunscreen. Her hair spray. And I know when I walk through that door, I'm in big trouble.

Think Three Mile Island.

Think Chernobyl.

Think *Ishtar*.

At least the heated emotion I encountered from the human souls on my last visit is gone. Part of that has to do with the fact that Hostility is in North Korea, joining forces with Anger and Arrogance to see what they can stir up. Plus I'm impersonating Indifference, so everyone pretty much ignores me.

When I walk into Jerry's office, he's on the computer, typing so fast his fingers are a blur of white light. "Have a seat," he says, not looking up.

I tiptoe across the floor in my socks, trying not to look down. When you're suspended above the heavens in a big glass box, acrophobia takes on a whole new meaning.

Jerry finishes up what he's doing and looks me up and down.

"That's a different look for you," he says, noting my drab, nondescript appearance.

"I'm traveling incognito," I say, trying to pretend I don't know why I'm here.

Probably wasn't a good idea to flaunt my relationship with Sara in public.

"What have you been up to, Fabio?" he says.

"Nothing much," I say, forcing a smile. "Just the usual."

"The usual," says Jerry, still not smiling. "Is that so?"

I nod, continuing to feign ignorance. It's pointless, of course. Even if Destiny hadn't ratted me out, this is the so-called supreme being we're talking about.

Sometimes I really hate the fact that Jerry's so fucking omniscient.

Jerry eyes me knowingly, then leans back in his chair and puts his Birkenstocks up on his desk, crossing his ankles. "How's Earth treating you these days?"

"Good," I say, after clearing my throat. "Can't complain."

"Really?" says Jerry. "That's not like you. You always complain."

"Just taking your advice," I say. "Doing my job better. Caring about it more."

"Is that so?" he says, juggling a couple of galaxies in one hand while text-messaging on his cell phone with the other. The show-off. "From what I can tell, it seems to me like you're caring a little too much."

"What do you mean?" I ask, putting on my best facade of innocence.

For a few moments he just stares at me—you know, the way God does when he knows you're not telling the truth? So I'm about to give up and confess, tell him it's true, that I've fallen in love with a mortal woman who's on the Path of Destiny, when Jerry turns his flat-screen computer monitor toward me and says, "According to the latest data I've received, it appears that over the past quarter, your clients have a seventy-nine percent success rate."

I stare at the charts on the monitor, too stunned to give an immediate reply. This isn't what I expected to be confronted with when I got called in to see Jerry, so the rebuttals I'd rehearsed won't work. That and I can't believe the numbers. Seventy-nine percent.

"Wow," I say, trying not to smile while wearing the same look of surprise I wore when Caligula's guards came to assassinate him. Like he didn't see that one coming.

"That's a lot of accurate life-path decision making for a bunch of recently evolved mammals," says Jerry. "Especially considering your previous benchmark was sixty-eight percent. And that was during the Age of Reason."

In addition to the belief that humankind possesses the ability to understand the universe, Voltaire and Descartes and the other great thinkers during the Age of Reason professed the concept of rational will, which postulated that humans make their own choices and therefore do not have a fate thrust upon them.

Voltaire and Descartes were pompous idiots.

"I must have had a lucky run," I say, flashing the smile I bought from Humility.

"Lucky, my ass," says Jerry, removing his feet from his desk and leaning forward on his palms so fast that my smile dissolves in an instant.

Fucking Humility. I'm going to ask for a refund.

"I'm not sure what you're talking about," I say.

"Don't bullshit me," says Jerry. "I'm the Creator, for Christ's sake. It's not like I was born in the last ice age."

Good point.

"There's only one explanation for a fate-conversion success rate this high," says Jerry. "You're breaking rule number one. And you should know better than to get involved with humans. The others have an excuse, like Courage or Jealousy or Pride. . . ."

"He's gay, you know," I say.

"Really?" says Jerry. "Well, that explains a lot. But that doesn't excuse you from getting involved in the lives of humans. You have to think about the consequences of your actions, Fabio. You're Fate, God damn it."

I just nod. There's really not much you can say when Jerry takes his own name in vain.

"Now, I don't want to have to call you in here again for this," says Jerry. "Otherwise, I'm going to have to take some punitive actions. Are we clear?"

I nod again.

"Good," says Jerry. "Now get the hell out of here. I have a universe to run."

CHAPTER 29

Over the past few months I've discovered how much work it is to try to help humans rather than just allow them to screw up their lives. I suppose this is kind of what it's like to be a parent, but since I've never taken care of anything other than a couple of woolly mammoths and a python that disappeared down the toilet back in the 1970s, I never realized how rewarding parenting can be. Or how difficult it is to stand by and watch your children make mistakes when your guidance could save them a lot of heartache and disappointment.

Technically, Jerry never told me to stop getting involved in the fates of my mortals. He just told me I should know better and that I had to think about the consequences of my actions. While that argument might hold up in the terrestrial world, Jerry tends to get a little pissy when you misinterpret his decrees. And disobeying a direct order from Jerry isn't exactly the best way to stay on his good side. Just ask Satan.

Of course, he did threaten me with punitive action. But then,

Jerry's always threatening someone. And though his bark can often be worse than his bite, Jerry doesn't tend to make idle threats. So while it's unlikely I'll get banished to the underworld, Jerry could suspend me without powers. And when you can't transport or go invisible, it kind of takes the shine off of being immortal.

But getting my powers suspended isn't the worst that can happen. If Jerry really gets pissed, he could strip me of my immortality. Which would suck. I'd have to get a job, a new place to live, and my man suit would eventually wear out. And when my man suit wears out, so will I.

Not exactly how I want to celebrate my 257,981st birthday.

So if I want to be able to maintain the lifestyle to which I've become accustomed, I'm going to have to give up my newfound purpose and allow my humans to continue to make the wrong choices.

This has been harder to accept than I expected, which has made for a sullen Fabio. Sara has tried to cheer me up by actually cooking a meal for me instead of reheating leftovers and by cleaning my apartment in a French maid's outfit, but when I'm depressed, I just want to lie on the couch and eat some Ben & Jerry's and watch reruns of *Seinfeld*.

So I decide I need a change of scenery. I need to go someplace tropical. Someplace relaxing. Someplace where I can get away from it all.

"Come on, Shadow Fury!"

I'm at the Daytona Beach Dog Track in Florida, watching the sixth race at the Wednesday matinee. I've already hit the daily double and one exacta. When Shadow Fury crosses the finish line first, that'll give me the winner in five out of six races. Of course, it doesn't hurt that Lady Luck is helping me place my bets.

"Come on, Shadow Fury!" she screams out, a half-finished cranberry and vodka in one hand and her race ticket in the other. If I didn't know any better, I'd swear she had no idea our dog was going to win.

We have to make a pretense of being excited; otherwise we're likely to draw more attention to ourselves than we already are. Which is why we had to throw the third race.

I know it's not exactly sporting. And watching enslaved animals chase a mechanical rabbit around a racetrack for the gambling and entertainment desires of humans makes me feel like I need to take a hot shower. But when you've been around for more than a quarter million years running day care for billions of inferior life-forms and their creator has just told you to stay out of their business, sometimes you need to enjoy the perks of your semiomniscient abilities.

"Hallelujah!" shouts Lady Luck in delight as Shadow Fury wins the race, finishing almost a full body length ahead of the other greyhounds. "Praise Jerry."

"Jerry?" says a disgruntled gambler sitting behind us. "Who the hell is Jerry?"

"The dog's trainer," I say, taking Lady Luck and heading over to the window to cash in our tickets.

"Oh, Fabio," she says. "Thank you for talking me into this. I haven't had this much fun since the 1980 U.S. Olympic hockey team."

After we cash in our tickets, we finish off our drinks, then give all our day's winnings to an old-timer who's had a hard day at the track. I let Lady Luck do it. That way, I'm not technically getting involved. And besides, it's what she does.

"Well, Fabio, it's been a real hoot," she says, giving me a kiss on the cheek. "But I think it's time I get back to work."

Indeed. While we were raking it in, a lot of the other patrons at the Daytona racetrack weren't as fortunate. I watch Lady Luck skip away, her gold lamé dress shimmering in the Florida heat as she brushes past men and women whose luck will immediately take a turn for the better.

One of those Lady Luck misses is Cliff Brooks, a career underachiever trying to parlay the hundred bucks he came here with into enough so he can afford to take his girlfriend out for a nice birthday dinner. Maybe Hooters or Robbie O'Connell's Pub. But after six races, all Cliff has to show for his efforts is one dog that placed and fifty bucks that went to the house.

If I don't do anything, Cliff is going to spend the rest of his life unfulfilled by his work, earning money for the sake of earning money, and failing to discover his optimal path. I know I should just turn around and transport out of there, go find a nice group of Buddhist monks or maybe hang out with the Dalai Lama, but after more than a week of not getting involved, I'm going through pathetic-human withdrawals. Jonesing for a crack addict or a homeless person or a criminal defense lawyer. And Cliff Brooks is the fix I need.

I know Jerry told me not to get involved, but it's just one little human. One pathetic soul. One mortal who has made a lifetime of wrong choices.

But today, he's got something going for him he isn't expecting. A bit of good fortune he won't be receiving from Lady Luck. Cliff Brooks is about to get a visit from (drumroll please) . . . Captain Fate.

Guardian of the destiny-challenged.

Defender of human ineptitudes.

Champion of uninspired futures.

I'm thinking I need to get myself a theme song. Maybe something like the opening title sequence of *Star Wars* or "The Peter Gunn Theme." Or maybe something original. I'd ask Beethoven or Tchaikovsky to write me something snappy, but, well, they're dead.

The problem with defending the fate of Cliff Brooks, other than the fact that it could cost me my immortality, is I'm visible. I could sneak into the bathroom or find a phone booth somewhere and remedy that situation so I could help him without his knowing it, but if he goes to lay any more money on the dogs before I can get to him, well, then, all bets are off, so to speak. So just as Cliff finishes reading the program for the next race and is getting in line to place his next doomed bet, I sidle up next to him and take him by the arm.

"You don't want to do that," I say.

"Do what?" he asks, making no attempt to remove my hand from his arm.

"Make that bet," I say, leading him away from the betting queues.

"Why not?" he asks.

"Because Shoot the Moon isn't going to win," I say.

"How did you know what dog I was betting on?" he asks as I lead him past the concession stands.

"Let's just say I'm psychic."

"Really?"

"Really," I say, leading him out the back entrance. He's so acquiescent. I could be a thief. I could be a paroled sex offender. I could be a serial killer and this guy would let me lead him to a soundproof room with meat hooks and utility saws.

"So you can read my future?"

"More or less," I say.

"Like what?" he asks.

"Well, for starters," I say, "you might want to reconsider your choices for your girlfriend's birthday dinner. Taking her to Hooters isn't exactly going to get you laid."

"Wow," he says as I lead him to a bench and sit him down. "You *are* psychic."

Yeah, well, it doesn't take an immortal entity of predestination to know that treating your girlfriend to Hooters for her birthday isn't the path to sexual gratification.

"What else?" he asks, looking at me with complete trust.

Humans are so simple. Especially human men. Tell them how to avoid spending their nights masturbating and they'll follow you anywhere. The only real difference between male humans and male dogs is that the humans generally won't try to hump your leg.

"Your name is Clifford Brooks," I say, sitting down next to him and telling him all about himself—where he lives (Ormond Beach), what he does for a living (stockperson), how many times a month he has sex (0.37), and what he had for dinner last night (Kraft macaroni and cheese).

"I also know that you're not on your assigned path," I say. "You're not doing what you're supposed to be doing."

"What am I supposed to be doing?" he asks.

From the eagerness in his eyes and the expression of worship on his face, I could give him a cup of Kool-Aid laced with cyanide and he'd ask for more.

What am I supposed to be doing?

Human beings have this innate desire to allow someone else to direct their own lives instead of figuring things out for themselves. It's like they don't want the responsibility of screwing things up, so they can feel free to blame someone else.

Their parents.

Their therapist.

Jerry.

So instead of spending some quality time alone and figuring out what they really want, they distract themselves with television and video games and pornography.

What am I supposed to be doing?

What Cliff Brooks is supposed to be doing is working as a financial manager at a bank and earning enough money to support his wife and daughter. But he dropped out of college after one year to pursue an acting career that peaked when he wore the Goofy costume for one summer at Disney World.

"Go back to college and get your degree," I say.

And quick as a flash, he's a twenty-seven-year-old fraternity pledge with a minor in alcoholism.

So I try again.

"Get married and raise a family."

He's an abusive father with a future in restraining orders.

For some reason I think of Nicolas Jansen and figure, if it worked for him . . .

"Join a monastery."

He's a wanted pedophile being extradited from Caracas, Venezuela.

This is more difficult than I thought it would be.

All the other humans I've tried to help have responded to my guidance with improved fates. Maybe not always ideal. I mean, who aspires to pump out portable toilets for a living? But at least it's an improvement over smoking crack cocaine or joining a religious cult.

Cliff Brooks, on the other hand, presents more of a challenge. No matter what I come up with, I keep shooting blanks. So I just have to keep trying until I find a chamber that fires.

It's kind of like playing Russian roulette, only with fates instead of bullets.

"Start your own business."

Click.

"Enlist in the armed forces."

Click.

"Start a volunteer organization."

Bang!

According to the reading I get, Cliff Brooks is going to become a champion for the cause of animal rights and for abolishing greyhound racing in the state of Florida.

Uh-oh.

Not only is this a complete departure from his current path, but it's a significant improvement over the path he was assigned at birth. Sure, he was going to be a successful finance manager and a serviceable husband and father, but this new and improved fate goes beyond the parameters of his potential.

From what I can see, he's going to develop quite a following, even garner national attention, and will have a great deal of success for the foreseeable future. And by "foreseeable," I don't mean very long. Not that he's going to burn out or suffer a heart attack or get whacked by the greyhound Mafia. It's just that I can't see clearly past the next few years. It's literally blurred, as if a heavy fog has rolled in off the cosmic shore and obscured my vision.

I shake my head in an attempt to clear it, because I can't possibly be seeing what I think I'm seeing, but when I take another look, I still can't clearly see the fate of Cliff Brooks.

He's not quite there yet, but I'll be damned if he's not on his way to the Path of Destiny.

CHAPTER 30

"**Another one of** these," says Karma, waving his empty bottle of Kingfisher Lager at a passing waiter.

We're upstairs at Curry in a Hurry on Lexington and East 28th in Manhattan, which is packed with the weekday lunchtime crowd. Hanging plants and watercolor paintings of snake charmers and Indian romance adorn the walls. In the back, next to the bathrooms, a flat-screen television plays something from Bollywood.

The ascension of Cliff Brooks isn't something I can just ignore. It's unprecedented. An anomaly. A mutation of the cosmic order. I need to figure out how to set him back on the proper path.

Problem is, I was never much of a student, and Jerry's lectures in Path Theory and Predestination Law always put me to sleep, so I need some help. Dennis didn't have to take the classes as core requirements, since all paths eventually lead to him, Sloth slept through more lectures than I did, and Gluttony frequently ate his own homework. Even though Karma ditched school almost as often as I did, he somehow managed to score near the top of the class.

Fortunately, Karma was in town for his annual visit to George Steinbrenner, so it wasn't too hard to track him down.

"So," I say. "I have another question about paths."

"You mean like the Path of Fate, the Path of Destiny, all that metaphysical bullshit?" says Karma, his eyes a bit glassy from the two Kingfishers he's already put away.

"Yeah," I say, wondering how many beers he drank before I showed up.

"Man, I don't know," he says. "That was more than two hundred and fifty fucking thousand years ago."

The Japanese woman at the table next to us stops with her fork halfway to her open mouth and looks over at us.

"Listen," I say, as the waiter returns with another Kingfisher. "Just help me out on this and I'll get lunch."

"Okay," he says. "But I never was much of a student."

"Oh, come on," I say. "You aced Predestination Law. Got the highest final score of anyone in the class."

"I cheated," says Karma before downing half of his beer. "Bought the answers from Deception. Never even cracked a book."

Great. I come looking for clarity and wisdom and instead I get folly and crapulence.

"Do you remember anything about your schooling?" I ask. "Anything at all?"

"Some of it," he says. "I remember gym class and stealing Injury's wheelchair during Greek Week and filling Celibacy's locker with naked pictures of Confidence. Oh, and I remember the visualization techniques we learned in Virtual Theater."

Pageantry taught that class. The idea was to imagine yourself as an inanimate object that represented your abilities. My visualization, my inanimate object that represented the Fate of the human race, was a gasoline pump.

Before I can stop him, Karma is climbing up and sitting on our table, his ass in his lunch.

"What are you doing?" I say.

"I like to think of myself as a scale," he says, striking a pose with his legs crossed in the lotus position and his arms held out to the sides, elbows down and wrists bent, palms facing up.

I hate it when he does that.

"People are staring," I say.

"Let them stare," he says in a loud, commanding voice. "I am Karma. I weigh the outcome of your decisions. Heed my wisdom."

"Heed this," says a balding thirty-five-year-old New York native with a future in failed opportunities who gives Karma the bird.

Not a wise decision.

Karma places the tip of his middle finger against the inside of his thumb and makes a flicking motion at the balding man. The next moment, the man is tripping over his own feet and falling face-first into a table occupied by a married couple who just ordered the chicken curry.

Instant karma.

At the back of the restaurant, the manager of Curry in a Hurry, a forty-year-old Indian with a future in heart attacks, is pointing his finger at us.

"Get off the table! Get off the table and get out or I'll call the police!"

Karma isn't moving.

"Can we get back to my question about paths?" I ask.

"It's all about cause and effect," says Karma, ignoring me and addressing the two dozen or so patrons of Curry in a Hurry. It's fast-food philosophy for a fast-food crowd.

"If you do good things, good things will happen to you." Karma lowers his right hand and raises his left. "If you do bad things, yada yada yada."

I look around, expecting the other restaurant customers to either be laughing and shaking their heads or ignoring Karma completely. After all, this is New York City. Stuff like this happens all the time. Instead, other than the balding guy with a face full of chicken curry and the couple whose meal he ruined, I discover most of the customers are paying attention. More than that. They're almost transfixed.

I've seen this reaction before, back during the Classical Age, after the exodus and before the birth of the Roman Empire, when the vast majority of humans were hungry for messiahs and spiritual leaders. Karma would sit down on a hill or under a tree and just start talking and the people would flock to him, asking him to lead them out of whatever persecution or injustice they suffered. When he got them all good and worked up, right where he wanted them, he'd spontaneously combust and they'd run away screaming.

Afterward, we'd have a good laugh about it over some wine and unleavened bread.

But now, human beings seem to have eschewed their pursuit of spiritual saviors for the pursuit of corporeal rewards and material goods.

Glycolic-acid peels and breast implants.

Prada handbags and Hugo Boss suits.

Luxury SUVs and home theater systems.

Even when they do seek out internal guidance, they've traded in the ascetic for celebrity. Their messiahs are pop singers and movie stars, their spiritual leaders television evangelists and radio personalities. But then I look around this Indian fast-food restaurant on Manhattan's East Side, at the people transfixed by Karma, and I think maybe humans are hungrier for guidance than I thought. Maybe they want more than a paycheck and a bedroom set from Ethan Allen to define who they are. To measure their success.

Or else Karma just knows how to work a crowd.

"He who speaks in a nonhurtful, truthful manner creates positive karma," he says, his eyes closed, espousing the philosophy of karma in Buddhism.

"Engage in wholesome action, avoiding that which would do harm.

"Pursue a livelihood that does not harm others or oneself.

"Do not answer injustice with injury. Answer injustice with kindness."

I'm pretty sure that last one's Lao Tzu, not Buddha, but these people don't know the difference.

"What about the Path of Destiny?" I ask.

"Man creates his own destiny," he says. "The path you seek is your own."

It's really frustrating when he talks in philosophical axioms.

"What if I'm not seeking a path but am sending others down a path that isn't meant for them?" I ask, trying to remain patient while the manager of Curry in a Hurry is on the phone, calling the police. "Does Karma say anything about that?"

"To understand another's path, you must first understand yourself."

Whatever that means.

Before I can pursue my line of questioning, a young man, just turned twenty and on his way to a series of dead-end jobs, approaches our table holding his baseball cap in his hands.

"If I apologize to my girlfriend, will she forgive me?"

"Deeds, not words, define the man," says Karma. "Apologize with actions and you will reap the rewards."

The young man thanks Karma and leaves the restaurant.

"Is it too late to make something right?" asks a twenty-five-year-old female who steals money from her parents to buy drugs.

"It's never too late to atone for one's offenses," he answers.

She starts to cry, then also leaves.

"Will I be able to find happiness?" asks another customer.

"Happiness is found within."

"Can you offer salvation?" asks a forty-two-year-old woman who will continue an extramarital affair for the next seven years.

"Screw salvation," says Karma, opening his eyes. "If you want salvation, talk to Jerry."

In the distance I hear sirens. They might not be for us, but just in case . . .

"I think we should leave," I say.

Karma polishes off the rest of his Kingfisher. "But I'm on a roll."

I guess that depends on how you define *roll*. Half of the patrons who were here when he started are gone and the manager is cursing Karma in Hindi. When I glance back at Karma, he has this smirk on his face.

"Please don't tell me you're thinking about spontaneously combusting," I say.

"It crossed my mind," says Karma. "What do you think?"

"Probably a bad idea," I say. "But if you're going to do it, can you at least wait until after we talk about Destiny?"

"What is all this Path of Destiny stuff about, anyway?" he asks, waving his empty beer bottle in the air again, seemingly unaware of his current status as Least Favorite Customer.

"I think we should talk about this someplace else," I say, as the sirens grow louder.

"But I haven't finished my lunch," he says, grabbing a piece of naan from under his left thigh and scooping some lamb curry off his pants.

"Come on," I say, taking him by the hand and pulling him down from the table. "Let's get out of here before the police show up."

"Too late," he says.

A police car pulls up in front of the restaurant as the remaining patrons, the spell apparently broken, go back to their meals and avoid eye contact with us. A few moments later, the manager appears at the top of the stairs, followed by two uniformed officers.

"Them!" the manager yells, pointing at us. Like I did anything wrong. "They disrupt my business and drive my customers away."

"Is that what happened?" asks the first police officer, a twenty-seven-year-old unmarried man who is fated to stay that way.

"Not exactly," I say. Though I have no idea what I'm going to say to follow it up. This is one of those times when I wish I could just blink out of existence. Maybe transport myself to Hawaii or Santorini or Jamaica. I hear Hedonism II is nice this time of year.

The forty-two-year-old woman whom Karma told to "screw salvation" points to him and says, "He thinks he's the incarnation of karma."

"Is that so?" says the officer.

"The conquest of karma lies in intelligent action and dispassionate reaction," says Karma, and then belches in the officer's face.

Like that's going to help us.

"And what about you?" asks the officer, looking at me. "Who do you think you are?"

"I'm someone in the wrong place at the wrong time."

"You got that right," says the officer. "Let's go outside and have a little chat, find out who you two really are."

"I am Karma," announces Karma, climbing onto another table, knocking over glasses and plates as he assumes the lotus position. "I am like a scale. . . ."

"Let's go, buddy," says the first officer, reaching over and grabbing Karma by one arm.

Karma isn't budging, which brings the second officer over to the other side of the table, where he takes hold of Karma's other arm.

"Your actions will have consequences," says Karma. "You must obey my law!"

"Yeah," says the first officer, pulling out his handcuffs. "And you must obey mine."

Faster than you can say *samsara*, Karma is turned around on his chest, his face to one side in a plate of palak paneer, his wrists handcuffed behind him.

"You're going to be sorry!" he says as they pull him to his feet, spinach and cheese dripping from his face. "It's a bad idea to fuck with Karma!"

"And it's a bad idea to fuck with the NYPD," says the officer.

The second officer escorts me down the stairs and out the door, where a crowd has gathered on the sidewalk to watch the show. Behind me, Karma shouts, "Cause and effect! Cause and effect!" as he's dragged out of the restaurant in handcuffs.

CHAPTER 31

The last time I was incarcerated, human beings still believed the sun revolved around the Earth and public executions of heretics were good, wholesome, family entertainment. Back then, prisons were generally referred to as *dungeons* and it wasn't uncommon to have to share your eight-foot-by-six-foot luxury suite with half a dozen condemned men, most of whom needed a bath and some of whom needed a proper burial.

I have to say, the accommodations have improved significantly since then.

Our cell is twenty by ten, with a bench running along the back wall and a single toilet with a sink in the far corner. Instead of dirt and rocks littered with human excrement, the floor is a clean, concrete slab. There's even central air-conditioning. And the only one of us who needs a bath is Karma.

"Can I have a grande double latte?" Karma calls out, his face pressed against the bars, spinach and cheese coagulating in his hair and on his shirt. "No, wait. Make that a chai iced tea."

"Hey, pal," says the thirty-nine-year-old insurance salesman who just lost his job and is sharing the spacious cell with us. "Can you order me a cappuccino?"

"What size?"

"Tall," says the man.

"And one tall cappuccino!" shouts Karma.

Where we are is the drunk tank at the 13th Precinct, which isn't really fair, considering I'm completely sober. But I couldn't leave Karma on his own for fear he'd decide to either pull a disappearing act or spontaneously combust, so I told the officers who arrested us that I'd eaten some special brownies courtesy of Alice B. Toklas and they threw me in the tank with Karma.

It's similar to the circumstances that preceded my last trip to prison in the early sixteenth century, when Karma got drunk at a pub in Cologne, Germany, and started talking about how he'd spoken with Satan. Sure, it was true. We'd had dinner with him just a couple of centuries before. But you don't go around sharing information like that, especially not in a country caught up in a mass hysteria of witch hunts. Needless to say, since I was the heretic's traveling companion, I was guilty by association.

But getting out of the dungeon in Cologne was easy. When the guards weren't looking, we just transported out of Germany to a beach in Barbados. The men we shared our cell with were tortured until they admitted they used witchcraft to help us escape, but they were all going to be tortured and strangled and burned at the stake anyway, so it wasn't like we made things any worse for them.

"Do they have any biscotti?" asks the drunk insurance salesman, whose name is Alex Dunbar and who is on his way to spending the next two decades discovering the limits of his intelligence and developing adult diabetes.

Karma looks up and down the empty hallway outside the holding cell. "I think all the baristas are on break."

"This isn't Starbucks," I say.

Karma turns around and looks at me as if I'd just said there was no Santa Claus.

"It isn't?" says Alex.

"No. This is a prison cell. We've been arrested for being drunk and disorderly and we're in prison, where they don't serve lattes or cappuccinos or biscotti."

Alex Dunbar starts to cry.

"Now see what you've done," says Karma, who walks over and sits down next to Alex and puts an arm around him. "It's not enough he lost his job today, but now you have to go and take away the only thing he was looking forward to."

Sometimes I don't understand Karma. I really don't.

"It's okay," says Karma, giving Alex a one-armed hug and offering comfort. "The woman who fired you is going to get hit by a bus on her way home from work today."

"She is?" says Alex, brightening up, his sniffles tapering off.

"She is?" I say.

Karma gives me a quick shake of his head that Alex misses.

"She sure is," says Karma. "She's going to get nailed by the forty-two bus in Times Square."

"Cool," says Alex.

"Now I want you to lie down on the bench and get some sleep," says Karma. "And when you wake up, we'll have cappuccino and biscotti."

"We will?" he asks.

"You bet."

"Cool."

Karma gets up and Alex lies down on the bench, curling up on his side with his sweater under his head. "Hey," says Alex. "How do you know about the bus?"

"Because I'm Karma."

"Oh," says Alex, who puts his hands between his knees and closes his eyes. Less than a minute later, he's snoring lightly.

Karma comes over and stands next to me. "So you ready to get out of here?"

"What do you mean?" I say.

"You know," he says, folding his arms like Barbara Eden in *I Dream of Jeannie* and blinking. "Let's go."

"This isn't the sixteenth century," I remind him. "The police have our IDs. They know where we live. Plus we're being video-taped. We can't just disappear."

"Bummer," he says. "So what do we do?"

"I already called Justice," I say.

"You did?" says Karma. "When was that?"

"Right after they brought us in," I say. "You were still carrying on about cause and effect and trying to get the palak paneer out of your hair."

"Oh, right," he says, running his fingers across the side of his head and picking out a couple of pieces of spinach. "So what did Justice say?"

"He said he'll be over as soon as he takes care of a problem in the Senate."

"That could be a while," says Karma, taking a seat on the bench.

I sit down next to him. "Are you still drunk?"

He looks at me with bloodshot eyes. "Not really sure."

"Can you answer a question for me?"

He nods. "I'll give it a shot."

A few feet away, Alex begins to snore louder.

"What happens if someone who was born on the Path of Fate ends up on the Path of Destiny?"

Karma looks at me the way Ramses II looked at Moses when he asked the pharaoh to release the Israelites from slavery.

"And you asked *me* if *I* was drunk?"

"Well, what happens?" I ask.

"It can't happen," says Karma. "Predestination Law clearly states that those born to their path are bound to it. Unless, of course, Fate or Destiny intervenes."

"I thought you said you never cracked open your textbook."

"I didn't," says Karma. "But I spent three days memorizing the answers for the test."

"And you still remember them?"

"Sure," he says. "I mean, come on. That was only two hundred and fifty thousand years ago."

Sometimes I wonder if Karma is bipolar or just a smart-ass.

"But what if it could happen?" I say. "What if it *did* happen?"

Karma picks a glob of cheese out of his hair. "Is there something you're not telling me?"

So I tell him about Cliff Brooks. And Sara. And all of the other humans I've helped. And about the time I watched Marie Curie take a milk bath. It just comes out. I get that way sometimes when I'm confessing. Kind of an all-or-nothing thing.

"You know you're not supposed to get involved," he says.

"This coming from someone who just climbed on a table at an Indian fast-food place and revealed himself to a restaurant full of humans," I say. "Two of whom changed their fates based on your advice, by the way."

"Sorry about that," says Karma. "My bad. But it shouldn't be permanent."

"Hello," I say. "I can see their paths. And it looks pretty permanent to me."

"The universe corrects," says Karma.

"What's that supposed to mean?"

"It means that while their journey might be temporarily altered," he says, "they should eventually find their way back to their original paths. Same thing with all of the other mortals you've helped, including this loser you sent off onto the Path of Destiny. Chances are he'll end up back at Hooters trying to impress his girlfriend."

"Are you sure?" I ask.

Karma nods. "You can't fight the universe, Fabio. It's self-correcting, self-fulfilling, and self-serving. Sooner or later, everyone ends up where they're supposed to be. Don't you remember this from Universal Law?"

I kind of ditched that lecture.

"It's the same as the box theory," says Karma.

The box theory contends that humans are creatures of habit

who become comfortable with their lives and circumstances, with the boxes they've built around themselves. If something in their life changes to take them out of their box, they tend to do whatever they can to get back to their comfort level. To get back inside their box.

I've seen it enough times with my humans to know it's more than just a theory. It's a pattern of self-destructive behavior.

Professional athletes and lottery winners who are suddenly thrust into a world of wealth and end up bankrupt. Single men and women who drive love away because they're more comfortable being miserable. Aspiring artists and talented writers who have grown so used to the struggle that they let golden opportunities slip away.

Failure is often easier for humans to accept than success.

Although I should be relieved to know that I probably don't have to worry about the ramifications of changing the cosmic path of Cliff Brooks, I can't help but feel as though I've let him down in some way. And I start to wonder if all of these humans I've been trying to help are just going to end up back where they were.

Desperate. Unfulfilled. Lost.

I think I'm beginning to understand why humans have such a difficult time dealing with disappointment.

"What if the universe doesn't correct?" I ask, more hopeful than worried. "What if Cliff Brooks remains on the Path of Destiny?"

"Well," says Karma, "Predestination Law doesn't specifically address the issue, since it's not supposed to be possible, but I suppose it could be covered by cosmic theory."

"Which says . . ."

"More than likely you'll just cause a cosmic shift that will require divine intervention," says Karma. "Or else cause a black hole to appear and suck all of existence into oblivion."

Well, that makes me feel better.

"But," says Karma, getting up from the bench and walking over to the front of our cell, "it's only a theory."

For a few minutes there's nothing but the sound of Alex Dunbar snoring and distant voices from beyond the closed door at the end of the hall. Then Karma sighs, grasps the bars, presses his face between them, looks out at the empty hallway, and says, "Where's my latte?"

Justice shows up about a half hour later, dressed in a black pinstripe suit, sporting a pair of black Gucci wraparound sunglasses, and carrying a black titanium walking stick.

The thing about Justice is that he's a sociopath.

Personally, I think the whole visually impaired image is all for show, but I've never been able to prove it and I'm not about to try to expose him now. At times like this, it's good to have connections who know how to work the system.

Within minutes of Justice's arrival, Karma and I are released from the drunk tank and cleared of all charges. Naturally, Justice requires a payoff for his assistance and for his silence, so I give up my box seats at Wrigley Field while Karma offers to set up a private meeting with the Dalai Lama.

"Just make sure you don't stare at his third eye," says Karma. "He's really self-conscious about it."

Once outside, Justice takes off to deal with some voting machine problems in Florida, leaving Karma and me on the 13th Precinct steps.

"Well, that was fun," I say. "Let's do it again in another five hundred years."

"I'd better get going," says Karma, looking at his watch. "I've got a bunch of unsettled karma that needs to be balanced."

"That's an understatement," I say, making my way to the sidewalk to hail a cab.

"Hey, Fabio," says Karma.

"What?" I snap, turning around. Getting arrested and having to deal with Justice always puts me in a mood.

"Don't get too close to humans," he says. "They're contagious."

Human beings are technically a virus. That was one of the first things we learned in Primordial Soup 101. But knowledge like that is the kind of thing you tend to suppress when you've fallen in love with one of them.

"Thanks," I say. "Anything else?"

"Just be careful," he says. "And for Christ's sake, stop helping them. You never know what you'll catch."

CHAPTER 32

A couple of days later, I'm checking on the paths of some of the mortals whose fates I've redirected, just to keep on top of things, when I discover that Cliff Brooks isn't as much of an anomaly as I thought.

The future of Nicolas Jansen, the fine young drug addict who stabbed me in Amsterdam and joined a monastery in France, has started to fade from view.

George and Carla Baer, the previously doomed couple with a future in bondage and discipline, are drifting off my radar.

Even Darren Stafford, the ex–biology teacher and would-be bird molester, is destined for something beyond my reach.

As I mentally sort through my case files, I discover that in addition to Cliff Brooks, Nicolas Jansen, Darren Stafford, and George and Carla Baer, I've managed to set more than a dozen other humans on the Path of Destiny.

I have to admit, I'm surprised by my powers of suggestion. I was just shooting for paths that didn't involve drug addiction or pedophilia.

Apparently, I'm better at this than I thought.

Of course, when it was just Cliff Brooks whose future I'd changed, I stood a better chance of getting away with what I'd done. But the last time anyone had a positive impact on humans like this was Josh, and he didn't exactly maintain his anonymity.

Even if Karma is right and the universe will eventually correct and help my humans find their way back to their original paths, he didn't mention how long that might take. I don't know if Destiny will realize I'm the one responsible for increasing her workload, but eventually someone is bound to notice. Humans don't just change their stars, so to speak, without some sort of cosmic push. And if Jerry finds out I'm the one who did the pushing, there's a good chance I'll lose my frequent-flier privileges.

I wonder if I can plead temporary insanity.

I wonder if Jerry will cut me some slack.

I wonder if air travel has improved much since the *Hindenburg*.

I think I need to lie low for a while, though it's not like I can exactly hide. Damn Jerry's omnipresence. So instead I decide to head out to Los Angeles. At least there I can take cover in the smog. And the superficial glare from all of the designer clothes, luxury vehicles, and cosmetic enhancements is hard for Jerry to look at ever since his laser eye surgery.

"Will you be gone long?" asks Sara in bed the night before I leave.

"Just a couple of days," I say.

I can't tell Sara I'm off to hide from God in the superficiality and pollution of Hollywood, so I tell her I have some clients I have to see on the West Coast.

"I love that you care so much about your clients, Fabio," she says. "That you work so hard to try to help them. It's one of my favorite parts about you."

"What are the other parts?" I ask.

She smiles and raises an eyebrow and disappears below the covers.

And I've suddenly forgotten what we were talking about.

I wasn't lying to Sara when I told her I was going to see someone, though you'd think Truth and Wisdom would live at the top of some hallowed mountain in the Himalayas and require a sherpa and two weeks' worth of suffering just to reach them. Instead they live on Mulholland Drive in the Hollywood Hills and require a personal fitness trainer and two weeks' worth of tanning salons just to look like them.

Why they chose to live in Los Angeles, I don't know. Probably got sucked in by the whole City of Angels crap. But then, I can't think of another place on the planet that can use more truth and wisdom than Tinseltown.

It's the epitome of retail therapy. A microcosm of consumer culture, of how the constant pursuit of *more* prevents humans from discovering their true inner nature and from directing their lives to their most optimal fates. Nowhere are there more material distractions and social pressures that influence humans and prevent them from finding their paths than in Hollywood. Some would argue for that distinction to go to Las Vegas, but if you ask me, Vegas is more of an adult theme park than a cultural ecosystem.

I just hope Truth and Wisdom haven't succumbed to the pressures of the Hollywood lifestyle.

"Fabio!" says Truth, greeting me at the front door of their $12.5 million estate with an automobile courtyard, tennis court, swimming pool, sauna, and a sweeping view of the San Fernando Valley.

Truth releases me from a big bear hug. "It's great to see you," he says, all whitened teeth and artificial tan.

So much for keeping it real.

Although it's been a while since I've seen him, his face looks unnaturally smooth. He either got an upgrade on his man suit or else he's getting Botox injections.

"You look great," he says, then draws me inside and walks with me down the hall. When he's not looking, I check to make sure I still have my wallet and keys.

The thing about Truth is that he's a kleptomaniac.

"So what's new in the Big Apple?" he asks.

I fill him in on all the gossip that's fit to spill as I follow him out back, where Wisdom is sitting poolside with a copy of *The Power of Positive Thinking* and a mojito. He doesn't look much different from Truth, except he has gold hoops through both earlobes.

"Well, if you ask me, you look great," Truth says to me, then turns to Wisdom. "Isn't that the truth? Doesn't he look great?"

Without looking up, Wisdom says, "Expressions of praise are nothing more than the reflection of your own perceptions. They have nothing to do with truth."

The thing about Wisdom is that he has an inferiority complex.

"Can we play nice for today," asks Truth, "in honor of our guest?"

"I always play nice," says Wisdom, putting down his book and getting up from his lounge chair to give me a hug. "Can I get you a mojito, Fabio?"

We spend the next couple of hours getting drunk on white rum and mint leaves and reliving old times, though to be honest, there's a lot more getting drunk than sharing of memories, since most of the humans on my path don't deal too much in truth and wisdom. Once we're good and hammered, Truth suggests we head down to the Formosa Café.

An unimpressive red-and-ebony Chinese-themed Hollywood watering hole in a run-down section of Hollywood, the Formosa offers a full dinner menu, though most of the people in the dimly lit café are here for cocktails, sitting at the bar or in the red leather booths beneath the black-and-white autographed photographs of stars who dined here in the past: James Dean, Marilyn Monroe, Clark Gable, Paul Newman, Jack Benny, Elizabeth Taylor, Marlon Brando. You half expect one of them to come strolling through the door at any moment.

"A lot of the people who come here are regulars," says Truth, sipping his martini between Wisdom and me at the bar as he palms an ashtray. "But you still get a good mix of new couples and first dates, which makes for an entertaining evening."

"What do you mean?" I ask, trying not to notice that the woman sitting on my left is thinking about taking a role in a porn film where she has sex with a Great Dane.

"He does this every time," says Wisdom. "It's childish, if you ask me."

"I don't hear you complaining about the results," says Truth.

Wisdom just responds by taking another sip of his mojito.

"This couple behind us," says Truth.

I glance over my shoulder and see a man and a woman in their early thirties, both dressed in white, sitting at a booth sharing a bottle of cabernet. They're not married, but it's in their future, followed by an ugly divorce.

Maybe coming to Los Angeles wasn't such a good idea after all.

"They're celebrating two years of nonmarital bliss," says Truth, slipping an empty shot glass into his coat pocket. "She's hoping he's going to propose tonight, which he actually plans on doing. Except there's one little problem."

Truth holds his right hand up like a shadow puppet of a bunny rabbit, points its ears at the couple over his shoulder, then opens and closes his other three fingers as if mouthing silent words. Two seconds later, the man sitting behind us says, "I slept with your sister."

I'm not sure who's more surprised at his admission—him or his girlfriend.

"What?" she says.

He looks around as if trying to figure out what happened. Obviously, this isn't a confession he intended to make. But he makes it again.

"I slept with your sister," he says.

He probably wasn't expecting to have a full glass of red wine thrown in his face either; otherwise he wouldn't have worn all white.

"But we had sex only three times," he says, following his sobbing girlfriend out of the booth, past the bar, and out the front doors.

No sooner have they vacated the booth than Truth and Wisdom have claimed it for us.

"Never fails," says Truth, leaning back into the soft red vinyl.

A busboy comes by with a towel to wipe up the wine and remove the bottle and glasses.

"You did that just to get a booth?" I ask, sitting down.

"Well, that's not the only reason," says Truth, sliding the salt and pepper shakers off the table and into his man purse. "I mean, come on, the guy had to come clean sooner or later. Might as well be at a time when it benefits us. Am I right?"

Wisdom pretends not to care, though he looks much happier in the booth than on a bar stool.

"But you changed their fates," I say.

They're not going to get married now, which means they won't get divorced. Instead, the boyfriend will attempt a futile reconciliation before sleeping with the sister again, knocking her up, then splitting and moving to Aspen to become a ski instructor, while the girlfriend will end up in a series of relationships that don't end up much better than this one.

It's all I can do to sit still and not go after the doomed couple, but I can't risk taking that chance. Maybe if I were with Sloth and Gluttony, but Truth and Wisdom are pretty much in Jerry's back pocket.

"Sorry about that," says Truth. "But nothing good would have come from that relationship anyway. Better they know the truth now rather than keeping it hidden."

"Oh, so now you're waxing wise," says Wisdom. "How quaint."

"I was just making a point," says Truth. "Why does this always have to be about you?"

"I'm just saying that you might want to think about sticking to what you know," says Wisdom. "And to be quite honest, I have my doubts about that."

"Are you questioning me?" asks Truth.

Their incessant banter fades into the background as I look around at the other patrons in the Formosa, leaning against the bar or huddling in the red leather booths beneath the watchful eyes of dead movie stars—their fates blending together in discordant disillusion, in a cacophony of failure.

Undiscovered.

Unrequited.

Unemployed.

These are not bad people. Except for the sexual predator at the end of the bar who's posing as a director and slipping some GHB into the cosmopolitan of the would-be starlet he's scamming.

I should really put Dennis back on my speed dial.

But the rest of these humans, these helpless mortals, are just trying to find a way to be happy, and most of them are struggling to make that happen. While a lot of it has to do with the unreasonable societal expectations placed on them, most of it has to do with the hand they were dealt. With the path they were born on. With me.

I turn back to Wisdom and Truth, who are still engaged in their never-ending discussion about who is the more important of the two. Like it matters. There is no wisdom in the needless suffering of my humans. And the truth is, I'd rather spend my time helping them than hanging out with a couple of petty, manipulative immortals.

"So you're actually saying you believe Plato was a moron?" says Wisdom.

"I don't believe anything," says Truth. "I know it."

I excuse myself and pretend to go to the bathroom, then sneak out the back door into the warm Los Angeles night, where the traffic of Santa Monica Boulevard drones past, heading west into Beverly Hills and east toward Hollywood. Although the traffic is relatively loud and heavy, it can't drown out the memories of the ghosts that haunt this town.

Just a few miles from the Formosa, twenty-three-year-old River Phoenix collapsed and died outside the Viper Room from an overdose of heroin and cocaine. A mile away on Sunset Boulevard, John Belushi died from the same lethal combination when he was thirty-three. And around the corner, F. Scott Fitzgerald finally succumbed to complications brought on by alcoholism and smoking at the age of forty-four.

Three of my favorite celebrities of the twentieth century, and all of them ended their paths with me within a mile of one another.

There was a time when I would have found a coincidence like that amusing. Now it fills me with an overwhelming sense of failure. I could have saved all three of them, enjoyed their continued contributions to film and literature, helped them to live longer, more fulfilling lives. Instead, I stood by and watched them self-destruct.

Across the street attempting to hail a cab is the woman whose fiancé slept with her sister multiple times. The present and future disappointment of a partner lurks behind his jilted lover, attempting to talk her out of leaving, apologizing with a sincerity that smacks of desperation. I should just let them go, let them make their mistakes and move on. Except I can see a future where they'd be good together. Where they would be happy. Where they would enjoy a partnership of love and respect.

Every human being has a choice.

They can choose happiness or they can choose misery. They can choose forgiveness or they can choose resentment. They can choose love or they can choose anger.

There are no absolutes. Every situation requires a choice. And every human chooses how he or she wants to react. But too many times, humans choose to be miserable. Too many times, they choose not to forgive. Too many times, they choose anger.

I know Jerry told me to stop interfering, but I've walked through a door that has closed and locked behind me. I can't ignore my choice-challenged humans any longer.

CHAPTER 33

The Westfield Mall on Market Street in San Francisco is an upscale nine-floor urban shopping center, home to a collection of 170 fashionable stores and boutiques that cater to the trendy and stylish consumer.

Calvin Klein, Hugo Boss, and Ann Taylor.

Banana Republic, Tommy Bahama, and Lucky Brand Jeans.

Beard Papa Sweets, Godiva Chocolatier, and Juicy Couture.

True, Juicy Couture sells fashion accessories rather than confections, but when thirteen-year-old girls walk around wearing the word *juicy* on their asses, it kind of sends a mixed message about what's on the menu.

Within its 1.5 million square feet of consumer indulgence, the Westfield Mall also boasts a Bloomingdale's, a Nordstrom, three Bebe stores, nine sunglass retailers, seventeen separate shops that provide health and beauty services, and twenty-six jewelry stores. The mall even has concierge services, valet parking, and a day spa.

You'd think with all of the money they sank into this place, they would have managed to find room for a Hot Dog on a Stick or an Orange Julius, but the lowest common denominator of nourishment I can find in the food court is a Panda Express and a Jamba Juice.

So as I sit on a leather recliner eating my orange chicken and drinking my Orange Dream Machine smoothie with a soy protein boost, I watch all of the mall addicts wander past with their bags of eight balls and acid tabs to distract them from their futures.

The fifty-two-year-old housewife who hasn't had sex with her husband in six months and who is considering having an affair just to feel the loving, hungry touch of a man again.

The twenty-nine-year-old store manager of Banana Republic who can't get enough of his wife but who wonders if they have enough in common outside of the bedroom to keep the marriage together.

The forty-year-old divorced mother of two who would prefer to stay with a boyfriend whom she's not in love with rather than taking a chance and opening her heart to another man who truly loves her.

Relationships seem to be the flavor of the day.

I see this all of the time: men and women who remain in stagnant relationships or who opt not to enter into new ones because it's easier than being alone or starting over from scratch. They'd rather remain in the comfort and familiarity of something that doesn't work than find the courage to take the chance on something that might bring them happiness. Something that might lead to the future they've always wanted. Something that might actually involve the risk of heartbreak.

They prefer the comfort of their box.

So they settle for less than what they want. They settle for mediocre relationships and tepid romance and distant bedmates. And they eventually end up here. Or someplace like here. Maybe someplace with a Hickory Farms or a JCPenney or a Beck's Shoes rather than Bristol Farms or Bloomingdale's or Kenneth Cole. But regardless of the brand name, the places all serve the same purpose.

Shopping helps to hide what's wrong with a relationship. Maybe not as much as good sex, but if you can buy something nice for yourself, treat yourself to a new pair of shoes or that watch you had your eye on or a few hours in a day spa, you feel better about yourself and that helps you feel better about your relationship. At least for a while. Until you realize you're just masking the cause of your own suffering.

I'm here to put an end to that.

"Ladies and gentlemen," I say, standing up in a planter box in the center of the lounge area. Probably not the most subtle way for me to get my point across, but I've got a lot of relationship-challenged humans to fix and I don't want to do this piecemeal. "Can I have your attention, please?"

A few bored customers look my way. The rest just ignore me and head off to Aveda or Banana Republic or the Sunglass Hut International. So I try again, but in my best impersonation of Jerry.

"Can I have your attention, please?"

This time I get their attention and most of them not only look my way but stop what they're doing and start walking toward me. It's amazing what you can accomplish when you sound like God.

The problem is, there's a big difference between sounding like

Jerry and being Jerry, who has an aura I just can't emulate, no matter how much omni-whatever I try to project. So I have a limited window of opportunity to get my point across. Eventually, these humans are going to realize I'm a fraud and I have to convince them of their emotional ineptitude before they reach that point of realization. Or before the mall security shows up.

"You don't have to suffer," I say. "You don't have to live a life of self-delusion. You are the masters of your own happiness."

While not entirely true, it sounds good. Or at least it did when I heard it on NPR. But from the blank expressions of the humans staring back at me, they have no idea what I'm talking about.

So I figure I should just dumb it down.

"Look," I say. "You don't need all this crap to make you happy. To make you feel more attractive. To fill the emotional void in your lives. You don't need your Roberto Cavalli shirt or your Dior sneakers or your Versace sunglasses to compensate for your failed relationships. Okay, well, maybe he does," I say, pointing to a thirty-two-year-old reproduction of a Ken doll who's wearing all three. "But for the rest of you, there's still hope."

One floor above me, I see the flicker of mall security heading toward the escalator.

"You," I say, pointing to a thirty-year-old chronic screwup who just bought his girlfriend a pair of diamond earrings to make up for the fact that he's emotionally challenged. "She doesn't want jewelry. She just wants you to be honest and compassionate."

He looks around, smiling self-consciously.

"You." I point toward a young married couple who have regular shouting matches over toilet seats, grocery shopping, and the alphabetical order of the CD collection. "It doesn't matter that he's anal retentive or that she leaves her crap everywhere. What matters is that you accept each other because of your faults, not in spite of them."

"He's right," she says, looking up at her husband.

"Whatever," he says, then turns and walks away as his wife follows, the beginnings of an argument blooming from her lips.

At least I tried.

Out of the corner of my eye, I see the security guards are making their way down the escalator.

"And you," I say, this time leveling my index finger at the divorced forty-year-old mother of two who has chosen safe mediocrity over the risk of true love. "Dump your underachieving live-in boyfriend and open your heart to emotional intimacy."

And that's all I have time for before the two mall security guards arrive and ask me to step down out of the planter box.

"Well, it's been fun," I say. "You've been a wonderful audience. I hope you enjoyed the show. Just remember, don't go to bed angry, never settle for less, and always eat your vegetables."

With that, I bow, doff an imaginary hat, then follow the lead of my invisible chapeau and blink out of existence.

CHAPTER 34

"I have a surprise for you," says Sara as she takes me by the hand and leads me across Fifth Avenue.

I'm not really that big on surprises. Go figure. But the day I get back from California, Sara tells me she has to take me somewhere and I'll love it.

I hope so. I could use some cheering up. Not that I didn't have a good time in San Francisco, but after transporting to Manhattan, I do a quick checkup on the humans I've recently sent down the Path of Destiny and discover that Cliff Brooks is dead.

I don't know how this happened. I sure as hell didn't see this coming. Maybe if he'd been destined to die while fighting for a noble cause or saving someone's life, I could understand. But humans on the Path of Destiny don't just up and get attacked by a pack of starving greyhounds while eating a Big Mac and fries.

I haven't felt this bad since the Donner party.

At least with them, it wasn't like I offered advice on their travel itinerary or suggested something on the menu. They made their own mistakes and I let them. But with Cliff Brooks, I'm the one who put him on the Path of Destiny. I'm the one responsible for directing him to his own death.

"Here we are," says Sara, shortly after we cross the street, and I realize we're going to the Met.

At first I have no idea what she could possibly have planned for my surprise. Then I see the signs posted at the ticket windows and at the front doors advertising the Met's new temporary exhibit:

The Nature of Fate.

"You're always talking about fate and destiny," says Sara, as we walk into the museum. "About the concept of the multiplicity of fate and how people make choices without considering the possible consequences, about the inevitability of their fate. So I thought you'd appreciate this."

I don't know if *appreciate* is the word I would use to describe how I feel about seeing a collection of artwork representing my nature.

"Surprised?" asks Sara, squeezing my hand.

"That would be the word," I say, then flash a convincing smile and give her a kiss. "You're the best."

As a general rule, I tend to stay away from museums. Not that I don't have an appreciation for art. It's just that so many of the pieces that hang in the world's museums are depictions of people and events I've known and experienced, memories I'd prefer not to revisit, especially in my current state. Apparently, they've brought them all to the Met so that I can enjoy the Nature of Me.

Surprise.

There's *The Death of Socrates. The Last Supper.* The discovery of the New World.

The storming of the Bastille. The sinking of the *Titanic*. The Great Depression.

There are mythological paintings of Sisyphus and Oedipus and Prometheus. Of Pandora's box and *The Judgment of Paris* and *The Death of Achilles*. And there are dozens of other paintings and portraits and sculptures depicting men and women as they're about to make a life-changing decision or at the moment when they realize the fatal significance of their actions.

Yes. This is just what I needed to cheer me up.

In my defense, a number of these works of art represent Death, Envy, Lust, Cruelty, and War. Still, it's rather humbling to see myself portrayed in such a collection of mayhem and mistakes and despair.

"What do you think?" asks Sara.

I think I'm going to throw up.

Instead, I hear myself say, "It's overwhelming."

I don't think I ever imagined myself in this light. These paintings make me seem like an insensitive, careless bastard who forces unpleasant circumstances upon innocent humans. Sure, the circumstances are dictated by the choices my humans have made, but no one likes to see their true nature depicted in the soft glow of museum lighting.

"What do *you* think?" I ask.

"About the collection?" asks Sara.

I nod. "What do you think about the nature of Fate?"

"I think Fate is capricious," she says. "I think he enjoys the pain and suffering he inflicts upon people. Like it was something he was born to do."

Apparently, that was the wrong question to ask.

"You said *he*," I say.

"What?"

"You referred to Fate as *he*. As if Fate were a man."

"Well, of course," she says. "Only a man would be the cause of so much misery and gloom and appear to take so much pleasure in it."

"You've never met Cruelty," I say.

"Who?"

"Nothing."

I really have to stop saying things in my outloud voice.

We continue past paintings of mistakes and bad judgments. Of lost hopes and lost opportunities. Of failures and disappointments. By the time we've made it through the exhibit, I feel as though I've gone ten rounds with Mayhem and been raped by Aggression.

CHAPTER 35

Two days later I'm sitting in my apartment watching television with Sara, lying low while trying to come to terms with the death of Cliff Brooks, when Sara says, "Honey, is that you?"

I glance at the flat-screen television, where the news anchor on CNN is talking about some miracle that took place in California. In the corner of the screen is a grainy photo of a figure standing in a planter box, his mouth open and his arms outstretched as if preaching. From this distance, it's hard to get a good look at the figure's face. But when another image of the figure appears on the fifty-inch, high-definition screen, enlarged and digitally enhanced, it's apparent the figure looks a lot like me.

Well, this is awkward.

Turns out my impersonation of Jerry and subsequent disappearing act made the national news. Dozens of men and women have come forward to say they were touched by the divine, by a presence that spoke to their hearts and filled them with love.

This is me we're talking about, right?

Disappearing in front of a large group of people—in broad daylight in a shopping mall—probably wasn't the smartest thing for me to do. But at least I know I made a difference, convinced a lot of relationship-challenged consumers to reexamine the way they relate to one another.

Fortunately, the Miracle on Market Street, as they're calling it, took place in San Francisco, which everyone knows is full of gays, heathens, and liberals, so you can't believe anything that happens there. Besides, Jerry doesn't pay attention to reports of supernatural events unless they involve locusts, resurrections, or the Chicago Cubs.

But at the moment, Jerry isn't the problem.

Sara picks up the remote control and stops the playback using TiVo, leaving my somewhat blurry but clearly recognizable face displayed on fifty inches of flat-screen, high-definition digital technology.

"Tell me that's not you," she says.

"That's not me," I say.

Is it technically lying if you tell someone what she asked you to tell her?

Sara walks up to the television and points to my larger-than-life image. "That's not you?"

"Um," I say, and then start to laugh. I get that way when I'm nervous sometimes. Or when my immortal identity is discovered by my mortal girlfriend.

"Do you think this is funny?" she asks.

"No," I say, shaking my head. And I'm wondering if this is a good time to spontaneously combust or if that would only make things worse.

Relationships with humans are so complicated.

"Fabio?"

Maybe if I just ignore her she'll go away.

"Fabio?"

Maybe I can get Memory to do a selective purge.

"Fabio!"

"Yes," I say, blurting it out. "Yes, it's me."

So much for spontaneously combusting.

Sara looks at me, her stare shifting from my face to the flat-screen television, then back again. I feel like I've been caught doing something inappropriate. Like that time when Disappointment walked in on me masturbating to an eight-by-ten glossy of Virtue.

"Is it true what they said about what you did?" asks Sara.

"Is what true?" I ask, still holding out hope she'll just drop the whole thing.

She hesitates, as if she's not really sure she wants to know the answer to her next question. "Did you just vanish into thin air?"

After dealing with humans for countless centuries, I've discovered when it comes to mortal women, there are certain questions you should never answer truthfully.

Does this make me look fat?

Do you fantasize about having sex with other women?

Did you just vanish into thin air?

While I suppose there are situations where honesty is actually appropriate for the first two questions, like at an all-you-can-eat buffet or at the Playboy Mansion, the last one should be a no-brainer. But I can't seem to find the words to lie to Sara. And I know that if I don't tell her the truth, any future we have together is likely to involve a lot of counseling and a lot less sex.

So I just nod.

"How is that possible?" asks Sara.

I could go into the physics of molecular transportation and how my genetic structure allows me to jump around the globe and the solar system at the speed of light, but that would probably just bring up more questions, and I never really had the patience for scientific explanations. So instead I decide to give a demonstration.

"Like this," I say.

When I reappear an instant later behind Sara and tap her on the shoulder, she screams and turns around and falls to the floor in an unconscious heap.

Okay, maybe that wasn't such a good idea.

When Sara regains consciousness a few minutes later on the couch, I flash my most charming smile and hope she doesn't scream or call the police or kick me in the face. Sure, the warranty's still good on my man suit for another nine months, but I'm not covered for dental.

"Did that really happen?" she asks.

I nod, still smiling.

"And you can do that whenever you want?" she asks. "Go wherever you want? Just vanish from one place and appear in another?"

I nod again.

Several long moments pass in which Sara doesn't say anything but just stares at me, her expression as unreadable as her future.

Not a muscle twitches. She barely blinks. Just as I'm beginning to think she's suffering from the onset of shock, she says, "Well, I guess that explains why you never ask me to pick you up from the airport."

I let out a laugh, thinking things are going to be okay, that I'm not going to have to share all of the secrets of my existence, until I realize Sara's not laughing but is still staring at me with that same blank expression.

"Are you from another planet?" she asks.

"No," I assure her. "I'm not from another planet."

How do you explain you hail from the ether of the universe without sounding like a lunatic?

I just hope she doesn't ask me if I'm human.

"Are you human?" she asks.

I don't immediately respond, hoping that by my stalling for time she'll forget the question.

"Fabio?"

I could just transport out of here, go hide someplace and hope this eventually blows over.

"Fabio?"

I could pray for a natural disaster to provide some temporary distraction, but Jerry would want an explanation, and I hate paperwork.

"Fabio!"

"No," I say. "I'm not human."

From the expression on her face, I can tell this isn't an answer she ever expected to hear.

"Then what are you?"

So I tell her all about me. About my existence and my abilities. About my history and my future. About my man suit and my list of sexual partners. Sure, finding out your boyfriend has had sex with more than a hundred thousand women can be a little overwhelming, but I'd rather she hear it from me.

"A hundred *thousand*?" she says.

I shrug. "Give or take."

I mean, really. Homo sapiens appeared barely more than two hundred thousand years ago. True, I've been fooling around with human women for only the past five thousand years, but spread out over the existence of modern man, a hundred thousand women averages out to one every other year. Of course, that number doesn't include Destiny or Lust or Secrecy, or any of my other numerous dalliances. But I don't see any reason to upset Sara.

"How do I know you're not making this all up?" asks Sara. "How do I know you're telling the truth?"

I obviously can't prove it to her by telling Sara about herself. So I tell her about her older brother who drowned in a pool when she was three. And her parents who got divorced when she was seven. And her best friend who got pregnant when Sara was thirteen. And her college boyfriend who cheated on her with a stripper.

After a few more minutes of staring at me in silence, she finally says, "So you're really Fate?"

I nod.

"Which means you can see how my life is going to turn out?"

"Not exactly."

"What do you mean?" asks Sara.

This is where things get tricky.

Confessing to Sara that I control the fate of more than five and a half billion humans is one thing. And I haven't even considered telling her about Jerry. She'd want to meet him, which of course is impossible, and that would just lead to arguments about her feeling like I don't think she's good enough to meet God, which is a conversation I'd prefer to avoid altogether.

But telling someone they're destined for a future greater than the mass of the human population can have an adverse impact on their destiny. They start looking for signs. Altering their habits. Thinking about what's going to happen. All it takes is for one moment to shift, one cosmic wheel to get out of alignment, and their destiny can veer off in another direction. As I look at Sara, waiting for me to give her an answer, I know I don't have any choice but to tell her the truth.

"I can't read your future," I say.

Okay. Mostly the truth.

"Why not?" asks Sara, a concerned expression on her face. "Is there something wrong with me?"

"It's not like that," I say. "You're not on my path."

"Path?" she says. "What path? What does that mean?"

I take a deep breath, then blurt it out. "It means you're on the Path of Destiny."

I follow up my latest confession with an explanation of path theory, detailing the difference between Fate and Destiny while leaving out the fact that I got a C in the class. Jerry was very disappointed in me.

"So what am I destined for?" she asks.

"You'd have to ask Destiny," I say. "But I'd advise against bringing this up with her. You're kind of not supposed to know about her. Or me. Or any of this. I could get in big trouble. Plus she's already not real happy about the fact that I'm your boyfriend."

"Well, it's not like I'm going to have lunch with her tomorrow," says Sara.

"You'd be surprised."

After a moment, Sara sits up on the couch and wraps her arms around me, holding me tighter than she's ever held me.

"Thank you for sharing this with me," she whispers in my ear. "I won't tell anyone."

I feel like a superhero who's just revealed his secret identity. Clark Kent confessing he's Superman. Peter Parker divulging his inner Spider-Man.

Sara Griffen. My Lois Lane. My Mary Jane Watson.

Still holding me tight, Sara says, "How come Destiny doesn't want you to be my boyfriend?"

"Because she's a selfish whore," I say. It's just an automatic response. "And she feels like I'm preventing you from fulfilling your destiny."

Sara pulls away and looks at me. "Maybe it's like I said before," she says, her smile radiant. "Maybe you're my destiny."

In the mirror behind Sara, I see my grainy image reflected on the flat-screen, captured on a cell phone camera, the evidence of my identity sent in by an anonymous source, and I find myself wondering what Destiny was doing Monday afternoon.

Sara turns around to see what I'm looking at. "How much trouble are you going to get into for this?"

"I don't know," I say. "But Jerry watches CNN religiously, so I'm pretty sure he's going to find out."

"Who's Jerry?" asks Sara.

"Who?" I say, playing dumb.

"Jerry," she says.

"I don't know what you're talking about," I say.

"You've mentioned him before."

"No, I haven't."

"Is he your boss?"

"No."

"You mentioned once he reminds you of God."

"No, I didn't."

Her eyes suddenly grow wide. "Is he God?"

"No."

"He is God, isn't he?"

"No."

"Can I meet him?"

CHAPTER 36

In addition to her constant badgering for a face-to-face with Jerry, to which I finally caved and told her I would see what I could do, Sara wants to know everything about me.

Where I've lived.

What I've seen.

Whom I've slept with.

"You don't really want to know," I tell her.

"Yes, I do," she says. "I want to know everything about you. And that includes your sexual history."

So I tell her.

About the women from ancient Greece who introduced me to Minoan massage. And the Egyptian slaves I boned during the construction of the Great Pyramid of Giza. And how Helen of Troy wasn't as good in bed as you'd think.

I barely make it more than halfway through the Classical Age and don't even get to Cleopatra before Sara tells me that's enough.

"I told you so," I say.

So we steer clear of the remainder of my one hundred thousand sexual partners, which is just as well. Even the most well-adjusted human woman is going to struggle with her self-esteem once she finds out you've slept with Cleopatra, Marie Antoinette, and Queen Elizabeth.

Instead, Sara asks me how I manage to stay so fit and free of physical blemishes. Even being immortal, she figures the daily wear and tear and the exposure to the elements over a couple of hundred thousand years would leave me looking a little weather-beaten.

So I explain to her about my man suit.

"You mean it's not flesh?" she says, poking at my bare, sculpted chest as I stand there, completely naked, for her to inspect.

"No," I say. "It's kind of like advanced silicone, but with properties beyond anything humans have developed."

She keeps poking me, then runs her hands along my torso until they're below my waist.

Is it getting warm in here or is it just me?

"So this isn't real?" she asks, taking my aroused member in her hands with the curiosity of an unabashed virgin.

I feel like I'm a big toy on display. But I'm not complaining.

"It's not . . . really . . . a question . . . of real," I say, biting my lip as she runs her fingers along my erection. "It's more like . . . a matter of . . . a matter of . . ."

And I've lost my train of thought.

"It sure feels real," says Sara, crouching down to inspect me close enough that her eyelashes brush against me. "I can't even find a seam."

And I'm thinking I should have told her the truth a long time ago.

Sara continues with her perusal of my man suit, moving from my genitals to my feet, then up my backside, her hands caressing me as if she's a blind woman who's never touched a man's body before. Then she's back in front of me, standing on her tiptoes and looking into my eyes, back and forth from one to the other.

"What are you inside?" she asks.

And I thought explaining my man suit would be problematic.

While some of us are simply blinding balls of white energy inside our man suits and woman suits, others are fiery flying beings, or what some human religions would call seraphim. While there aren't really any angels, quite a few of us have wings—though most don't have the human or cherubic countenance often depicted in various religions. Some are actually nasty-looking creatures with the faces and bodies of constantly aroused boars or scaly amphibians or one-eyed goats with a faceful of teeth.

Take Anger and Hysteria and Cruelty. You wouldn't want to run into one of them without a man suit in a dark alley.

The rest of us come in various half-animal, half-human forms prevalent in the Greek and Roman mythologies. For some reason, humans were more tolerant of our natural forms back then. Just seemed to fit right in with their wild parties and Mount Olympus orgies. So we were occasionally seen cavorting around au naturel.

Centaurs and satyrs and gryphons.

Minotaurs and hydras and chimeras.

Lions and oxen and eagles with four or more wings, some of them covered with eyes.

I suppose that's for the all-seeing beings like Kindness and Honesty and Truth. But it's a nightmare if you end up needing contacts.

Me? I'm one of the blinding white balls of energy. Same for Destiny, except she gets her aura artificially colored so she can be a blinding *red* ball of energy.

When I explain all of this to Sara, she says, "Can I see you without your man suit?"

"What part of *blinding* did you not understand?" I ask.

"How about just a peek, then?"

"No."

"But how do I know what you really look like?" asks Sara.

"Imagine a hundred-watt lightbulb," I say. "Only a lot brighter and about the size of Napoleon Bonaparte's ego."

"Really?" she says, poking at me again and looking up my nose and in my ears. "It's hard to imagine something that big could fit inside this."

"You'll just have to take my word for it," I say.

As Sara inspects me for seams and zippers and an expiration date, she continues an endless barrage of questions—about my origins and my childhood and my favorite time periods.

My origins are pretty standard. Jerry created me and the others out of the cosmic goo a little over a quarter of a million years ago. Fortunately, by that time, he'd finally figured out what he was doing.

The Big Bang, as it's called by humans, was really more like the Big Accident. Nearly fourteen billion years ago, Jerry was screwing around in his lab, mixing up science, theology, philosophy, rubbing alcohol, drain cleaner, and some baking soda, when *poof,* the universe was born. Earth didn't come along for another nine billion years or so and modern man for another four billion years after that, so we just floated around in the cosmic goo until Jerry's little experiment finally began to show signs of intelligent life.

My childhood? I never really thought about myself as having been a child, but I guess technically the first twenty-five thousand or so years of my existence could be considered my childhood. Wasn't much to do other than sit around and wait for man to evolve. I got bored easily and made a lot of doodles. Sometimes Jerry took us on trips to Saturn or Mercury. He took us to Uranus only once. I think that's because every time he said *Uranus*, Karma and I would start to giggle.

Jerry really doesn't have much of a sense of humor.

Favorite time periods? Well, I really dug the early Classical Age, watching the Mayans perform ritual sacrifice, and making bets on the Trojan War. The fifth century was a lot of fun, what with Attila the Hun invading everyone, and the fall of Rome. And no list would be complete without the late Middle Ages, when leprosy reached epidemic proportions and the Black Death swept across Europe. But if I had to pick one time period to beat all time periods, the prehistoric era tops the list.

Call me old-school, but nothing beats the Stone Age for shits and giggles. True, the women weren't much to look at and the conversation was pretty limited, but watching Paleolithic man evolve from his apelike ancestors into modern-looking hunter/gatherers was priceless. Talk about your *Funniest Home Videos*. You haven't seen anything until you've seen a subhuman covered with hair set itself on fire.

Good times.

Somehow, I don't think that was the answer Sara was expecting.

"What about the Renaissance?" she asks. "Or the Golden Age of Greece? Or the scientific revolution? Or when Jesus was alive?"

"Yeah, I guess," I say.

While those might have been monumental eras in the artistic, philosophical, scientific, and spiritual evolution of humans, there really wasn't much for me to get excited about. Sure, I got to witness all of this amazing development, all of this history unfolding, but my participation was in a limited role. It was kind of like being the third-string quarterback on a football team with Joe Montana and Steve Young ahead of you on the depth chart and trying to get excited about the fact that your team just won the Super Bowl.

"Besides," I say, "Josh wasn't that much fun to be around."

It's true. He thought he deserved special treatment because his dad ran the company; he never remembered anyone's birthday and would throw a tantrum if anyone forgot his; and he *always* played the martyr card.

But when it came to stepping up and getting crucified, Josh definitely took one for the team, so I have to give him props for that.

By the time Sara's finished inspecting my man suit and grilling me about the last fifty thousand years of my existence, I figure I've managed to give her enough to think about that she'll forget all about the fact that I have God on my speed dial. Then she says, "So, when do I get to meet Jerry?"

As if having an immortal entity for a boyfriend isn't enough.

CHAPTER 37

I'm sitting at my computer just past midnight, assigning fates to my share of the two hundred and fifty thousand babies scheduled to be born today and reading an article on Wikipedia about fate and destiny, when I get another staff e-mail from Jerry:

> Urgent Memo! Please Read!

Chances are, Jerry's e-mail is just another piece of spam warning us about a computer virus or letting us know we can receive a cash reward by forwarding messages to test a Microsoft/AOL e-mail tracking system. But considering his big project, I can't take the chance and find out I've missed the memo about the apocalypse. So I start reading.

At first I think it's one of those spiritual memos Jerry occasionally sends out to remind us of his glory, because he starts off with some religious-sounding rhetoric about the Messiah. But then I realize this is serious, so I read it again:

On this day, let it be known that the return of the Messiah is imminent. Although the exact date and location of his return is yet to be determined, the time is near for a new savior to be born among the mortals. To lead them with wisdom and with patience and, I hope, with a sense of humor.

Effective immediately, all staff members are instructed by executive order to prepare for the Messiah's arrival sometime within the next eighteen months as indicated in your individual job descriptions. Those not directly affected are expected to plan the baby shower.

Thank you for your cooperation.

J

Wow. A new Messiah. I didn't see that one coming. Even among us immortals, a new Messiah is pretty big news. Bigger than a pandemic or even a nuclear holocaust. It's been a couple of thousand years since Josh had his shot, and now it looks like someone else gets to take a stab at it. Hopefully, this one will result in a happier ending.

Not that Josh didn't get the job done. He had a substantial impact on spirituality for the last two millennia. But even if you're the savior of mankind, crucifixion is a tough way to go to have to get your point across. Of course, in today's world, getting nailed to a cross and left to slowly suffocate is a violation of human rights, so chances are the new Messiah will just get crucified publicly and politically.

Call it the modern-day Golgotha.

Naturally, I won't have a whole lot to do with the Messiah.

Some of his adversaries and naysayers, sure. Maybe even a disciple or two, if I get lucky. But Destiny will be in charge of all the major players. Even Dennis and Lady Luck and Karma will probably get to play significant roles. Not me. Not Fabio. I get to sit on the bench with a clipboard and watch while the rest of the team takes care of business. My only hope for contributing is if any of the star players go down with an injury or if I get to take a few snaps during garbage time.

I really need to stop watching so much football.

I print up Jerry's e-mail and put it in my "Savior Pending" file, then return to assigning fates to my unborn humans, but my mind keeps drifting to the unborn Messiah.

I wonder if he'll be born in a third-world country or in an industrialized nation.

I wonder if he'll be born on December 25, just to keep things simple.

I wonder if he'll figure out a way to prevent movie studios from green-lighting films based on television series.

And I wonder if he'll be a she.

It's not entirely out of the question. Two thousand years ago, no one would have listened to a female Messiah. And although not a whole lot has changed, it wouldn't surprise me a bit if the next Messiah turned out to be someone like Jodie Foster or Linda Hamilton or Sigourney Weaver. Someone who can kick some ass and still project all of the compassion of the Madonna.

This gets me to wondering about who the Messiah's mother is going to be. After all, if you're going to have a Messiah, you need a vessel to give birth to him. Or to her. And this in turn gets me to thinking about Mary. Not Magdalene, who was a bit of a ball-buster, truth be told, but Mrs. Joseph of Nazareth.

Honestly, surnames back then were a little unwieldy.

Of course, I don't get any say in choosing the mother. But since there has to be someone to give birth to the Messiah, Destiny has to have advance knowledge as to the mother's identity. Not even Jerry knows his future one-night stand. He didn't know the identity of Mary until the night of the conception. Cuts down on the performance-anxiety factor. Plus Jerry's not much of a ladies' man. So this way there's no awkward courtship.

Anyway, even before she got pregnant, I remember how Mary would walk into a market or a synagogue or a bris and everyone would light up. Men, women, children. Even the Pharisees stopped looking so serious and would try to chat her up. She had this aura about her that tended to cause anyone within her vicinity to take notice and smile and forget whatever it was that troubled them.

And I'm thinking this sounds vaguely familiar.

For a few minutes I just sit there, trying to convince myself it's not possible. That I'm making connections that don't exist. That I'm letting my imagination get the better of me. Except the more I think about it, the less I believe it's just my imagination.

I get up from my desk and walk into my bedroom, where Sara is on my bed in her bra and underwear, leaning back against the pillows, watching *South Park* and eating cold pepperoni pizza.

She takes a bite of pizza and chases it with a swig of Pepsi, then notices me standing in the bedroom doorway, staring at her.

"What?" she says.

Somehow, I can't imagine paintings of her in repose looking quite like this.

"What do you think about children?" I ask.

Sara cocks her head as if she doesn't quite understand the question, then scrunches up her face and says, "They smell."

Funny. That's just what Mary said.

On the television, one of the characters in *South Park* is suffering from a case of explosive diarrhea and Sara bursts out laughing.

I watch Sara a moment longer, then head back to my office and sit down at my computer, where I sort through some files dating back to just before the turn of the first century in Galilee, making more comparisons. The more comparisons I find, the more it makes perfect sense.

Sara's effect on other humans.

Jerry's e-mail.

Destiny's suggestions that I not get involved with Sara.

Which would also explain why Destiny hasn't said anything to Jerry. She'd have to tell him about Sara, about who she is, about why she's so important, and Jerry can't know about her until it's time.

That's just my luck. Out of more than six and a half billion humans on the planet, I've fallen in love with the one woman destined to carry the savior of the human race.

My girlfriend.

The Virgin Sara.

CHAPTER 38

Coming to the realization that the mortal woman you've fallen in love with is destined to become fertilized by God tends to have an adverse effect on your ability to focus when you're having sex.

"Fabio?" says Sara, lying naked on the bed beneath me. "Is something wrong?"

"No," I say, looking down at her. "Why?"

"Because your clothes are still on."

Call me old-fashioned, but I'm feeling a little uncomfortable taking off my clothes. I know I shouldn't feel guilty about the idea of initiating sex with Sara, but I can't help myself. It's kind of like cheating with your best friend's girlfriend, only your best friend is the all-powerful creator of the universe.

Sara, on the other hand, doesn't suffer from any sexual dilemmas and rolls me over, then unzips me and slides my pants and boxers off before she climbs on top of me. I close my eyes and try to enjoy the moment, but my mind keeps wandering to thoughts of

Mary and Joseph and little baby Joshua looking at me and shaking his head in disappointment.

Of course, I don't have any definitive proof that Sara is actually the mother of the next Messiah. Still, that doesn't make it any easier for me to think about what this means if I'm right. It's bad enough to think I'm having sex with the future vessel for the Messiah. But I haven't been able to get rid of the image of Jerry in a black smoking jacket and matching satin bikini briefs, grooving to Barry White singing "Can't Get Enough of Your Love, Babe."

While Sara continues to ride my man suit, I try to distract myself from thoughts of Mary and Messiahs and Barry White by focusing on Sara and her naked body. But it's kind of hard to stay focused because I keep imagining Sara filled with the glory of Jerry.

Apparently, Sara notices I'm distracted and glances down at me. "Are you sure everything's okay?"

I nod and smile. "I'm perfect."

Sara continues to move her hips up and down, watching me. It's enough to make me tell her the truth, but that would be a bad idea. I mean, come on. If you thought someone was supposed to bear the next Messiah, would you want to be the one to tell them?

"What was Cleopatra like?" asks Sara.

"What?" I say.

"In bed," says Sara. "Was she any good?"

This is another one of those times when telling the truth is a bad idea.

"Not as good as you," I say.

Sara smiles, then closes her eyes, increasing her rhythm. "Pretend I'm Cleopatra."

This isn't the first time Sara has asked me to imagine she was one of the other mortal women I've slept with—Nefertiti, Catherine the Great, Marilyn Monroe. I indulge her because it makes her happy. But it's bad enough I've broken the rules about revealing my identity to Sara. Now I'm role-playing kinky sex with the future mother of the Messiah.

I wonder how this is going to look on my résumé.

CHAPTER 39

In Rockford, Illinois, there's an old shopping mall that's been converted into a church. A religious Christian center, actually. All denominations welcome.

Methodists. Mormons. Lutherans.

Baptists. Protestants. Catholics.

Out in front of the church mall, an electronic marquee proclaims:

CHURCH WHEN YOU WANT IT—SEVEN DAYS A WEEK!

The mall used to be home to more than a dozen stores— including a travel agency, a chocolate shop, a Mexican restaurant, and a JCPenney. Now it's home to more than two hundred thousand square feet of religion.

A mall of faith.

Consumerism as spirituality.

When you walk in through the front doors, you're greeted not by the smell of Cinnabons or pretzels but by several tables of doughnuts and stainless-steel coffee dispensers. You walk past what used to be a Swiss Colony and a Baskin-Robbins and a Stride Rite and instead you find the Ichthus Christian Book Store, the Garden of Eden Gifts, and the Jesus Christ Superstore.

Here you can buy books and Bibles, crucifixes and crosses, pictures and plaques.

Rosaries, statuaries, and nativities.

Music CDs, posters, and bumper stickers.

You can purchase John the Baptist bobble-head dolls, Moses water fountains, Jesus and Mary key chains.

Guardian angel visor clips, a set of the Twelve Apostles corn-on-the-cob holders, and a complete line of biblical action figures.

Moses. Abraham. Noah.

Judas. Paul. John the Baptist.

Cain and Abel. Samson and Delilah. David and Goliath.

Most of the action figures come from the Old Testament, which makes sense when you think about it. All of the best action and bloodshed took place back before Jerry became a kinder, gentler deity. I mean, what churchgoing preadolescent boy really wants to play the Last Supper or Forty Days in the Desert when he can play Exterminate the Canaanites or the Ten Plagues of Egypt?

My personal favorites are the God Almighty Action Figure with the Hallowed Cloak of Invulnerability and Kingdom Come Kalashnikov AK-47 Assault Rifle. Or the Deluxe Jesus Fighting Action Figure that comes with ninja-Messiah throwing nails and a Death Killer-Cross pump-action shotgun.

Once you make it past the gauntlet of stores peddling religious paraphernalia, you hit the church mall's courtyard, which used to be filled with fountains and benches and potted plants but is now home to a quartet of fifty-inch flat-screen monitors televising the current sermon being shown in the main auditorium. And all along the halls leading from the mall entrance to what used to be Bergners department store, where consumers once wandered carrying bags filled with shoes and clothes and home accessories, now wander consumers with bags full of Jesus sandals and Shroud of Turin sundresses and Adam and Eve bath towels.

The funny thing is, other than the mass-produced religious symbols being peddled in the stores, there are no crosses or iconic paintings or religious images anywhere else in the church mall.

Finally, when you reach the main auditorium, the converted Bergners department store, you find a cavernous room filled with metal folding chairs with vinyl seats, less than two dozen of them filled, while an evangelist in street clothes stands onstage next to an overhead projector and an eight-foot tall projection screen as he explains a flowchart from God to Jesus.

Most of the not-quite two dozen worshipers are spread out through the first five rows. No one is sitting next to anyone else. The congregation consists of five adulterers, four alcoholics, three unfulfilled housewives, two high-school dropouts, two premature ejaculators, one pedophile, one shoplifter, one crystal meth dealer, and one megalomaniac.

I sit down next to the megalomaniac, who has selected a chair in the back row and is eating a bag of fresh figs while watching the presentation. He's wearing a white wool overcoat. On the floor next to him are two shopping bags filled with souvenirs and gifts.

"Doing a little Christmas shopping?" I ask, trying to sound casual.

"Just a few things for the girls in the office," says Jerry, popping another fig into his mouth before offering me the bag.

"No, thanks," I say.

I don't have much of an appetite. Not surprising, considering Jerry texted me on my cell phone this morning and told me he wanted to see me. Now.

I'm wondering why he asked me to meet him here instead of in his office.

If he wants to discipline me, his office is much more private than this. And much more intimidating. Jerry's not much for making scenes in public or drawing attention to himself.

On the stage, the evangelist is saying that the path to God is through Jesus.

"This guy's horrible," says Jerry. "I have half a mind to smite him on principle."

Apparently, Jerry isn't in a benevolent mood.

"So," I say, forcing a smile that feels as contrived as a Hollywood sequel, "what did you want to see me about?"

"Now, what would I want to see you about?" says Jerry, popping in another fig. I hate it when he plays coy. "Well, for starters, how about this?"

On the eight-foot tall projection screen appears an image of me. Grainy. Taken with a cell phone. In a shopping mall in California. It's up there for a good ten to fifteen seconds, but none of the humans notice. It's one of Jerry's talents. I still don't know how he does it.

On the stage, the evangelist is saying God works in mysterious ways.

"Then there's also this," says Jerry.

The next image on the screen is of Cliff Brooks. This must be the "before" picture, since he's smiling and the lower half of his body hasn't been devoured by greyhounds.

"And this," he says.

Cliff Brooks's smiling face is gone, his image replaced by a picture of George and Carla Baer. Only they're not smiling.

They're both dead. Asphyxiated. Strangled. Hanged from the ceiling by leather restraints while wearing matching red rubber ball gags.

"And this."

The next image on the screen is of Nicolas Jansen wearing his monk's robe, impaled facedown upon a six-foot decorative cross.

On the stage, the evangelist is saying Jesus died for our sins.

"You've made a big mess of things, Fabio," says Jerry, as several more images of dead humans I tried to help appear in a slide show of mistakes. "Interfering with humans. Path disruption. Multiple premature human fatalities. Not to mention unauthorized public dematerialization and impersonating me."

The last image is of Cliff Brooks, the "after" picture, his face no longer smiling, his stomach torn open as several starving greyhounds eviscerate him.

I stare at the projection screen, numb, barely aware of my man suit. All of these humans I thought I'd helped, all of these lives I thought I'd improved, all of them dead and ended.

Violently.

Spectacularly.

Ironically.

Before I realize what's happening, tears are running down my cheeks.

"I didn't mean for this to happen," I say, pointing to the projection screen, where the image of the disemboweled Cliff Brooks has been replaced by the Virgin Mary holding her newborn child.

Chalk it up to bad timing.

"I don't care what you intended to do," says Jerry. "All I care about are the results. More than half a dozen humans are dead because of your actions. More than three dozen people saw you vanish before their eyes. And more than two hundred million humans saw your image on CNN before we could alter it. Do you realize we have to perform another memory purge because of you?"

Standard procedure for a memory purge is to adjust the truth first, presenting a modified version of events so people believe something other than what actually happened. Not really any different from what governments do on a daily basis. And it's amazing what can happen when twenty-four-hour news channels pound the general public with misinformation.

Humans tend to believe anything if they see and hear it enough.

So Jerry enlists the aid of Deception and Creativity, who alter the truth. In this case my image, which will end up looking like someone famous. Usually dead. Often mythical. The current default image for a preventive memory purge is Elvis, but we're going to have to come up with a new one eventually. The man's been dead for more than thirty years. But then, humans are gullible creatures.

"I warned you there would be consequences if you continued to interfere, Fabio," says Jerry. "So as of now, you're suspended without powers, pending a complete investigation."

"All of my powers?" I ask.

"All of them."

So no molecular transporting. No cloak of invisibility. No reading fates. I might as well be human, except I can't die and I have an awesome man suit. Which explains why Jerry wanted to meet me here instead of his office. It's kind of tough to get back to Earth when you have to take public transportation.

"Who's doing the investigation?" I ask.

"Integrity and Trust," says Jerry. "In the meantime, while the investigation is ongoing, Chance will take over your duties."

"Chance?" I say. "Are you kidding? You can't leave it up to him."

"Your actions have put the cosmic balance of this planet in jeopardy, Fabio," says Jerry, handing me the bag of figs while he reaches inside his coat. "You've given me no choice."

His hand comes out of his coat with a single white envelope, which he passes to me.

"What's in here?" I ask.

"Fifty bucks and an airplane ticket," he says, gathering up his shopping bags of souvenirs.

I open up the envelope and count the money, just to be sure. Jerry's not real good with currency. He can never get the exchange rates right. And he's notorious for undertipping.

"What about my Universal Visa card?" I ask. "Can I still expense to my business account?"

Jerry gives me an expression of disapproval that reminds me of how he looked just before he leveled Sodom and Gomorrah.

"Fine," he says. "Consider yourself grateful. But no unauthorized expenses. And you'd better maintain records of all charges if you don't want to get billed back."

I nod. Though I never was good about keeping my receipts.

"What am I supposed to do while the investigation is going on?" I ask.

"Nothing," says Jerry. "Just wait until you hear from me. And for Christ's sake, stay out of trouble."

Then he's gone, leaving me with cab fare, a one-way ticket to LaGuardia, and a half-eaten bag of figs.

CHAPTER 40

The last time I flew on any form of public transportation was back in the spring of 1937, when I was an undocumented passenger aboard the *Hindenburg*'s final flight. Not that I really needed to be in attendance for the thirty-six people fated to die. When you build an aircraft with a frame covered by cotton varnished with iron oxide, then you fill your creation with a highly flammable gas, "tempting fate" just doesn't quite cover it.

The entire ship was destroyed in under forty seconds.

I'm hoping my flight to Duluth, Minnesota, turns out with better results.

When I arrived at the Rockford airport, I fully intended to fly back to New York so I could be with Sara, maybe even see if Laughter or Humor was in town to help cheer me up. But as I was waiting in the security checkpoint line, I noticed a pair of teenage girls being noticed by a man easily twice their age and I got to thinking about Darren Stafford. His death hadn't been one of those shown to me by Jerry, which meant maybe he was still alive. Maybe there was still hope. Maybe I could save him.

So I switched my flight, billed it to my expense account, called Sara to tell her I wouldn't be home for dinner, and got Darren Stafford's phone number from information and called to make sure he was still alive. Then I boarded my plane bound for Duluth.

Or so I thought.

Turns out this flying isn't as simple as I expected. I thought I'd sit down, take an hour-long nap, and wake up in Duluth. Instead, I had to take a ninety-minute flight to Denver, where I waited more than an hour for my connecting flight, which is more like two hours of nonstop turbulence, to Minnesota, where I'll have to wait another hour for a fifty-five-minute flight to Duluth.

Rockford to Denver. Denver to Minneapolis. Minneapolis to Duluth.

Spending almost as much time waiting for my flight as I do in the air.

How do humans travel like this?

In the seven hours it'll take me to get to my destination, I could have bar-hopped across the globe and ruined the futures of another three hundred humans. Instead, I'm trapped inside this pressurized cocoon made of metal and plastic, crawling along at a speed of five hundred miles per hour on the second leg of my journey, stuck next to an insurance salesman from Iowa who hasn't stopped talking since before takeoff.

"And then she tells me—get this," he says, gulping down the last of his second gin and tonic. "Then she tells me she never wants to see me again. So you know what I do? I tell her to go to hell. I tell her Duncan Mayfield is meant for better things in life than a tramp like her. That's what I tell her."

I doubt that. With a name like Duncan Mayfield, the only thing you're meant for is ridicule and abuse, maybe an unwanted pregnancy or getting played by a con artist. The better things in life aren't on the menu.

The thing is, for the first time in my existence, I can't really be sure. Ever since Jerry disabled my fate radar, all of the voices I used to hear have been silenced. It's as if someone pulled the plug on a discordant symphony I'd been listening to for as long as I can remember. A symphony of mistakes and bad judgments, of failures and disasters, of unrequited love and unfulfilled expectations. Now all I hear is the muffled roar of the jet engines, the steady drone of hushed cabin conversations, and the incessant blather of Duncan Mayfield.

"Then there was the time I nailed this cute little housewife in Boston," he says. "Banged her all afternoon, and then, when her husband came home from work, I sold him a life insurance policy with an inflated premium."

I'd call Dennis and ask him to pay a house call, but I can't use my cell phone while we're in flight. I suppose I could kill Duncan myself, but that would probably just delay my connecting flight. That and I don't want to get blood on my man suit.

When you've recently discovered that your good intentions have caused the inadvertent deaths of more than half a dozen humans, you're not really thinking clearly. Throw in the fact that you've been stripped of your ability to instantly transport anywhere on the planet and you're now sitting in the window seat of the emergency-exit row next to a human whose fate you can't read but who makes you wish you'd lost your hearing in a hand grenade accident, and you might understand why I'm considering getting off before the next scheduled stop.

I suppose I could go through my files and find Duncan Mayfield, find out his story and how much of what he's telling me is fabrication so I can call him on it, maybe get him to shut up, but I don't really have the patience to sort through more than five and a half billion case files right now, especially since I still haven't gotten around to alphabetizing. So I just have to assume he's making most of his life story up.

Humans are like that. On average, less than forty percent of what someone tells you actually happened. The rest is just filled in. Fabricated. Made up to hide their shortcomings and make them look better.

A work of fiction.

A Hollywood movie.

Their entire life based on a true story.

It's disconcerting not being able to know which parts are made up. Not being able to read the fates of the other two hundred and forty-two passengers aboard this Boeing 757. I feel inadequate, incomplete, as if one of my senses has stopped functioning. Which, I guess, it has.

The woman sitting across the aisle glances at Duncan and all I see is her annoyance.

The captain comes over the intercom and all I hear is his voice.

The flight attendant walks past and all I get is a hint of White Linen.

I'm limited. Lost. Struggling with my identity. Questioning my purpose. If I can't read anyone, how can I tell what's bothering them? If I don't know what's bothering them, how can I help them?

Of course, most of the people I've helped lately have met with untimely and gruesome deaths, so maybe it's a good thing I can't help anyone. The last thing I want to do is kill any more humans.

"And then there was the flight attendant I nailed so many times I used up all of my frequent-flier miles."

Except for Duncan Mayfield.

When I finally land in Duluth, I get off the plane as fast as I can, then find the first available cab that accepts credit cards and give the driver the address for Darren Stafford. On the ride there, I'm rehearsing my delivery, trying to think of a subtle way I can warn Darren about his impending death without alarming him or motivating him to call the police. But when the cab pulls up in front of Darren's apartment building, it looks like Darren has already beaten me to the punch.

Two police cruisers and an ambulance are parked out in front, their lights flashing in the twilight. A crowd of people has gathered on the lawn and along the sidewalk, murmuring and speculating. Yellow Do Not Cross police tape is stretched across the entrance to Darren Stafford's first-floor apartment.

So much for subtle.

I get out of the cab and walk up to a couple of men who appear to be in their thirties: one who looks like he's going to spend the rest of his life drinking Pabst Blue Ribbon and blowing his retirement savings playing Texas Hold 'Em, while the other one looks like he has a future in necrophilia.

It's just a look some humans have.

"What happened?" I ask.

"Guy hanged himself," says the probable future necrophiliac. "Wrapped a tie around his neck and choked to death."

"Neighbor found him hanging from the ceiling fan," says the poker addict.

"Which neighbor?" I say.

"Over there," says the poker addict, pointing to a man standing outside the taped-off entrance to Darren Stafford's apartment, talking to the police.

The potential corpse violator says something else but I barely hear him as I stare in the direction of the neighbor talking to the police. Just beyond them is another figure, obviously unnoticed by anyone else. While the onset of twilight and the flashing lights from the emergency vehicles cast her face in flickering shadows, there's no mistaking the luxurious red hair and the sexual trappings of Destiny.

She doesn't see me standing in the crowd, trying to blend in with the underachievers and the sexual deviants. I'm about to duck behind an overweight woman who most likely has a future in high blood pressure and heart attacks, when Destiny glances my way. Her eyes narrow as if she's trying to tell if it's really me, and then she's gone.

Great. This is all I need. Not only am I suspended from duty without my abilities, but now another one of my humans is dead and Destiny knows about it. Which means she probably knows

Darren Stafford shouldn't have been on her path in the first place. Which means she's probably the one who turned me in to Jerry. Which means he probably knows about me and Sara.

I wonder how I'm going to explain this.

I wonder how I allowed myself to get into this situation.

I wonder how things could be any worse.

CHAPTER 41

It's just past dawn in Queens as I ride home in the back of a cab that smells like used condoms and stale sweat. I could have called Sara to come pick me up, but it's embarrassing enough to have to use a public bathroom and to be forced to take public transportation with a bunch of future-challenged humans. Asking my mortal girlfriend for a ride home from the airport would be downright mortifying.

While my flight from Duluth to LaGuardia took nearly half the time of my previous flight, I'm still in a bad mood. After all, if it takes you four hours to die a slow, agonizing death instead of seven hours, there's still not a whole lot to celebrate.

As my cab rolls along toward the Triborough Bridge, the silence that fills my head is unnerving. I can't read the cabdriver or any of the other humans in the cars on the interstate with us. I'm surrounded by more than eight million people, most of them on my path, and I can't hear a thing. It's as if they're all dead.

By the time we reach Manhattan, I'm feeling claustrophobic.

After hours of being cooped up inside small metal boxes, I need to get out. So I ask the cabdriver to let me off at the corner of 125th and Second and I start walking. Nowhere in particular at first. I just wander through the city, this place I've called home for most of the past century, visible to everyone. Unable to hide or seek refuge in my supernatural abilities. More like the humans I share this city with than the immortal that I am.

I wander along Fifth Avenue and through Central Park, then wind my way through Midtown and the Theater District before following Broadway to Lower Manhattan, finally stopping when I reach Battery Park. There I sit and watch the sun climb over Brooklyn as gray clouds roll in, threatening rain.

I've never felt like this before. Exposed. Vulnerable. Freezing my ass off. I never really realized how cold it gets in New York in December because I'm invisible most of the time. When you're invisible, your man suit creates enough body heat to keep you warm during a blizzard when you're streaking naked through Central Park. And don't think we don't enjoy doing *that* whenever we get the chance.

But now I'm just cold. Cold and anxious. I don't know what's going to happen to me, to my relationship with Sara, or to all of the humans I've tried to help. All I know is that I need a warm bed and some thermal underwear.

On my way back home, I stop to check on some of my humans, those whose fates I've influenced over the past few months, and discover that the slide show Jerry showed me was just a sample of the consequences of my hubris.

The bipolar homeless woman who argued with herself near the Flatiron Building.

Dead.

The schizophrenic street musician who played the banjo outside Madison Square Garden.

Dead.

The obsessive bag lady who collected gum wrappers and lived in Central Park.

Dead.

Career losers and part-time sociopaths. Sexual deviants and corporate whores. Drug addicts and compulsive consumers.

All dead.

More than a dozen of my humans, some set on the path of Destiny, others still struggling along the path of me, and none of them managed to see their next birthday.

The universe corrects, my ass.

I don't know what made me think Karma knew what he was talking about. I should have known better than to listen to someone who cheated on his final exams and ditched Cosmic Theory on a regular basis.

This isn't how I envisioned my own fate playing out. Stripped of my powers. Responsible for the deaths of nearly two dozen humans. Wandering the streets of Manhattan freezing my man suit off. To make matters worse, the gray Manhattan sky finally decides to make good on its threat and it starts to rain.

It's times like this I wish I'd selected more functional accessories when I ordered my new man suit. Like waterproof skin or self-drying hair. Six-pack abs and self-waxing genitals aren't much help when you don't have an umbrella.

I need a drink.

I'm still more than twenty blocks from home and the closest bar is Iggy's—a laid-back dive bar on the Upper East Side that always smells like stale beer. When I walk in through the narrow vaginal canal of an entrance, one of the walls is lined with brick while the other wall is lined with the bar. Beyond that, Iggy's opens up into a room with tables and chairs and a karaoke machine.

While the inside isn't much to look at, Iggy's is one of the hottest karaoke spots in Manhattan most every night of the week. But just past noon, the only music is Johnny Cash coming out of the jukebox singing "God's Gonna Cut You Down."

And I'm thinking maybe I should go someplace else.

Plus the only other patrons sitting at the bar are Ego, Boredom, and Guilt.

"Fabio!" says Ego. "You look like you gained some weight."

Boredom gives a halfhearted nod and a yawn before tipping back his Budweiser, while Guilt just smiles at me sheepishly, then pounds the rest of his Scotch.

Why couldn't I have found Humor, Laughter, and Cheer?

I order and down a Jack and Coke while Ego prattles on about his recent exploits. I finish another while Boredom drones on about how there's nothing to do in the twenty-first century. Then I pound a double during Guilt's rambling confession about his affair with Deception.

On the jukebox, the Clash is singing "Should I Stay or Should I Go?"

The longer I sit there listening to Boredom and Ego and Guilt and the more doubles I drink, the more I begin to wonder if my wandering into Iggy's was just an accident. The more I wonder if there's some sort of cosmic correlation going on here.

For years I'd lost interest in my job. Become apathetic. Grown bored. Then when I began helping my humans, my ego took over and I became convinced of my own greatness. Enamored with the wonder of Me. Now, I'm overcome with guilt at the way things have turned out. At all of the death I've caused.

This can't just be a coincidence.

"What the hell is this?" I say, turning to the three of them, the words coming out in a sloppy slur of saliva and whiskey.

They all three look at me as if waiting for the punch line.

"What's what?" says Ego.

"What are you doing here?" I say, shouting.

I realize I've probably had one too many double Jack and Cokes.

"We're just drinking," says Boredom.

"Yeah," says Guilt. "We're just drinking. That's all."

"No," I say with a shake of my head, waving my drink in the air. "You're not just drinking. You're here for a reason."

"Are you talking about me?" says Ego.

Boredom just shrugs and lazily drinks his beer, while Guilt looks like he definitely has something to hide.

"You," I say, pointing my glass at Guilt and spilling my drink. "I know what you're trying to do. I know what this is all about."

Guilt looks around, his expression filled with panic.

"Jerry sent you, didn't he?" I say. "He sent you here to spy on me. To teach me a lesson."

I realize I'm shouting. And slurring. And that the bartender and the other mortals who have wandered into the bar are starting to stare.

"Are you sure this isn't about me?" asks Ego.

I don't answer him. All I can see are the humans watching me. And I can't help but wonder if by just being here I'm affecting their futures. If I haven't already altered their fates. If they're all going to die because of me.

Guilt is swearing up and down that he didn't mean to do it, whatever it was, but I ignore him as I stumble out of the bar and onto Second Avenue, into a steady December rain, and bump into a woman struggling with her umbrella. She curses me and I scream and run away, wondering if I just killed her.

I stumble along in the opposite direction of my apartment, afraid to see Sara, afraid I'll somehow manage to kill her, too. I know she's on the Path of Destiny and that theoretically I can't affect her, but if I can send my own humans onto Destiny's path, what's to say it can't work both ways?

I realize that's not likely and that I'm probably overreacting, but when you've been drinking double Jack and Cokes all afternoon with Boredom, Ego, and Guilt because everyone you've tried to help keeps prematurely dying, you tend to believe in your own inevitability.

As I wander aimlessly through the East Side toward Lower Manhattan, I encounter men and women in the rain whom I'm afraid to come near. To brush past. To make eye contact with. I'm afraid if I do, I'll condemn them to their deaths.

At the corner of First and East 67th, I cross the street and almost get hit by a cab and I wonder if the driver has just collected his last fare.

I stagger past a homeless man urinating underneath the Queensboro Bridge on-ramp and I wonder if he'll develop a fatal bladder infection.

A diplomat from Syria makes eye contact with me out in front of the United Nations Headquarters and I wonder if I've just started an international incident.

I don't know how Dennis deals with this on a daily basis.

And then it hits me. All of these deaths. Dennis must know something about them. He might even be responsible for them. After all, he is Death.

I wonder if he's in town.

I wonder if he's been talking to Destiny.

I wonder if he's getting back at me for the past five hundred years.

The logical part of me—that quiet voice of reason that's been bound and gagged—is trying to tell me I should just go back to my apartment or find someplace to get dry and sleep off my drunk so I can contemplate these ideas with a clear head. Instead, I find myself stumbling through the East Village into the Lower East Side—where I fall down the stairs and arrive at Death's door.

I sit up and lean against the door. Although the fall didn't hurt, I've managed to damage my man suit on the way down. There's a tear in my left forearm that looks like it's going to need to be repaired. Of course, it doesn't really matter much, considering I can no longer transport. But my warranty doesn't cover Damage Under the Influence.

Sitting there in the rain, feeling sorry for myself, with my back against Dennis's windowless basement apartment door and my legs splayed out in front of me, I reach up and knock backward with my right hand.

"Open up," I say. "Open up or I'll huff and I'll puff and I'll blow . . ."

And then I vomit into my lap.

Just before I pass out, the front door opens and I fall backward inside.

CHAPTER 42

I wake up on my back on a full-size bed covered with a down comforter and a trio of feather pillows. The duvet is black satin and the pillowcases are three-hundred-thread-count Egyptian cotton. Plum colored. To match the bed skirt.

"Welcome back from the dead," says Dennis. "Start early today, did we?"

Dennis is in the kitchenette, brewing up the best coffee I've ever smelled. I forgot how much of a gourmet coffee snob he is.

I glance down and realize I'm wearing a pair of Dennis's black silk pajamas.

"Where are my clothes?" I ask.

"In the garbage," says Dennis, walking over and handing me a hot, steaming mug of bitter delight. "Drink this. You'll feel better."

I take a sip of coffee and the whiskey in my brain screams out in protest.

"How long have I been here?" I ask.

"About an hour," says Dennis, who pours himself a cup of coffee and sits down in a purple wing-back chair beneath a floor lamp with a red shade.

I glance around the studio apartment, where there is no collection of skulls on the built-in shelves, and the walls aren't painted black. There are no moldering rugs and no creepy organ music emanating from the Bose surround-sound speakers.

Instead, the shelves are filled with the teachings of Socrates, Plato, and Aristotle, along with books on quantum physics, collections of poetry, and everything ever written by Mark Twain. The walls are painted a soft sage green and the floors are covered by area rugs with accents of red and violet. Billie Holiday's rendition of "I've Got My Love to Keep Me Warm" flows from the speakers.

"So," says Dennis. "How's your day been?"

"Full of surprises," I say. "A regular red-letter day. I understand *you've* been busy."

"No more than usual."

"Is that so?" I say, my meaning implicit in the tone of my voice. Or maybe it's the way I'm glaring at him.

"Something on your mind?"

"Oh, as if you didn't know," I say. "As if you didn't have anything to do with it."

"What are you talking about?"

So I tell him.

About Darren Stafford and Cliff Brooks and all of the other humans on my path whom I killed. About my meeting with Jerry. About the time I got drunk and bet Samuel Adams he didn't have the guts to stand up to the British.

Well, he didn't.

"But it's not like you didn't know all of this already," I say.

"What's that supposed to mean?" he asks.

"Come on, Dennis," I say. "Don't play games with me. I know you're responsible for all of their deaths."

"Me?" he says. "What makes you think I'm responsible?"

"Oh, I don't know, Mr. Reaper," I say. "Maybe because it's your *job*."

"Hey, I'm not the one who decided to start altering the fates of his humans."

"Yeah," I say. "But you didn't have to kill all of them."

"I didn't kill anyone," says Dennis.

"Oh, right," I say. "Like I'm going to believe that one."

"Listen," says Dennis, leaning forward. "They were all dead before I got there."

"So you admit you know about them."

"Of course I know about them," says Dennis. "I'm the one who reported them to Jerry."

"You reported them?" I say. "Why did you report them?"

"Because none of these people were supposed to die."

"Really?" I say, the sarcasm dripping. "So that's why I had to fly coach to get home."

"No," says Dennis. "When someone is about to die, unless I'm getting a massage or a manicure, I arrive at the moment just before their deaths. But with all of these humans you mentioned, I didn't know about them until the *instant* of their deaths. By the time I showed up, they were already turning cold and starting to stiffen. And you know how much I hate rigor mortis."

Sometimes, during rigor mortis, muscles of the dead can contract in ways that make the limbs move, even though the body is dead. This really freaks Dennis out.

"I don't understand," I say, my head swimming with whiskey and caffeine. "How could you not know about them?"

"I don't know," says Dennis. "Why don't you tell me? You're the one who decided to play Jerry."

None of this makes any sense. But then, I have been fucking with the universe.

"I didn't mean for this to happen," I say. "I was just trying to help."

"Yeah, well, you helped them all to an early death," says Dennis. "None of these humans were in my day planner. I didn't have Cliff Brooks scheduled for another thirty-seven years."

"So you didn't have anything to do with the deaths of my humans?" I say.

"No," says Dennis. "That's what I've been trying to tell you."

"Oh," I say, taking a large sip of my coffee.

For a few moments there's nothing but the sound of me jumping to conclusions and the soft, fragile voice of Billie Holiday.

"So," I say. "What do you think of the Jets' chances against the Patriots this weekend?"

CHAPTER 43

"**Where have you** been?" asks Sara. "And why are you wearing black silk pajamas?"

I'm not sure which question is harder to answer, but I figure since I've already given up my identity and the existence of Jerry, I might as well come clean.

Like Honesty always says, she's the best policy.

"I went to see Jerry," I say.

"Really?" says Sara. "What was he like?"

"Pissed off."

"Oh," says Sara. "How pissed off?"

So I tell her.

About my dead humans. And my suspension. And my stripped powers. And the time I saw Charles Darwin naked.

Natural selection, my ass.

"So, no more transporting?" she asks.

I shake my head.

"No more blinking out of existence?"

I shake my head again.

"No more having sex while you're invisible?"

I have to admit, that was a lot of fun. I highly recommend it. But sadly, no more invisible sex, either.

Sara seems more disappointed about this than I am.

"How long will this last?" she asks.

"I don't know," I say. "Depends on when the investigation is complete."

"Who's doing the investigation?"

"Integrity and Trust," I say.

"That doesn't sound good," she says.

"You don't know the half of it."

Integrity and Trust are two of the biggest brown-nosers in the universe. The only one with his nose farther up Jerry's ass is Subservience.

"Oh, Fabio," says Sara, putting her arms around me and squeezing me tight. "I'm so sorry."

She holds me like that, close and intimate, our bodies fitting against each other, my face buried in her hair. In spite of the circumstances, my man suit is suddenly ready to go.

Sara leans her head back and looks up at me, a growing smile on her face. "So what's with the pajamas?"

"I threw up on my clothes and had to borrow these from Dennis."

She looks at me, her brow furrowed. "Who's Dennis?"

"He's Death."

"Death?" she says, letting go of me and taking a step back. "You're wearing the Grim Reaper's pajamas?"

"Is that too weird?" I ask.

She stares at me, looking me up and down a few times before the smile comes back. "Well, considering invisible sex isn't going to happen, I suppose Death's pajamas will have to do."

She steps back up to me and runs her hand along the black silk, then presses her face against my chest and inhales. "They smell like you," she says. "Can I wear them?"

Somehow I don't think Dennis is going to get his pajamas back.

An hour later we're lying in bed, me naked on my back and Sara curled up next to me wearing Dennis's unbuttoned and rumpled pajama top.

"So how long will the investigation take?" asks Sara, her fingers caressing my hairless chest.

"I don't know," I say. "Maybe a couple of days. A week, tops. Integrity and Trust are pretty reliable. And uncompromising. That's why everyone else hates them."

Integrity and Trust live together in a $9.25 million penthouse loft on the Upper West Side with hardwood floors, soaring ceilings, and breathtaking views of the Hudson River. It also has a fifteen-hundred-bottle temperature-controlled wine room, a suspended glass staircase, two wood-burning fireplaces, an oversized spa bathroom with deep soaking tub and double walk-in steam shower, and a twelve-hundred-square-foot rooftop garden with an outdoor shower and a Viking kitchen.

"What happens when the investigation is complete?" asks Sara. "What happens if they determine you're guilty?"

Guilty. It's such a harsh word. No one is ever truly guilty in

Jerry's eyes. Condemned, yes. Expelled, sure. Turned into pillars of salt, you bet. But found guilty? That's just not his style. Still, Sara's question is a valid one.

"Well," I say. "In addition to being stripped of my powers, it's possible I could be excommunicated."

"Excommunicated?" says Sara. "Isn't that from a church?"

"Well," I say, "we are talking about God. But however you want to put it—excommunicated, banished, disavowed—it all amounts to the same thing."

"Which is?" asks Sara.

This isn't really something I want to discuss. It's embarrassing. And depressing. You just never expect to have your immortality revoked. It's bad enough to think about being forced to take the subway instead of just doing it for kicks. But when you have to start thinking about applying for unemployment and looking for a job, the prospect of becoming mortal gets overwhelming.

Plus there's the whole transformation process. I hear it's rather unpleasant. Kind of like having your arteries pumped full of liquid lead.

So I've got that to look forward to.

"What do you think about the idea of living together?" I say.

Sara props her head up with one hand and leans on her elbow. "What are you talking about?"

Somehow, I doubt I'll be able to afford $3,990 a month for rent on unemployment. And as far as I know, there aren't a lot of job opportunities for disgraced immortal entities.

"Well, let's just say I might need a place to live."

"You'll lose your apartment?" she asks.

"Among other things," I say.

"Such as . . . ?"

"My Universal Visa card, my Garden of Eden health club membership, my immortality . . ."

"Your *immortality*?"

The way she says it makes it sound so permanent.

"You mean you'll grow old?" she asks.

I nod.

"You'll get sick?"

I nod again.

"You'll go gray and develop love handles and need reading glasses?"

Somehow, this conversation isn't making me feel any better. But I nod again.

Sara drops back down to the crook of my arm, her head nuzzled against me. "That doesn't sound so bad."

"Doesn't sound so bad?" I say. "I've been around for more than two hundred and fifty thousand years and now I'm about to find out what it's like to get sick and struggle with my weight and die of old age and you're telling me it's not so bad?"

"So we'll grow old together," says Sara, her voice vibrating against my chest. "When you get sick, I'll take care of you. When you start to go gray, I'll tell you it looks distinguished. When you develop love handles, I'll tease you about them. And when you need reading glasses, I'll adore the way you look in them."

"Really?" I say.

She rises up again and looks me in the eyes. "Really."

"But when I lose my immortality, I'll become human. I'll become flesh and blood. Which means no more man suit."

Which I've grown particularly fond of, by the way. You just don't appreciate the convenience of wick-dry technology until you have to contemplate buying antiperspirant.

"Fabio, as much as I love your perfectly sculpted and well-endowed body and the heights of pleasure it brings me to, I love you for the blinding ball of light you are inside your man suit."

She's staring at me with those big, gorgeous eyes of hers that both captivate me and fill me with courage.

"You love me?" I say.

She smiles and nods. "Undeniably. You are the best thing that has ever happened to me, Fabio. And I can't think of anyone else I'd rather spend the rest of my life with."

I smile back and tell her that I love her, too, and that if I have to lose my immortality with someone, I would want it to be with her.

Sara smiles and says, "I think that's the most romantic thing I've ever heard."

CHAPTER 44

Of course, in addition to the regular bumps most couples encounter, being in a mortal relationship with Sara could present some other problems.

My lack of experience as a human.

The inevitable depression I'll encounter at the loss of my immortality.

The fact that Jerry might be paying a house call.

While it's true I can't get Sara pregnant in my current form, if I become human, all bets are off. And if she's destined to become impregnated with the future savior, I'm thinking Jerry and the rest of the board of directors might frown upon our shacking up together.

I don't know what path I'll be put on if I become human, but I'm hoping if Sara is going to play the part of the Virgin Mary, I'll get to play the part of Joseph. Except I'm not much of a handyman. Or a role model. And my friends don't have the best table manners.

Gluttony belches and wipes his face with his sleeve. "Can you pass the soy sauce?"

I'm in Chinatown, having dim sum with Sloth and Gluttony. Gluttony has just finished sabotaging a Weight Watchers' conference along with his third helping of har gau, while Sloth is coming down from an apathy high and a three-hour nap.

Having dim sum with a compulsive overeater and an unmotivated slacker while you're waiting to find out if your immortality has been revoked might not seem like the best way to spend your morning, but Sloth and Gluttony always manage to make me feel better about myself.

"Dude," says Gluttony, his mouth filled with half of a char siu bao. "That sucks that you were stripped of your powers."

"Totally," says Sloth, yawning.

Of course, I didn't have to tell Sloth and Gluttony I was suspended. Gossip and Rumor made sure of that. The entire community knows.

I have to say I've been a little overwhelmed with the response. Faith and Hope and Love called to say they were there if I needed them. Karma sent me an inspirational singing telegram. Lady Luck e-mailed to say she was sending a little of herself my way. And I got a text message from Failure to join him at the Paradise Club in Midtown for the nude fire-breathing show.

Needless to say, I'm a little disappointed I haven't heard from Truth or Wisdom or Serendipity and that my calls to Honesty have gone unreturned. But I guess you find out who your real friends are when you've been censured by God.

"What's it like not to be able to read humans?" asks Gluttony.

"It's kind of creepy," I say. "A little too quiet, if you know what I mean. But I sleep a lot better at night."

"Sleep is so important," says Sloth. "It's, like, the most important meal of the day."

"Sleep isn't a meal, dude," says Gluttony.

"Yeah, well, it should be," says Sloth.

"If sleep were a meal," says Gluttony, shoving a taro cake in his mouth, "I'd so eat you."

"Dude, that is not cool," says Sloth. "Now I'm going to have that image in my head for the next century."

In addition to sleeping better at night, I've discovered that being suspended and having my powers stripped has helped me to improve my meditation, allowed me to take up yoga, and enabled me to relate better to my humans. Over the past couple of days, I've found myself riding the subway or walking through Central Park or hanging out in the Manhattan Mall and discovering how much more I understand people.

Before, when I was tapping into the fates of all of my humans, I couldn't focus on anything but a few superficial aspects of any one individual, which made it difficult to get to the root of the problem. It was like having sixty seconds to impart two hundred and fifty thousand years' worth of wisdom to someone who's worried because they're having a bad hair day.

Now, without the distraction of the other five and a half billion students, even though I can't read them, I'm able to focus on each person and get a sense of what makes them tick. I'm able to relate to them one on one. I'm able to appreciate how much we have in common.

True, they're inferior bipedal life-forms in fragile, biodegradable shells, and I'm a blinding ball of light in a technologically advanced suit with a half-life of two thousand years, but deep down, we all come from the same cosmic goo.

And I'm wondering if there might be a future for me in career counseling.

"So who did Jerry say was going to take over while you're suspended?" asks Gluttony between spring rolls.

"Chance," I say.

"Chance is a pussy," says Sloth.

I won't argue that. And if you ask me, he'll do a piss-poor job of managing my humans. He's just a possibility. An accident. The absence of any obvious design. How is that supposed to help direct anyone to a better future?

Of course, it's that kind of thinking that got me into this predicament in the first place.

"So how many humans did you kill, anyway?" asks Sloth.

"Dude," says Gluttony, with jook dripping down his chin.

"What?" says Sloth.

"You can't ask him that," says Gluttony.

"Why not?"

Gluttony lets out a belch. "Because it's rude."

Most of the customers in the restaurant are looking at us. Some of them, the ones closest to our table, have left or lost their appetites.

"It's okay," I say. "It's not like I have anything to hide."

Sloth sits up. "Then is it true you told Jerry he was a two-bit deity with delusions of grandeur?"

Rumor. That little bitch.

"No," I say. "That's not true."

Not that the thought of telling Jerry off hasn't crossed my mind.

Almost all human children, at some point in their emotional development, decide they know how to manage their lives better than their parents. Usually this behavior manifests itself during their teenage years and continues into adulthood. We're not any different. Most of us have felt for aeons that we could all do a better job of running the universe than Jerry, that he's been out of touch with reality ever since Moses, and that when confronted with a reasonable challenge to his authority, he becomes childish and overbearing.

I can't tell you how many times our discussions have ended with: *Because I'm God and I said so.*

"So how many?" asks Sloth.

I think about it a moment, counting them off on my fingers. "I've killed at least two dozen," I say. "Maybe as many as forty."

"Forty humans?" says Sloth. "Dude, that's, like, nothing compared to all of the humans Jerry's offed."

While it's true Jerry has become a kinder, gentler deity, he used to smite humans left and right. Jezebel. Saul. Lot's wife. Blasphemers and whores and complainers. He even killed a man who picked up sticks on the Sabbath. Talk about nitpicky.

"So what happens next?" asks Gluttony.

"I don't know," I say. "Depends on what Jerry does when he gets the report from Integrity and Trust."

"Narcs," says Sloth, coughing the word into his fist.

"But there's a good chance I could get my immortality revoked," I say.

"Dude, that's totally harsh," says Gluttony, waving down one of the dessert carts and getting two of everything.

"Totally," says Sloth. "If I weren't immortal, I don't know what I'd do."

"Probably the same thing you're doing now," says Gluttony. "Nothing."

"Good point."

At the table next to us, a little girl is staring at Gluttony as he pops a couple of egg custard tarts in his mouth. "It's not polite to stare," I tell her.

The little girl looks at me, sticks out her tongue, then turns around in her chair. I look at Gluttony and shrug. He smiles, then belches and blows in the direction of the little girl. Moments later, she's grabbing at all of the food on the table as her parents scold her.

"So what are you going to do if you get kicked out?" asks Gluttony, egg custard tart crumbling out of his mouth and onto his shirt.

"I don't know," I say. "I still don't understand why the universe didn't correct itself. Karma said that in spite of the impact I had on their fates, my humans would eventually find their way back to their original paths."

"That's usually how it works," says Sloth.

"How would you know?" asks Gluttony.

"Dude, I didn't sleep through *every* class."

Sloth proceeds to explain path theory and the Tenet of Universal Correction, much as Karma did, only it sounds a lot different coming from a narcoleptic pothead. Mostly, there's a lot less spiritual emphasis and a lot more *dude*s.

"That still doesn't explain why my humans started dying," I say.

"Maybe something else happened," says Sloth. "Maybe it wasn't your fault."

"Like how?" I say.

"I don't know, dude," says Sloth. "I'm just saying maybe there's something you haven't considered. If it were me, I'd want to make sure."

"If it were you, dude," says Gluttony, "no one would have died. They would have all just fallen asleep."

"Totally," says Sloth, yawning. "On that note, you guys mind if I take a little nap?"

Before we can respond, he's out cold, his mouth open, snoring.

"Check, please," I say.

CHAPTER 45

The holidays are usually my favorite time of year to behold humans at their most indulgent.

Christmas baskets filled with Beluga caviar, foie gras, and pink cashmere socks.

Department stores filled with come-ons, temptations, and merchandise pimps.

Shopping malls filled with men and women spending beyond their means.

In the past, I'd sit and watch the parade of gluttonous humans spend and consume as their futures revolved around the meaning of their Christmas presents. But this year, I just can't seem to get into the holiday spirit. At least, not in the way I used to.

Instead, as I sit on a bench at the South Street Seaport mall across from Abercrombie & Fitch and observe the throng of holiday revelers in their frenzied state of consumption, I think I'm beginning to understand why humans go into debt and run up credit card bills they're still paying off in June.

It's not because their lives are empty and they're trying to fill the void of their existence with Godiva and Cartier and Victoria's Secret. It's because they have people in their lives, friends and family and lovers, who are important to them. Someone they want to spoil. Someone they want to do something special for. Someone they want to show how much they love them.

True, most of them are misguided when it comes to expressing that love in the form of chocolate, jewelry, or lingerie rather than demonstrating it on a daily basis without the use of something with a Universal Product Code, but at least their intentions are in the right place.

I realize this because for the first time in my two hundred and fifty thousand odd years on this planet, I have someone special to spoil. Someone whose existence has enriched my own. Someone I can't wait to see wearing the purple lace flyaway baby doll with matching silk panties I got her from Victoria's Secret.

And I'm wondering how I can write this off as a business expense.

My face breaks open in a smile as I imagine Sara's expression when she opens the box. As I imagine her reaction and her smile. As I imagine how good the color will look against her fair complexion. Then a voice says, "Well, if it isn't Mr. Happy."

And suddenly I'm imagining a different scenario.

Think beheadings.

Think drawn and quartered.

Think Salem Witch Trials.

"Aren't we in a good mood?" says Destiny. Then she notices my smile has vanished. "Or maybe not."

Before I can protest, she's taken a seat next to me on the bench.

"So what's it like being stripped of your powers?" asks Destiny.

The thing about Destiny is that she's visible.

All around us, human men glance our way. The ones with wives and girlfriends try to pretend they're not staring, but it's kind of hard not to notice Destiny, who looks like a prostitute elf.

She's wearing a red Santa hat, a red velour mock turtleneck, a red micromini plaid schoolgirl skirt, and red midcalf patent-leather platform boots.

"Aren't you going to wish me a Merry Christmas?" she says.

My first reaction is to tell her to go to hell, but that wouldn't be in the holiday spirit and I don't want to let Destiny ruin my good mood. Besides, she's been to hell. We all have. It's just one of those places you have to visit at least once.

"You're very festive," I say, playing nice, indicating her jingle-bell wrist cuffs.

"I thought they were a playful touch," says Destiny, shaking one of her wrists. "I can play just about any holiday song. My favorite is 'A Holly Jolly Christmas,' but only when I'm in the missionary position."

"That's very Burl Ives," I say.

"You want to play some reindeer games?" she asks, stroking her thighs. "I'm not wearing any underwear."

Big surprise.

"Maybe I could borrow some of yours," says Destiny, peeking inside my Victoria's Secret bag. "Gift for someone? Or is this part of the new Fabio?"

"It's a gift," I say, sliding the bag around to my other side.

"Who for?" she asks, arching her left eyebrow.

As if she didn't know.

Destiny just stares at me, smiling that Cheshire-cat grin of hers, waiting for an answer.

"You really care about her, don't you?" she asks.

"Care about who?" I say, playing dumb. We both know what we're talking about. I'm just not willing to admit anything in case Destiny's wearing a wire. I don't want to get into any more trouble than I already am.

"You realize you can't be with her," says Destiny.

A little boy, no more than six years old, is pointing at Destiny and asking his mother if he can go sit on Santa's lap. The father looks like he wants to ask the same thing.

"It's sad, really," says Destiny, shaking one of her wrists and jingling her bells. "We used to have so much fun together, you and I. Controlling the futures of humans. Keeping the cosmos in balance. All those millennia we spent having noncontact sex. On the Great Wall. During the Trojan War. In the Vatican . . ."

An elderly woman sitting on the bench across from us glares at Destiny with disapproval.

"In spite of everything, I'm going to miss you, Fabio."

"Well, I haven't been permanently stripped of my position," I say. "So don't get all sentimental on me."

"Oh, come on, Faaaaabio," says Destiny. "You really think Jerry's going to give you your job back after the thirty-eight humans you killed?"

"I didn't mean to kill them," I say, a little too loudly.

The elderly woman sitting across from us gets up and walks

away, glancing back with a look that makes me think I should get out of here before she calls mall security.

"Well, it's been fun, Fabio," says Destiny, standing up and jingling. "But if you'll excuse me, I've got a date with Chance."

I sit on the bench and watch her walk away, heads turning, men and women captivated by Destiny's allure, until she's gone—her long, red, seductive body gliding through the crowds.

I remain on the bench for a few minutes, trying to recapture the festive mood I had before Destiny showed up. But whatever holiday cheer I had is gone, so I take my Victoria's Secret bag, make a quick exit out of the mall, and walk over to the Fulton Street Station to catch the subway uptown.

The train is packed with Ebenezer Scrooges and Tiny Tims. With George Baileys and Henry Potters. With Kris Kringles and Susan Walkers. Getting on and off at Bleecker Street and Astor Place and Union Square. True, it's Christmas, so everyone could just be in the holiday spirit, but all of the humans on the subway seem to be wearing Destiny's favorite color.

Women with red berets and red leather gloves. Teenagers with red tennis shoes and red knit beanies. Men with red wool scarves and red silk ties. Even the homeless guy who rides the subway all day and smells like urine is wearing a red bandanna.

Maybe they're just festive. Or maybe humans wear red all the time and I just never noticed. But for some reason, this triggers something Sloth said to me at breakfast the other morning. About how maybe there's something I haven't considered. Something I haven't noticed. Something about how maybe all of these humans who died weren't my fault.

As the train passes the 23rd Street and then the 28th Street stations, I find myself thinking about something Destiny said at the mall, something about the number of humans I killed, and I find myself counting off the humans on my path who died after I intervened in their fates. Going back to Nicolas Jansen, my first convert, I come up with a count of thirty-eight. So I count again, just to be sure, going from Nicolas to the most recent and back again and come up with the same number.

Thirty-eight.

And I'm wondering how Destiny knew the exact number of humans I've killed.

Sure, she could have heard it from Rumor or Gossip, but that would have been a lucky guess. And I doubt Jerry would have publicized any of the details about my transgressions. While he can be dogmatic and vengeful at times, you can't question his integrity. Besides, as far as I know, he wasn't aware of the humans on my path who died, other than the ones he showed me on the projection screen at the church in Rockford.

On the other end of the subway train stands a middle-aged man who, if I could read him, would probably be fated to a future of giving in to temptation. He just has that look. On cue, I catch him staring at the pair of underage high school girls sitting across from him.

And this gets me to thinking about Darren Stafford.

I'm thinking about what Destiny was doing hanging around outside of Darren's apartment the other night when I showed up. Sure, she had every reason to be there. After all, Darren Stafford was technically on her path, even if it was illegitimate. But Destiny isn't the sentimental type. Especially if she realized Darren Stafford was originally one of mine. Then I think about the way she transported out of there as soon as she saw me.

I wonder what happened to Darren Stafford between the time I called him and when he decided to hang himself.

I wonder if Destiny's presence at his apartment was standard procedure.

I wonder if Destiny knows about all of the humans I've been sending her way.

When we get to my stop, I exit the station and call Dennis on my cell phone. I know he doesn't like to be disturbed when he's working, but this can't wait.

"Yeah," he says.

Dennis never was much on small talk.

"Do you remember anything out of the ordinary about the death of Darren Stafford?"

"Who's Darren Stafford?" he says, sounding annoyed.

In the background I hear sirens.

"You know, the guy in Duluth who killed himself."

"Do you have any idea how many people in Duluth commit suicide?" he says. "You're going to have to be more specific."

So I get more specific.

"Oh, right," he says. "That guy. Dumpy apartment. Brown carpeting. Hanged himself with a tie."

"That's the one."

"So what do you want to know about him?" he asks.

In the background I hear gunfire.

"Did you notice anything strange?" I ask. "Anything at all?"

"You mean other than the fact that he wasn't supposed to be dead yet?"

Obviously, Dennis is still a little bitter.

"I mean anything that would indicate he didn't actually kill himself," I say.

"You mean like it was an accident?"

"I mean like someone else helped him," I say.

"As far as I could tell, the guy grabbed his red power tie and strung himself up," says Dennis. "If anyone helped him, I couldn't tell."

In the background I hear something explode.

"Did you say a red power tie?" I ask

"That's right," he says. "JCPenney. Microfiber polyester. Made in China. Real quality craftsmanship."

In the background I hear a woman screaming.

"Look," says Dennis, "I gotta run. I'll talk to you later."

And then the line goes dead. Figures.

I hang up my cell phone with the image in my mind of Darren Stafford hanging from his ceiling fan by his tie.

His red tie.

And I'm thinking about the pictures Jerry showed me at the church in Rockford, Illinois. All the humans on my path who died. The ones I allegedly killed with my own hubris.

George and Carla Baer with the red ball gags.

Cliff Brooks devoured by a greyhound wearing a red collar.

Nicolas Jansen, impaled on a cross, his monk's robe tied closed with a red sash.

In every picture, on every dead human, something red.

Red shoes. Red lipstick. A red bowling ball.

It's so subtle but so obvious. Something I wouldn't have thought to look for. Something I wouldn't have imagined but that makes perfect sense. Something that explains why the universe didn't correct.

Destiny has been killing my humans.

CHAPTER 46

You'd think that being an all-knowing, all-seeing, all-powerful deity, Jerry would be able to keep track of what his immortal charges were up to on a regular basis.

Starting wars.

Spreading disease.

Killing innocent humans and framing me.

Of course, he had no idea what I was up to for months, so I can't exactly fault him for not noticing what Destiny was doing with her personal days. And he does have a pretty full schedule, what with answering prayers and planning for the Messiah and hosting the Golden Globes. Still, I'd like to think he would have noticed *something*.

True, I don't have any tangible proof that Destiny is responsible for the deaths of my humans, but I know it's true, just as I know Sara is destined to bear Jerry's offspring. I feel it in my man suit. And although I'm sorry about what happened to Cliff Brooks and

Nicolas Jansen and all of the others, at least I know their deaths weren't my fault.

Except that's not entirely true. Had I not interfered in the fates of my humans to begin with, none of this would have happened. None of them would have been sent down the Path of Destiny. None of them would have died. But while I'm willing to accept responsibility for my role in all of this, I can't accept that I'm the only one to blame.

Before I realize what I'm doing, I'm picking up my cell phone and dialing Destiny.

"Faaaaabio!" she says, picking up after the first ring.

"We need to talk," I say.

"Hold on," she says.

In the background, I hear murmuring voices and the sound of laughter and an orchestra playing "Winter Wonderland."

"Where are you?" I ask.

"I'm where everyone is," she says. "At Jerry's."

Oh, right. The company holiday party. The one I couldn't attend because I don't have the ability to transport anymore. That one.

"Sorry you couldn't be here," she says, the background noises fading. "The party's just not the same without you."

"Yeah, well, no thanks to you," I say.

"What do you mean?"

"Don't play games with me," I say. "I know what you did. And I'm not going to let you get away with this."

"Get away with what?" she says, so coy I almost believe she doesn't know what I'm talking about.

"Cliff Brooks. Nicolas Jansen. Darren Stafford. Any of those names ring a bell?" I say.

"Should they?"

"Yeah," I say. "Considering you killed them."

"Now, why would I do that?"

"Because you're a heartless bitch."

"Do you have any proof?" she says.

"About you being a heartless bitch?" I ask.

"About these humans you think I should know about."

"I don't need any proof," I say. "You're the one who's going to need the proof."

"Hold on," she says. "There's someone who wants to say hi to you."

I figure she's just ignoring me, blowing me off as she grabs someone else to put on the phone. But a few moments later, a voice comes on and says, "Hey, Fabio. What's your excuse for not being here?"

Although I haven't seen her in a while, there's no mistaking the voice of Alibi.

The thing about Alibi is that she's airtight.

She's the perfect excuse. Always believable. Never indefensible.

She's the star witness. The girl next door. The one that every jury and every investigative committee will believe.

And if that's not enough, she just so happens to be Trust's little sister.

Perfect. Not only can Alibi provide a believable account of Destiny's whereabouts on the occasions of any of my humans' deaths, but she's related to one of the agents investigating me.

"You were saying?" says Destiny, coming back on the line.

I know it's childish and that I'll probably regret doing it, but I can't stand the sound of Destiny's voice any longer. So I hang up on her, then sit and stare out my window at the East River, trying to figure out what I'm going to do.

Maybe I could conduct my own investigation, see if I could turn up some evidence that would implicate Destiny in spite of everything. Snoop around. Talk to some people. Except with my frequent-flier privileges revoked, I don't have the time to make that work.

Maybe I could get Dennis or Lady Luck or Karma to investigate. Follow Destiny around and see if she makes a mistake or gives up anything that could help me. Except I know that would be asking a lot, since they barely have any time for themselves. Plus at this point, I doubt Destiny is going to do anything stupid.

Maybe I could have a sit-down with Jerry, come clean about everything and hope he believes me. But that would mean admitting to my relationship with Sara. Even if she wasn't supposed to be the mother of the next Messiah, chances are he'd put an end to us. And as much as I enjoy my man suit and having the ability to go invisible and being able to zip around the globe without having to go through a security checkpoint, I would rather be mortal with Sara than immortal without her.

So I don't really have any choice. I have to accept my circumstances and hope for the best. The problem is, Jerry's probably going to find out about my relationship with Sara sooner or later. And when that happens, I'm the one who's going to get screwed.

CHAPTER 47

My hearing is taking place in Jerry's private chambers.

I was kind of hoping for an Earthside location. Someplace neutral like Switzerland. I would have even settled for east L.A. or Afghanistan. But Jerry comes down to Earth only for special occasions, like stripping me of my powers or impregnating my girlfriend.

Naturally, I couldn't make the trip on my own, so Jerry sent Hermes down to escort me.

Hermes is the only one of the ancient Greek gods who stuck around once the Greeks eschewed their Olympian deities and got on the Christianity bandwagon. He didn't have a problem being relegated to the status of lesser god and taking a position as a glorified messenger and part-time chauffeur.

Most of the other Greek gods couldn't handle their loss of celebrity and their perks and their Mount Olympus address, so they just sort of faded into ignominy. Last I heard, Zeus and Hera were running a con game with Apollo in Turkey, while Aphrodite and

Athena were turning tricks in Poland. The rest ended up home-less, addicted to crack, or on welfare.

And I'm thinking that after today, I might have more in common with them than I'd like to admit.

Jerry is sitting behind a solid oak desk in an overstuffed, white wing-back chair the size of New Jersey. His desktop is completely empty except for a handmade leaded crystal gavel and a single stack of papers about half an inch thick. On the right side of his desk sit Integrity and Trust, looking smug and self-righteous, while on the left side of his desk sits an empty, cushioned, red vinyl chair.

I'm sitting across from Jerry, on the opposite side of his desk, one level down in a straight-backed wooden chair.

Unlike his office, Jerry's private chambers aren't made of glass and they don't have a 360-degree view of the universe. Still, it's kind of intimidating when you're sitting at eye level with the top of Jerry's desk and he's dressed in his Sunday whites staring down at you over the top of his reading glasses.

Jerry's already gone through the report from Trust and Integrity, the half-inch stack of papers on his desk. He didn't say a word, just read through the report with a lot of *hmm*s and a few *mmm-hmm*s and an occasional glance at me with a look of disappointment.

And I'm wondering if I can bribe Jerry with the pictures I took of him and Indiscretion at the last company hot tub party.

"Well, it looks like everything's in order," says Jerry, nodding to Integrity and Trust. "Guess we'd better hear the first witness."

Jerry flips open his cell phone and presses one of his speed dials. An instant later, Secrecy is sitting in the red vinyl chair.

She nods to Jerry, then turns to me.

"Hey, Fabio," she says, with a look of resignation.

I just nod. There's not much to say, considering she's here to corroborate my guilt. I don't blame her. It's just an awkward situation.

Jerry sits there expressionless as Secrecy recounts the incident in Amsterdam where she helped to stitch up my man suit. Although she never saw him stab me and never explicitly mentions his name, she effectively ties me to the death of Nicolas Jansen.

"Sorry, Fabio," she says, and then she's gone.

Jerry presses a button on his cell phone and a moment later, Lady Luck appears.

"Hey, sugar," she says to me. "How you doin'?"

"Great," I say, forcing a smile. "Never been better."

She responds with a radiant smile that only Lady Luck can give, and I almost believe everything's going to be okay.

Then she starts talking.

About the day she and I met at the Daytona Beach Dog Track, which just so happened to be less than a week after Jerry told me not to interfere in the life paths of my humans. It doesn't take long for her testimony to connect me to Cliff Brooks.

After Lady Luck comes Karma, a bottle of Dos Equis in one hand as he confesses about how I admitted to interfering in the fates of my humans and to sending one of them down the Path of Destiny. I can tell he doesn't mean to give me up. It just comes out. Like an unexpected belch. You get that way when you're asked to testify before God. It doesn't help that Karma's been drinking.

Once he's finished, Karma walks over to me and gives me a hug. "Sorry, Fabio."

"It's okay," I say.

He gives me a sheepish smile, drains the rest of his Dos Equis, then disappears.

More than a dozen others take the stand, including Sloth, Gluttony, Honesty, Truth, and Wisdom. Some of them testify about my character. Others corroborate my whereabouts in relation to the humans whose paths I altered. And Honesty lets the proverbial cat out of the bag about my relationship with Sara, prompting Jerry to look at me and shake his head as if he'd caught me dancing around a golden calf.

I'd object to her testimony on the grounds of doctor/patient confidentiality, but, well, she is Honesty.

The next one to take the stand is Dennis.

He shows up wearing a black Armani suit, with a black satin shirt and a black tie. His shoes are so shiny you can see my desperation reflected in them.

Dennis nods to me, expressionless, then turns to Jerry.

"Ready when you are, Big Guy," says Dennis.

Jerry smiles. He loves being called Big Guy. That and the Great and Powerful Oz.

The two of them proceed to chat for several minutes about death and pestilence and the good old days when plagues were in vogue. Dennis even gets Jerry to laugh. With the way he's dressed and the manner in which he seems to be softening up Jerry, I'm wondering if Dennis is here to back me up.

"Do you swear to tell the truth, the whole truth, and nothing but the truth?" asks Jerry.

"So help me You," says Dennis.

At first Dennis talks about my character and my compassion and how I seem to have developed a real love for humans, and I'm beginning to think I was right about him having my back. Then he proceeds to tell Jerry about how he happened upon me saving a human from his scheduled death.

So much for having my back.

Destiny is next, testifying further as to my involvement with Sara. She doesn't reveal the nature of Sara's destiny, but the fact that I developed a romantic relationship with a mortal on the Path of Destiny is damning enough.

Destiny and I don't exchange any pleasantries and I don't accuse her of killing my humans. What would be the point? She'd just deny it and Jerry would call in Alibi and I'd end up looking like I was trying to deflect blame. And even if my humans hadn't died, I'd be in this chair anyway, being investigated for everything else I've done. Besides, if there's any cosmic balance, Destiny will eventually get what's coming to her.

I just have to trust in the system.

After Destiny leaves, Jerry calls Surreptitious to the stand. I'm not sure why she's there, considering I haven't seen her since the Trojan War, until she testifies how she overheard me reveal my true identity to Sara, along with several universal secrets and some previously unknown dirt on Jerry.

I am so busted.

Once Surreptitious has finished raking me over the coals, Jerry confers with Integrity and Trust, who both nod and glance my way wearing self-satisfied expressions. Then they're gone, transporting to some state of moral perfection that would probably make me break out in a rash, leaving Jerry and me alone in his chambers.

"Well, that was fun," I say. "Maybe we could do this again next week."

"This isn't a joking matter, Fabio."

Nothing's ever a joking matter to Jerry.

"I know," I say. "I was just . . ."

"Trying to lighten the mood," says Jerry.

I shrug.

Jerry lets out a deep sigh and shakes his head. "Do you have any idea of the seriousness of what you've done, Fabio? Not only have you broken the covenant of the secrets of the universe by revealing yourself to a mortal woman, and purposely altered the fates of more than three dozen humans who have consequently died, but you've created a domino effect that will have repercussions for decades. Perhaps even centuries."

The way he says it makes it sound so catastrophic.

"Did you even consider the consequences of your actions?" he asks.

"Of course I did," I say. "But I didn't think anyone would get hurt. I didn't think anyone would die."

"The problem is, they did die," says Jerry. "But even if they hadn't, you knowingly broke the rules about getting involved with hundreds of mortals. That's grounds enough for being stripped of your powers."

"I know," I say. Like he has to rub it in.

"And yet that didn't stop you."

I shrug. I don't know what he wants me to say.

"What I don't understand," says Jerry, "is why you would continue to try to help them if you knew it could cost you your immortality."

"I don't know," I say. "I guess I just wanted to help my humans discover something better."

Jerry studies me for several long moments, his fingers tapping against his solid oak desk.

"While your intentions were admirable, that still doesn't excuse your actions," he says.

I figure it's best for me to just remain silent. The only thing I can accomplish by speaking is to make things worse.

"I'd like to let you off with a warning," says Jerry. "Give you six months' suspension to teach you a lesson."

I nod appreciatively, thinking maybe this isn't going to be as bad as I thought.

"But that would be sending the wrong message," he says. "If I let you off with a slap on the wrist, what kind of precedent would I be setting?"

"One of compassion?" I say, hoping to appeal to his New Testament side. "One of forgiveness?"

"And if I did that, how many others would try the same thing?" says Jerry. "Sloth? Arrogance? Vanity? Where would it end?"

"I don't really think—"

"No," says Jerry. "You don't really think. That's what got you into this mess. And that's why I have to do what I don't want to do."

Uh-oh. I'm getting a definite Old Testament vibe here.

Jerry comes around his desk and leans against it facing me, his arms folded. "You're one of my favorite immortals, Fabio," he says. "You always have been. But I didn't make my rules to be broken. In spite of your motives, you still have to answer for what you've done. And as much as it pains me to do this, I have to make an example of you."

I just sit there, unable to believe it's actually going to happen. That I'm actually going to become mortal.

"It's going to sting, isn't it?"

"A little," says Jerry.

I nod. "When?"

It can't happen now. Mortals aren't allowed up here. Plus, they can't survive teleportation. We found that out the hard way.

"One day. Maybe two," says Jerry. "That should give you enough time to set your affairs in order and to make sure you're in a safe place for the transformation."

"Will I be able to keep the apartment?" I ask.

"Not unless you get a job," says Jerry.

"What about Sara?"

"Unfortunately, due to the sensitive nature of the information you've imparted to her, we're going to have to schedule a memory purge, effective immediately."

"No." I say. "Please."

"I'm sorry, Fabio," says Jerry. "But without a memory purge, it won't be possible for Sara Griffen to fulfill her destiny. She'll be too influenced by what she knows to be able to continue effectively down her path."

"At least give me some time," I say. "Let me say good-bye. Just one day. Twenty-four hours. That's all I ask."

Jerry laces his fingers together in front of his face and stares at me. I can't tell what he's thinking, but if you've never been stared at by God, it's kind of unnerving. He always looks so judgmental.

After what feels like an ice age has passed, he nods once, unlaces his fingers, looks at his watch, and says, "Twenty-four hours. The memory purge will take place at eight a.m. After that, she won't know you from Adam."

CHAPTER 48

The trip back to Earth takes longer than expected due to some collapsed dark matter on the Terrestrial Highway, restricting transportation to one lane in each direction, which gives me time to think about how I'm going to break the news to Sara.

Honey, remember when you said how you'd never forget the first time we met?

Somehow, I don't think she's going to take the news well.

I just wish there were some way for her to remember at least one thing about me. About us. But with a memory purge, everything is wiped out. All memories. All associations. All feelings. There's nothing left but the previous reality that existed.

Kind of like *Eternal Sunshine of the Spotless Mind*, only without Jim Carrey or Kate Winslet or Kirsten Dunst dancing on a bed without a bra in her underwear and a white T-shirt.

The worst part about all of this is that *I* don't get a memory purge. I get to remember everything I had. Everything I lost. I get to experience the pain of unrequited love. I get to embrace misery.

Jerry told me it was all part of becoming mortal, of accepting the human condition. A crash course in empathy.

He told me it would build character.

Right. Like Jerry knows anything about building character. He smote 14,700 Israelites just because they complained about the way he went about his business, for Christ's sake. Not to mention the seventy thousand men he killed just because David took a census.

Obviously, I have some resentment issues I'm going to have to work through.

By the time we finally get through the cosmic construction zone, I've come to the conclusion that I'm not going to tell Sara about what happened. About my getting fired. About her memory purge.

What would be the point? She'd just get upset and start to cry and then we'd spend our last day together watching the clock, counting down the hours, waiting for the end of us.

So I decide instead to tell her I've been let off with a warning. After I serve my suspension I'll be reinstated to full immortality and get all of my abilities back. That way, rather than bemoaning our fate, we'll have a reason to celebrate.

I just hope I can manage to pull it off.

Speaking of fate, before Jerry evicted me from his chambers, he informed me that after I'd made the transformation to human, even though I hadn't technically been born, I'd be placed on the Path of Fate. Which is really now the Path of Chance, but I didn't think Jerry was in much of a mood for semantics.

So in preparation for my becoming human, Jerry is having the necessary documentation drawn up—birth certificate, work history, and a preapproved Mileage Plus Visa with fifty thousand frequent-flier miles.

While I appreciate all of the effort Jerry is making to help to prepare a solid foundation to begin my human existence, I can't help but bemoan the permanent loss of my ability to transport and go invisible, not to mention my Universal Visa Card and my membership to the Garden of Eden Health Club.

The steam baths there are paradise.

When Hermes drops me off at my apartment at just past eight in the morning and leaves in a huff when I don't give him a tip, Sara isn't home. All I have is a message on my cell phone that she went to the gym before work and probably won't be home until after six.

Great. Our last day together and Sara's going to be gone for most of it.

You'd think she would have stuck around to find out what happened. After all, it's not every day your boyfriend has a hearing before God to determine the status of his immortality.

Or maybe I'm expecting too much.

I also need to take into account the fact that although the hearing took less than an hour in Jerry's chambers, in Earth time I've been gone for almost three days.

I guess maybe Sara got tired of waiting.

So I call and leave a message on her voice mail, telling her I'm home and apologizing for being gone so long and that I have some good news and to come home as soon as she can.

I'm tempted to tell her the truth so she'll come home and we can spend the full extent of our last day together. But I don't want to upset her. And I don't want to play the selfish card. After all, even if Sara would want to know the truth so she could treasure our last twenty-four hours together, she wouldn't remember any of it. It's not as if she'd be missing out on something she'd regret later.

I'm the one who'll remember.

I'm the one who'll be missing out.

I'm the one with the regrets.

I wonder if this is what it's like to be human. To make decisions in someone else's best interests rather than your own.

I'm thinking this should at least earn me some fate points, maybe get me started out on a respectable path. A fate that doesn't involve prostitution or working eight hours a day in a cubicle. Although at least with prostitution, I could set my own hours and get a chance to work outdoors.

And while I realize the odds are against it, I can't help but wonder if I could manage to talk Jerry into placing me on the Path of Destiny.

Somehow, I don't think Destiny would appreciate the irony.

I wander around my apartment for a few minutes waiting for Sara to call back; then I take the elevator to her apartment and use the extra key she gave me. Once inside, I put on her favorite Sheryl Crow CD and wander through her place, remembering all of the time we spent together, smiling at all of the take-out containers in her refrigerator, inhaling her scent on the dresses hanging in her closet.

I lie down on her bed.

I dab on some of her perfume.

I slip into a pair of her silk pajamas.

Thirty minutes later I'm standing in front of her dresser with the top drawer pulled open and a pair of her boy shorts in my hands, when a voice from the bedroom doorway says, "No wonder you didn't answer your cell phone."

I turn to find Sara standing there, still in her workout clothes, her sweat-dried hair pulled back and her face unadorned with makeup, and I think she's never looked so beautiful.

I drop the underwear and walk up to Sara, take her in my arms, and kiss her for so long, I lose track of everything but us. The apartment around us ceases to exist and all I know is Sara—her scent and her touch and the way she feels pressed against me. When we finally pull apart, she looks at me, her lips inches from mine.

"Wow," she says. "What's gotten into you?" Then she looks me up and down. "Or should I say, what have you gotten into?"

I run my fingers through her hair; then I cup her face in my hand and smile. "You have no idea how much I love you."

She smiles and we kiss again and before I know it, our clothes are off and we're climbing all over each other, falling into her bed, and I'm exploring Sara as if I've never known her. Touching her as if I've just discovered her. Delighting in her as if this were our first time.

When we're finished and she's curled up next to me beneath the sheets, Sara says, "So what happened to put you in this mood?"

So I lie. I tell her I'm suspended. That I'm in a lot of trouble. That I have to perform community service. But in another few months, I'll be immortal again.

"And you were so certain you'd be made into a lowly mortal," she says.

I laugh and hope it doesn't sound like I'm choking to death.

"Though I have to admit," says Sara, "I was kind of looking forward to growing old together."

"Well," I say, forcing a smile, "I guess you'll just have to get used to being married to a younger man."

She smiles and kisses me, then glances over my shoulder.

"Oh, shit," she says, looking at the clock. "I have to take a shower and get to work."

She starts to get up and I reach out and take hold of her wrist. When she turns back, I'm almost overwhelmed with how beautiful she looks, halfway turned around, one breast exposed, her dark hair falling across her bare back.

"Don't go," I say.

She looks at me and starts to say something, then stops. There must be something in my face that changes her mind, because she nods and smiles and says, "Okay."

After a phone call to her office to reschedule her appointments, Sara rejoins me in bed, where we spend the rest of the morning and the afternoon and most of the evening talking and making love and eating leftover Thai food.

Eventually, sometime before midnight, Sara drifts off to sleep and I spend the next few hours just looking at her face—at her eyes and her lips and the way her hair falls across her forehead. When she rolls over, I stare at her neck and her back and the soft, gentle slope of her shoulders. I reach out to touch her and she lets out a little purr of contentment. Then I curl up next to her and inhale her scent and listen to her breathe.

At some point, I fall asleep.

CHAPTER 49

I **wake up** alone in Sara's bed.

Faint light filters in through the bedroom window and I can see the beginning of a gray, overcast Manhattan day in the waxing light of dawn. When I turn to look at the bedside clock, the green digital numbers glow 7:37 in the subdued light.

At first I think Sara's gone, that she woke up and went to the gym and in twenty-three minutes I'll be erased from her memory forever. Then I hear the unmistakable strains of Mozart's Piano Concerto No. 27 coming from the living room and the sound of someone knocking around in the kitchen and before you can say, "*L.A. Confidential* should have won the 1997 Best Picture Oscar," I'm out the bedroom door.

I know what I said about not being selfish, but I need Sara to know she's not going to remember anything about me or us. And in spite of the odds against its happening, I need her to try to remember. To try to hold on to something, anything, just one memory, and maybe, just maybe, if she can do that, there will be a chance we can still be together.

I realize as I walk into the kitchen that it might have been more appropriate to make this appeal wearing some clothing. Or at least a bathrobe. Plus I have a morning woody.

Well, at least I'll look earnest.

Sara is sitting at the kitchen table in a pair of Lucky Brand jeans and a red cashmere sweater I've never seen before. Her back is to me as she eats leftover pad thai with a fork.

"Sara," I say. "I have something important to tell you."

She turns halfway around in her chair to look at me, swallows a bite of pad thai, then looks me up and down with a smile and says, "Apparently."

"No," I say. "This is serious."

She looks at me, obviously amused, then turns her chair all the way around and leans forward with her elbows on her knees and her chin in her hands.

"Okay," she says. "I'm listening."

I'm not sure how to tell her, so I just blurt it out.

"In another twenty minutes, you're not going to remember me."

She just sits there staring at me, wearing that same amused smile.

"I don't know," she says, checking out my man suit. "You're a tough one to forget."

"You don't understand," I say, crouching down in front of Sara and taking her hands in mine. "You're going to forget about everything. About me. About us. About Jerry . . ."

"Jerry?" she says, her eyes opening wide. "Oh, my God! Did we have a threesome?"

"Sara, I'm not kidding around."

"Neither am I." She gets up and walks over to her bedroom door and looks inside. "Did we have a threesome? Because I honestly can't remember."

Oh, no. I look at the kitchen clock. I should have nineteen more minutes before the purge. Unless Memory got here early.

"Sara," I say, standing up. "Sara, do you know my name?"

She looks at me from the bedroom doorway, then glances up as if trying to remember something before she looks back at me with a sheepish grin. "I take it you're not Jerry."

"No," I say. "I'm not Jerry. You really don't know my name?"

Sara smiles again and shrugs. "I know. It's bad. But to be honest, I don't remember anything about last night. I must have had one too many shots. Though I don't feel hungover."

Memory did come early. Damn her. Why can't she be more reliable?

"So what's your name?" asks Sara.

"Fabio," I say with a sigh, my morning woody deflated. "My name is Fabio."

"Really?" she says, laughing. "You don't look like a Fabio."

That's exactly what she said to me the first time we met, only without the laughter. Still, it makes me wonder if there's a chance.

Naked and flaccid, I walk over to Sara and take her hands in mine again. "Maybe it's not too late. Maybe you can still remember."

"Look, Fabio," she says, laughing again. "Is that really your name?"

I just nod. If I weren't deflated already, I'd go limp.

"Look. You're a very attractive man with an incredible body," she says, giving me my hands back. "And I'm sure we had a lot of fun last night. But the truth is, I'm not looking for a relationship right now. So I think it would be best if we just call it what it is."

"And what's that?" I say.

"A one-night stand."

Great. They gave her a memory purge with a commitment-phobic chaser.

I start to respond, to say something that will make her remember me. That will change her mind. I have no idea what I'm going to say, but when I open my mouth, what comes out is, "Ow!"

"I'm sorry," says Sara. "But I'm just not ready for anything serious right now."

I wave her off with one hand, then bend over and put both of my hands on my knees.

Suddenly I don't feel so good.

"Are you okay?" asks Sara, with more suspicion than concern as she takes a step back.

I shake my head. It feels like someone has turned on an electric mixer in my stomach.

Either this is what it feels like to have your heart broken, or else I'm starting my transformation early.

Doesn't anyone stick to a schedule anymore?

A cramp hits and I let out a groan. Then another cramp doubles me over. Sara is saying something about doctors and help and putting my clothes on but I can barely hear her. The electric mixer in my stomach is spinning faster, spreading down to my groin and up to my chest.

The transformation from immortal to mortal is about as painful as you can imagine. Granted, I've never gone through it before, but we all read about the case studies of Lucifer and Azazel during Introduction to Immortality.

First comes the sensation your insides are churning. The electric-mixer syndrome. This continues for several minutes, spreading throughout your entire man suit until you're one giant mixing bowl of cosmic goo.

Shortly thereafter, your insides implode.

Imagine all of your internal organs and blood vessels and cartilage and bones suddenly going supernova, exploding within the confines of your skin. Now imagine that in reverse.

When I implode, the blinding white ball of light contained inside my man suit will expand, giving me the appearance of an over-inflated balloon. Then it will collapse and start to cool, forming bones and organs and blood vessels while my man suit transforms into human flesh. Except since the blinding white ball of light that was my immortal self has three times the mass of the internal components contained inside a typical mortal man, there's going to be a great deal of waste that's going to have to be released.

Think food poisoning.

Think stomach flu.

Think the Johnstown Flood.

The electric mixer is already working its way down my legs and up to my head and I realize I'm not going to have time to get back to my place.

Before I lose the ability to walk, I stagger past Sara, nearly knocking her over as I stumble into her bedroom and head for her bathroom.

"Hey," Sara shouts from behind me, her voice muffled by the roaring in my ears.

I ignore her and lurch toward the bathroom, hoping I make it before the implosion. I barely get inside and close the door when the electric mixer stops. For a moment, there's nothing. No cramps. No discomfort. No mixing. Just a preternatural stillness inside of me.

"Fabio?" says Sara from the other side of the door. "What's going on?"

Before I can answer her or make it to the toilet, my insides implode.

I collapse on the floor, writhing and screaming, my insides on fire and freezing cold, my excess immortality pouring out of every orifice until I think I'm going to die. Until I start to wish I were dead. I don't know how long this goes on. Maybe thirty seconds, maybe thirty minutes, but when it finally stops, I'm left gasping and mortal on the bathroom floor in a steaming, coagulating pool of foul-smelling inhuman detritus.

Somehow, I don't think this is going to help me to get a second date.

CHAPTER 50

Over the next two weeks I call Sara every day, apologizing for the mess I made in her bathroom and offering to take her out to dinner to make up for it, but she doesn't return my phone calls. So I send her flowers and candy. I send her bottles of champagne. I send her lingerie from Victoria's Secret because I know how much she loves silk panties.

For some reason, I don't get a thank-you card.

It's hard enough to deal with the rejection of your former girlfriend on a daily basis, but when you also have to get used to moving around in a cumbersome, hairy, 175-pound human body that doesn't come with self-cleaning flesh or optional air freshener, you tend to get a little irritable.

Not to mention I haven't been able to find a job. Part of that is probably because I tend to come off as a know-it-all during my interviews. But when you've been around as long as I have, it's kind of hard not to tell people that you know more than they do.

This being mortal is a lot harder than it looked. I don't know how these humans manage to do it. It's one hurdle and obstacle and disappointment after another. It was so much easier when I could pretty much do whatever I wanted.

Of course, that's what got me into this mess in the first place.

So the New Year comes and goes and I keep trying. I go to interviews. I learn to bathe regularly. I get a wig and a fake mustache so I can stalk Sara without her recognizing me.

The day after I surprise Sara at her work with a dozen roses, two NYPD officers show up and arrest me on charges of harassment. As they're taking me out in handcuffs, I complain about the fact that it's not fair and how stalking women used to be such a normal part of my existence.

While I'm in jail, I discover I can't count on Justice to come bail me out. Since my company cell phone was confiscated, I can't remember the phone numbers for Karma or Lady Luck or even Dennis, because I had them all on speed dial. The only number I know by heart is Sara's, and I don't think she's in the mood to hear from me. But I call her anyway, just in case. She hangs up before I can get out any more than, "Hi, Sara. It's Fabio. . . ."

So much for my one phone call.

During the hearing, all of the gifts I sent to Sara are presented as evidence against me, along with the pictures of what I did to her bathroom and the letters I wrote describing all of the intimate details I know about her. It doesn't take long for the judge to issue an order of protection against me, stipulating that I'm not to attempt to contact Sara in any manner for a period of one year.

And I'm wondering how things can get any worse.

When I get back to my apartment, I discover that as result of my order of protection, I've been evicted. There's a notice on my door. I have until the end of January to vacate the premises. If I don't, formal eviction proceedings will commence.

So I have to find another place to live. I don't see why that should be such a big problem. Besides, I couldn't afford the $3,990 a month, considering I'm not earning an income. And with my Mileage Plus Visa already maxed out, it's probably a good idea for me to find someplace cheaper anyway. Problem is, it turns out it's kind of tough to get a landlord to rent to you when you're unemployed, carry $10,000 in credit card debt, and have an order of protection on your record.

Being human is so complicated.

For the rest of January I spend most of my time looking for a place to live and for some kind of employment, both without any success. I even apply for a job as a guidance counselor, figuring that might be right up my alley, but apparently you need a master's degree for that, and on my résumé, Jerry fabricated only a BA in liberal arts.

What the hell am I supposed to do with that?

Because of the order of protection and the consequences I'd face if I broke the terms of it, I keep an eye out for Sara wherever I go. I don't want her to think I'm stalking her, but Manhattan is an island. It's tough not to bump into someone in New York even if you're not legally supposed to be within two hundred yards of them. Turns out I don't have to worry about running into Sara in the building because she's moved out until I'm gone.

Still, I think about her every day. Every minute. Every second. Which makes it kind of difficult to focus on myself. How am I supposed to enjoy being human if the only good thing about my mortality will call 911 if I send her a Valentine's card?

So I ache and I pine and I get evicted from my $3,990-a-month apartment with parquet floors and views of the East River and a full-service twenty-four-hour doorman and concierge service and a health club and a rooftop garden. I sold as many of my belongings as I could just so I could afford to eat. The rest of my stuff I leave in my apartment. It's not like I could take it with me. Besides, most of it reminds me of Sara.

With no place to go, I head over to the East Village to see if Sloth and Gluttony can put me up. I call on Lady Luck in her Chelsea flat. I knock on Dennis's Lower East Side basement apartment door. I even hit up Failure in his dumpy Battery Park City studio.

Nobody's home. Nobody answers. Nobody offers me a helping hand.

So here I am, on the last day of January, with the sun going down, and no place to go.

I don't know what I expected.

I guess I expected my friends to still be my friends. I guess I expected to be able to depend on the relationships I've had all of these millennia. I guess I expected someone would help me to figure out what I'm supposed to do.

And I realize I'm more like my humans than I ever imagined I'd be.

I'm in charge of my own fate now. My own future. I know that perhaps more than anyone else in the universe. And so far, I'm doing a piss-poor job of making my life better.

I'm jobless, homeless, and friendless. And to top it all off, in less than six weeks of mortality, I've managed to acquire a criminal record.

I'm not sure what my optimal fate is supposed to be, since I obviously can't see it anymore, but I think I'm beginning to understand why humans have such a difficult time staying on their paths. With so many obstacles and distractions to deal with, maybe they need their iPods and their BMWs and their DKNY to keep themselves sane.

For the first time in a month I laugh. Not a chuckle or a guffaw or a little burst of staccato laughter, but full-blown, gale-force laughter that sounds forced but isn't. The kind that turns people's heads and makes them wonder if the man in the knee-length black overcoat with the disheveled hair and the two days' worth of whiskers is in complete control of his mental faculties.

I'm kind of wondering that myself.

As I wander back through Lower Manhattan and into Midtown, carrying the extent of my personal belongings on my back in a North Face hiking pack, my laughter echoes along beside me, billowing out of my mouth in white bursts of breath. The sun has set and another midwinter Manhattan evening has come, filling the streets with shadows and sodium lights, in and out of which move men and women and children who are all trying to avoid the laughing lunatic marching along the sidewalk.

Occasionally, I stop on a street corner and shout out to anyone who will listen that I used to be Fate. That I used to be immortal. That I used to be in charge of their lives. No one listens. No one cares. No one believes me. Why would they? After all, I'm not

Fate anymore. I'm just Fabio. Fabio Delucci. A human with a fake name, a false past, no friends, and a Central Park address.

After grabbing a cup of coffee and a couple of items off the dollar menu from McDonald's, I wander into Central Park, past the zoo and the Mall, then find a nice little out-of-the-way patch of dry, sheltered, grassy ground in the Ramble and unroll my sleeping bag. There I sit and drink my coffee and eat my double cheeseburger and fries and wonder what I'm going to do. Where I'm going to go. How I allowed myself to get into this mess.

I don't know what I imagined would happen when I lost my immortality, but this isn't exactly what I had in mind.

CHAPTER 51

The morning after my first night sleeping outside, I'm sitting on a bench in Central Park, wondering if it's considered stalking if I'm homeless and living here and Sara just happens to come jogging past, when I'm approached by a homeless woman pulling a two-wheeled cart and wearing about five layers of clothing and a pink knitted beanie. At first I figure she's going to ask me for money, until she sits down next to me and says, "You're a new one, aren't you?"

I'm not sure if she's talking about my being homeless or mortal, but I guess it doesn't really matter. "How can you tell?"

"I can always tell the new ones," she says, nodding.

I look at her in her layers of clothing and her wiry hair sticking out of her pink knitted beanie and I wonder how long she's been on the streets.

"You been sleeping in the park?" she asks.

"Just last night," I say. "I didn't sleep much."

She nods. "Hard to sleep in the park. And it's not always safe. You should go someplace safer."

I sit there, waiting for her to tell me where this someplace might be, like the Plaza or the Four Seasons or the Trump Tower, but she just sits there, smiling and nodding, rocking back and forth to the beat of her own personal drummer.

Finally, she gets up and starts to walk away, hauling her cart packed with her belongings, then stops and turns back to me. "Come on," she says. "I don't have all day."

After a moment's hesitation, I get up and follow along at her side as we walk through the park toward Fifth Avenue.

"Would you believe me if I told you I used to be immortal?" I say.

She looks at me and smiles with a nod. "We all used to be."

Mona is her name, short for Ramona, and she takes me to the Neighborhood Coalition for Shelter on East 77th—a drop-in center seventeen blocks from my old apartment, where I get a hot meal and a warm shower and assistance finding a safe place for me to sleep.

It's also where I catch my first cold.

I'm not sure if I caught it when Mona gave me a hug or when Paul, the homeless guy sitting next to me at the dining table, sneezed all over my meat loaf and mashed potatoes or when I slept on a mattress-cot in a nonventilated shelter with a hundred other homeless people, half of them coughing all night long. But when I wake up two days later, I have this strange feeling in the back of my throat. Like there's something coating it. When I sit up, my head feels like it's full of sand. Then my nose starts to tingle and before I know it, I'm sneezing and spraying saliva and snot all over myself.

Apparently, all I have is a common cold, but to me it feels like I'm dying. I can't breathe. My head feels like it's filled with concrete that's hardening and splitting my skull. And my throat is so sore I can't eat.

The volunteers at the coalition provide medical care for me, which involves pumping me full of fluids and making me take this disgusting-tasting syrup. But the fact that they would even take an interest in me, that they would bother to feed and clothe and shelter and provide medical care for someone they'd just met, fills me with gratitude. With hope. And I wonder if this is how my humans felt after I helped them.

Maybe this is what being human is all about. Connecting with others. Providing a sense of fellowship. Sharing in the experience of existing rather than hoarding your success or struggling alone.

Maybe we all have something to contribute.

So a couple of days later, when I finally begin to feel like I'm not going to die, I decide to start helping my humans again. Even though I'm no longer Fate, I still think of them as mine. But instead of helping the serial shoppers and the consumer addicts and the credit card junkies who populate the malls and shopping centers and department stores, I focus on the homeless who share the shelter and the streets with me. Besides, I got kicked out of Macy's before I could even make it to housewares.

True, I can't see their paths. I can't see what decisions they've made to get here or what choices they'll make tomorrow. I can't see their mistakes or transgressions or behavioral patterns. But I realize that doesn't matter. I don't need to know someone's past in order to make them feel better about their future.

I don't need to know why someone's hungry in order to get them some food.

I don't need to know why someone's cold in order to make them warm.

I don't need to know why someone's depressed in order to give them hope.

So I tell the young homeless man who sleeps on the cot next to mine that things will turn around if he just believes in himself.

I help a middle-aged woman I meet in Tompkins Square Park who hasn't eaten in two days to get a hot meal.

I give my gloves to a homeless kid panhandling in the snow outside of McDonald's on Broadway.

Over the next week I offer support and guidance and suggestions to my humans, but I can't tell what effect I'm having on them. It's weird not knowing where my humans have been or where they're going, not knowing if I've actually helped them to find their way to a better path, but the more I help them, the better I feel about myself. The more I help them, the more it feels like I'm doing something right, like I'm finding my own optimal path. The more it feels like I'm relevant again.

And I'm thinking that maybe this mortality thing isn't going to be so bad.

Then one day, while I'm sitting on a bench at the Bethesda Terrace, eating a hot dog and watching a street magician perform tricks for money, wondering if I could earn a living reading people's fortunes, Destiny sits down next to me.

"I've always loved this spot," she says. "Remember how we used to have noncontact sex in the fountain?"

I've suddenly lost my appetite.

Destiny is wearing red sunglasses, a red silk sweater, red tights, and red midcalf boots, while I'm wearing a wool ski cap, a sweatshirt, a rain slicker, used khakis, long underwear, two pairs of socks, and sneakers.

"Are you here to gloat?" I ask. "Or is the magician going to discover a cure for herpes?"

"Him?" says Destiny, pointing to the street performer. "He's not one of mine. Must be on your path. Oops, silly me. I mean on Chance's path."

This is one of those times I wish it weren't impossible to kill an immortal.

"What do you want?" I ask.

"I was just in the neighborhood and thought I'd see how things were going."

I spread my arms wide, still holding my unfinished hot dog. "Well, as you can see, this is my office and I'm just finishing up my gourmet lunch. . . ."

"There's no need to be flip, Fabio."

"Really? I thought I had a pretty good need."

Destiny doesn't respond, just sits there smiling at me with that Cheshire-cat grin of hers.

"What do you want?" I ask again.

"I want to help you with Sara," she says.

I haven't laughed this hard since the Red Sox traded Babe Ruth to the Yankees.

"I'm serious," says Destiny. "I feel bad about what happened and I want to try to make things right."

"Well, in case you didn't hear, Sara has a restraining order against me," I say, regaining my bitterness. "I can't go anywhere near her for another eleven months. Not to mention that she doesn't remember me."

"Minor details," she says. "You forget how influential I can be."

"So you're saying you can get the order of protection lifted?" I ask. "You can get her to fall in love with me again?"

"All I'm saying is that I want to help get you and Sara back on good terms," she says. "The rest is up to you."

I look at her, sitting there all red and immortal, and I want to believe her. I want to believe she wants to help me, that she's offering to make things right. The problem is, I don't trust her.

"No, thanks."

"Suit yourself," she says, standing up. "I'm just trying to make amends. But if you change your mind, all you have to do is wait for Sara behind the Met."

She saunters away toward the shadows of the Terrace Arcade as I struggle for a snappy comeback. Before I can come up with anything, Destiny's gone.

A few days later, I see Sara jogging through Central Park. She doesn't notice me, probably because I haven't shaved and I'm wearing clothes I got from the homeless shelter and I'm taking a leak behind a tree. But just the sight of her is enough to make me realize how much I miss her. How much I love her. How much I can't stand my existence without her.

Damn that Destiny.

In spite of my common sense telling me it can't work, I keep hearing Destiny's voice saying she can get Sara and me back on good terms, saying she wants to make things right.

Maybe she's just fucking with me, wanting to have fun at my expense, watching me and laughing at my mortality, but I realize I can't give up on this. I have to find a way to get Sara back. To get her to fall in love with me. To get her to lift the order of protection.

So I go back to the shelter and get cleaned up. I talk to one of the volunteers about the employment referrals they offer. I inquire about their programs for helping me find permanent housing.

After all, I can't exactly bring Sara back to the shelter to watch *Letterman*.

While the coalition does offer employment and housing services, their waiting list is longer than I want to wait. So I panhandle on every available street corner. I go shopping for something I can afford. I practice what I'm going to say when I see her. And I hope Destiny was serious.

Three days before the end of February I'm sitting on a bench in Central Park behind the Met across from the Greywacke Arch. I'm wearing the clothes I got evicted in, though I had them laundered at the cleaner's down the street from the coalition, so with the shower and fresh shave I had this morning, you'd never guess I've been homeless for the past month. And while I'm still getting the hang of being human, I figure it's probably best if the woman you're trying to convince to fall in love with you doesn't know you're living in a shelter.

It's early in the morning and the sun has just begun to creep up over Queens. Other than a few people walking past and an old man sitting on a bench across from me, there's no one else around.

I wrap my left hand around the bouquet of daisies I bought, then look to my left and wait for Sara's confident, feminine form to come jogging into view.

This is one of the places where I first saw Sara jogging. I don't know how Destiny knew that. Or maybe she didn't. Maybe it was just a lucky guess. But I know Sara still runs past here regularly, because I've been stalking her again.

Old habits die hard.

I think about how we first met on the subway. The silent introduction. The way she smiled at me and held my gaze, disarming me and captivating me at the same time. I think about how my heart races whenever I think about her. About how, whenever I look into her eyes, nothing else matters.

She's in my marrow.

She's in the air that I breathe.

And every breath I take of her intoxicates me.

I don't have to wait long before the object of my intoxication appears. At her approach, my heart pounds and my palms sweat and I'm consumed with both fear and joy at the same time.

When she's less than twenty feet away, I stand up and hold out the daisies.

I can tell by the expression on her face that she sees me, but instead of stopping or running the other way, which I thought might be a distinct possibility, she keeps jogging toward me as she pulls something from her fanny pack and holds it up in her right hand as if to show me what it is.

And I'm thinking maybe she has a present for me, too. Maybe Destiny was right. Maybe everything will be okay.

"Hi, Sara," I say, raising my right hand in a greeting, my left hand wrapped around the flowers.

Before I can say anything else, Sara is reaching out toward me with her right hand and spraying me with something.

After that all I hear is screaming, most of it mine.

I stagger away, wiping at my eyes, and somehow manage to stumble through the Greywacke Arch and over to the Turtle Pond and stick my head under the frigid water, trying to put out the fire in my eyes, which only seems to make it worse. When I finally manage to open my eyes a little, I hear sirens in the distance along Fifth Avenue, drawing closer.

Fucking Destiny. I knew I shouldn't have believed her.

I can barely see as I scramble away from the Turtle Pond and make my way west through Central Park, past the Delacorte Theater and the Romeo and Juliet statue. Parting is such sweet sorrow, my ass. More like bitter agony, if you ask me.

I never cared for Shakespeare. The pompous prick.

By the time I make it out to Central Park West and head down to catch the subway, I can't hear the sirens anymore and my eyes have opened enough so I actually have some peripheral vision, but it still feels like I have a thousand needles jammed into each eyeball.

I take the B train downtown and get off at Rockefeller Center, then wander into St. Patrick's Cathedral, where I sit in one of the pews near the back and strike a pose as a dutiful worshiper while I come to grips with the fact that I'm an idiot and that the love of my life has just blasted me in the eyes with pepper spray.

I'd like to think it was just a knee-jerk reaction. That all Sara needs is a little more time to come around, to remember me, to realize she loves me. Except I know a memory purge is irreversible. She'll never remember me. And at this point, it's unlikely she'll ever love me.

As my tears continue to wash the pepper spray from my eyes, I get up and wander around the cathedral, checking out the stations of the cross, until I'm standing in front of the pietà. I don't go into churches much. When you used to take regular meetings with God and he had you on his speed dial, you tend to get your fill of him. But it's kind of creepy looking at Josh like this, dead in Mary's lap, frozen in a moment I witnessed.

While he wasn't quite as beautiful as most artists depict him and while no one ever gets his expression just right (Josh always tended to have this look of amusement on his face, even when he was in mortal agony), seeing the savior like this, through my pepper spray–induced tears, makes me realize the selfishness of my romantic endeavors.

Even if I could get Sara to remember me or to fall in love with me, I'd be disrupting her destiny. She's supposed to be the mother of the coming savior, the Madonna of the new millennium, and I'd be getting in the way. Not exactly the notoriety I'm looking for. Plus since I'm mortal now, I could theoretically get Sara pregnant before Jerry took his shot. And I don't know how good I'd be as a father, let alone the surrogate dad of Jerry's bastard Messiah.

So in spite of my love for her and how painful it is for me to admit it and the fact that I'm totally pissed off at Destiny, I realize I have to let Sara go. For the good of the humans I tried to help and for the cosmic wheel of the universe, I have to give her up.

The tears that were once washing away the pepper spray are now washing away my grief.

I leave St. Patrick's and head toward Second Avenue, stopping at a corner store to pick up a forty of Country Club malt liquor, which I finish off in less than half of the twenty blocks back to the Coalition for Shelter. By this time, morning has passed the midway point and is near to running itself out, so I figure I might as well stop off and grab another forty, since the first one went down so easy.

The second one goes down easier. And suddenly I'm feeling better.

I'm reminded of another one of my favorite artists of the late twentieth century, the band Sublime, which seemed headed for greatness until lead singer Brad Nowell died of a heroin overdose. Like so many other musicians on my path.

On their first album, "40 Oz. to Freedom" was the title song that seems to capture my current frame of mind: "Forty ounces to freedom is the only chance I have / To feel good even though I feel bad."

I'm less than two blocks from the shelter, blissfully drunk and beginning to understand why forties are so popular, especially since they're so cheap and I'm on a limited budget, when I see a police car drive past on 77th a block and a half ahead of me.

Instead of continuing along Second Avenue, I head east on 76th to First, then north to 77th, where I peer around the corner and see the police car parked out in front of the shelter, its driver talking to another police officer leaning in through the passenger window.

As if I didn't have enough problems.

I don't know how they found me. Probably through the NYC Department of Homeless Services computer database. But my guess is that after I broke the terms of the order of protection, they've issued a warrant for my arrest.

That's what I get for listening to Destiny.

I glance back down the street through my eighty ounces of inebriation and wonder what I'm going to do now. I have no girlfriend, no possessions, no place to sleep, and the cops are looking for me. So I do the only thing I can.

I walk into the nearest liquor store and buy another forty ounces of freedom.

CHAPTER 52

The next month passes by in a bleary-eyed blur of forty-ounce fixes and cheap wine chasers. I drink pretty much all day, mostly alone, every once in a while with another homeless person who happens to be sharing my bench or plot of grass or piece of cement.

When I need food, I get a ninety-nine-cent double cheeseburger from McDonald's or I hit up the occasional soup kitchen. When I need a place to sleep, I find an alley between some Dumpsters or a nice bench out at Battery Park. And when I need money, I panhandle in the Village or SoHo or occasionally up in Chelsea, but never any farther uptown than Penn Station. I don't want to risk going near the East Side or anywhere I might be more likely to run into Sara.

I avoid Central Park altogether.

My coat is filthy and my clothes stink, as do I most of the time, since I haven't bathed in a month. My hair is oily and matted and my beard soiled and scraggly, with more than a few ingrown hairs. I have dirt under my fingernails and blisters on my feet and my shoes are stained with water and wine and urine. When I cough, my lungs rattle. When I throw up, my throat burns and my stomach feels like it's trying to escape.

Any pleasure I once derived in helping my less fortunate humans has been lost beneath a thick, crusted-over layer of loss and despair and self-pity.

When I'm not begging for money, most of my days are spent with a bottle in a brown bag and whatever food I can afford, hanging out underneath the Williamsburg Bridge or down at Battery Park, watching the ferries come and go. Though I do treat myself to Riverside Park on days when I'm feeling adventurous. Sometimes, on clear days like today, just before sunset, I'll take a walk along the promenade, then head down to the pedestrian footpath that skirts the Hudson and I'll sit on a rock and stare at the George Washington Bridge.

Lately, I've been thinking about getting a closer look.

It's bad enough when you go from being vice president at Morgan Stanley to scrounging through garbage cans in Central Park. But when you fall as far as I've fallen and lose as much as I've lost, hope becomes a word you don't even dream about because it's so impossible to imagine. Eventually, you forget what it even means.

And I realize I have become the epitome of all I despised when I was Fate. A drunk, pathetic, worthless human. A waste of a carbon-based life-form.

I think again about how so many humans have such a difficult time staying on their paths. How they fail to live up to their potential. How they divert themselves from their optimal futures with possessions and alcohol and other distractions. Maybe they're not so much distracting themselves from their fates as from the struggle of being human.

I laugh. Not a sick or desperate laugh or one born from the onset of madness, but a brief burst of laughter filled with bitter irony.

I'm sitting on a rock in a copse of cherry-blossom trees, staring at the George Washington while New Jersey sits across the Hudson like a shadow of Manhattan. Behind me, traffic roars along the Henry Hudson Parkway while the river laps at the rocks fifteen feet below. During the height of spring, the cherry-blossom trees are rich with pink-and-white blossoms, but in the last week of March, at the end of a long, lingering winter, the trees are as barren as my future.

As I take another swig of cheap wine, half of which dribbles down my beard and onto my coat, a voice appears on the pedestrian path behind me.

"Fabio?"

I don't even have to look to know who it is.

Destiny steps around a cherry-blossom tree to stand in front of me. "Jesus, Fabio. You look horrible."

"No thanks to you," I say, taking a swig of wine.

"I'm sorry," she says. "I didn't realize . . . I'm sorry."

Destiny is wearing a red wool coat with a red beret and red jeans with red Doc Martens.

"That's kind of a subdued look for a slut, isn't it?" I say, aware that my sibilants have deteriorated.

"Haven't lost your charm, though," she says, sitting down on the rock next to me.

We sit there, not saying anything, just staring out at the sun setting over the Hudson and at the lights adorning the George Washington Bridge.

"You slumming again?" I ask. "Seeing how the other five and a half billion humans live? Or did you just come to laugh at me some more? Enjoy how far I've fallen?"

More awkward silence, followed by Destiny gasping as she gets a good whiff of me. Eventually, I pass Destiny the bottle of wine.

"What is it?" she asks.

"Cheap," I say.

She takes the bottle from me and takes a sip, then spits it out. "That's awful."

"Thanks," I say, taking the bottle back.

Another span of minutes plays out in silence. Finally, Destiny says, "I never meant for things to be this hard on you, Fabio."

"Yeah, well, that makes two of us," I say, punctuating my statement with a belch. "Maybe if you wouldn't have killed my humans, I'd still be immortal."

Although if I'm going to be honest, I have to admit that Destiny isn't to blame for what happened to me. I don't have anyone to blame but myself.

Still, that doesn't mean I'm not bitter.

"So is that why you came?" I say, wiping wine from my beard. "To tell me you're sorry? To clear your conscience?"

"Sort of," she says. "I just wanted to see how you were doing."

"Can't see me without a personal appearance, right?" I say. "Not exactly on your radar, am I?"

"I don't know what to say," says Destiny. "I can't undo what I've done and I'm not going to keep apologizing for killing humans who had no right being on my path in the first place. You can't mix up the cosmic gene pool, Fabio. It brings down the property values."

"Whatever helps you sleep at night," I say.

"Look, I didn't come down here to argue with you," says Destiny. "I just wanted to explain a few things."

"Well, thanks for the explanation," I say, tipping back the bottle to get the last of the wine. "By the way, thanks for the advice about Sara. I owe you one."

She opens her mouth to say something else, then closes it and stares out at the Hudson.

"I also thought you'd want to know that Jerry is making a trip to Earth tonight," she says.

Wine comes spraying out of my mouth and nose.

"Why would I want to know that?" I say, wiping a sleeve across my face. "How is that supposed to make me feel better?"

"I just . . . It seemed important," she says.

"To who?" I ask. "To you? So you could torment me some more?"

"I'm sorry, Fabio," says Destiny. "I only wanted to—"

"To what?" I shout. "To rub it in my face? To let me know that the woman I love is about to fulfill her destiny?"

"Look," she says, standing up. "I didn't have to come here, you know."

"Then why did you?"

She stares at me, then looks away. "I just thought you should know," she says, before she walks past me and into the deepening shadows along the edge of the river.

It's only a few seconds later when I realize I don't want her to go.

I turn around to ask Destiny to wait, to sit back down and tell me how everyone is doing, to see if she's talked to Dennis, to ask her about Sara, to just stay and keep me company, but she's already gone. And I'm alone again, sitting on my empty bench with my empty wine bottle and my empty life, surrounded by shadows and strangers and an existence that doesn't belong to me.

I stare out at the Hudson River flowing past, my eyes filling up with tears, and before I realize what I'm doing, I drop to the ground on my knees and I start praying to Jerry. I plead to the heavens, asking him to take me back, promising that if he gives me one more chance I'll be the model employee. I'll even take something like Obsequiousness or Sycophancy. Anything so I can have a chance to be immortal again. To help take care of humans. To have the chance to see Sara. To be near her even if she doesn't know who I am or what we used to share.

I wait for an answer as the sun disappears beyond New Jersey. I wait as darkness falls and the moon climbs up in the sky. I wait until the stars are all out and the night has officially turned the page to morning.

Then I start walking toward the George Washington Bridge.

CHAPTER 53

The George Washington is accessible on foot from Manhattan at 178th Street via a long, steep ramp that makes it ideal for bicyclists. At this time of morning, there aren't any bicyclists and the traffic is fairly light, so no one notices me climbing up the crisscrossed bracing of the bare steel tower on the New York side of the bridge.

As I make my way toward the top of the tower, I keep thinking these last three months have just been a long, bizarre, fucked-up dream and that I'm really in bed next to Sara or passed out in Truth and Wisdom's spare bedroom after a long night of drinking or that I dozed off while taking a hot mud bath at the day spa on Venus. And when I wake up I'll be so happy to discover I'm still immortal and that my existence is filled with love and meaning and the ability to spontaneously combust, I'll dedicate myself to being the best Fabio I can be.

I'm not sure if I think this to distract myself or to give me the motivation to keep climbing, since it's only a dream. But it definitely helps to block out the fact that I have to pee.

The height of the tower is more than six hundred feet above the Hudson River, so by the time I reach the top, my hands are raw and bleeding and my head is pounding. Probably not a good idea to climb to the top of a suspension bridge after drinking a bottle of cheap wine, arguing with Destiny, and being ignored by God, but sometimes people do stupid things.

I sit down on the edge of the tower and look south along the Hudson, my breath coming out in deep, panicked breaths. I didn't used to be afraid of heights, but there's something about the prospect of actually dying that makes you appreciate it's a long way down.

"You could have saved yourself the trouble of the climb," says a voice from behind me.

I turn around and see Dennis standing on the tower. If he were dressed in a suit or something casual or even an apocalypse cloak, I'd figure he was here to talk me out of this and treat me to a steak dinner, maybe give me a place to sleep and take a hot shower. Instead, he's wearing his black rain gear and blue mortician's gloves, so I know this isn't a social call.

"It's good to see you," I say.

"I don't get that very often," he says, sitting down beside me. "But thanks. You've looked better."

"Yeah, well, you try being human for three months and see how you look," I say.

Dennis nods. "The beard's sort of becoming, though. In an Attila the Hun kind of way."

We always thought Attila the Hun looked like he had pubic hair on his face.

We sit there on the tower in silence, two football fields above the water, looking out into the early morning darkness stretching toward the Atlantic. After a moment, Dennis glances down between his knees.

"You know, the fall from the upper deck would have been enough to do the job," he says.

"I figured as much," I say. "But I wanted to make sure I didn't just break all the bones in my body and maintain consciousness while I drowned."

"Well, I don't think you're going to have to worry about that," says Dennis.

More silence, while below us cars head east and west, oblivious to the fact that Death and the mortal previously known as Fate are sharing one last conversation on the tower above them.

"So how long have you known?" I ask.

"About you?" he says. "Since the transformation. As soon as you became mortal."

"And you didn't think to give me a heads-up?"

"You know I couldn't do that," says Dennis. "It would have had an impact on your future. You should know that better than anyone."

"Yeah, I guess."

"Besides," says Dennis, "Jerry gave us all strict orders not to interact with you."

I laugh. "The fascist bastard."

"You might want to reconsider your opinion of Jerry before you jump," says Death. "It might make things easier for you. Just a suggestion."

"I'll keep it in mind."

Another few minutes pass in silence, though I notice Dennis keeps looking at his watch.

"Got someplace you have to be?" I ask.

"Well, you know me," says Dennis. "My schedule's pretty booked."

I nod. "Well, then, don't let me keep you," I say, getting to my feet.

Dennis stands up and faces me. In the glow from the white lights that line the tower, his eyes look glassy, as if filled with tears. Either that or mine are.

"Thanks for coming," I say, my voice thick.

"No worries," he says.

"It's kind of weird, you know," I say. "After all this time, to think I'm going to come to an end. That I'm going to be no more. To think about my own mortality. Remember how we used to laugh about *Hamlet*?"

Dennis smiles and nods.

"'To be or not to be, that is the question,'" I say. "'Whether 'tis nobler in the mind . . .'"

"Fabio," he says.

"I know, I know. You have to go."

We stand there awkwardly a moment, neither of us knowing what to say; then Dennis steps forward and embraces me. "Headfirst is probably the best way."

"Thanks," I say.

He steps away and leaves me alone at the edge of the tower. I stand there looking south at the Hudson cutting a dark swath between Manhattan and New Jersey, at the lights spreading east and west to the horizons, then up at the stars and the moon in the endless sky above us.

I look back one last time and give Dennis a smile. And then I'm leaping out into nothing, tumbling slowly through the darkness, cold air whistling past my ears and the tower racing past in a blur of metal and white lights and I realize I'm not as scared as I thought I'd be. I don't know what I expected to feel, but this sense of calm surprises me, as if this were what I was supposed to be doing. As if the mistake were living. And I'm remembering Socrates, who said that death may be the greatest of all human blessings.

I glance up and catch a glimpse of Dennis peering over the edge, waving to me. I wave back and then he's gone and I'm falling past the upper deck and the lower deck, less than two hundred feet from the end and I'm suddenly craving some cinnamon rugelach from Zabar's.

Sara always preferred the chocolate.

I've heard that for humans, your whole life passes before your eyes in the moments before death. But for me, my last thoughts before I hit the water are of Sara.

Her laugh and her smile.

Her face and her lips.

Her voice and—

CHAPTER 54

I'm suspended in space. Or something like space. It's dark. And empty. And I'm all alone. Except it feels like I'm floating in water. And instead of drifting through some endless, cosmic void, I feel claustrophobic.

I'm not sure how long I've been in my current state. It seems like I've been aware of these sensations for only a few minutes. Except time doesn't really make any sense anymore. The last thing I remember is jumping from the bridge and turning over and looking back up and seeing Dennis waving to me and thinking about Sara just before I hit the water.

And then nothing.

No drifting away. No out-of-body experience. No tunnel of light or ethereal voices or Jerry waiting to welcome me into the afterlife with a pint of Guinness.

I never thought much about death. It's not something you tend to dwell on when you never have to deal with an HMO. All I know is I didn't imagine it would be like this. I guess I expected something more along the lines of Shangri-la or the Garden of Eden or the Elysian Fields—heavenly vacation destinations with lush vegetation and all-you-can-eat buffets and all-inclusive resorts. Maybe even complimentary massages with happy endings.

Instead, I'm floating in water with no happy ending in sight. And I can't see a damn thing.

I shift around and reach out, trying to determine where I end and where all of this empty space surrounding me begins, when my hands encounter some form of barrier. It's soft and pliable and it gives when I push, but it's too strong for me to break through. So I kick out with my feet, trying to escape, but the barrier holds.

I'm wondering if maybe after I jumped off the bridge I ended up getting eaten by a whale or some sort of enormous squid or octopus and I'm in its stomach, being slowly digested. Except as far as I know, there aren't any whales or giant squid in New York Harbor. And the clothes I was wearing have mysteriously disappeared. And there's some kind of long, snakelike parasite attached to my belly button.

If that isn't weird enough, I swear I keep hearing Sara's voice.

Sometimes she's just talking, her words muffled and unimportant, as if she's speaking to someone else. Other times, I swear she's talking to me. She doesn't say my name, but I detect an intention in her voice, just the same. Her warm, tenor saxophone voice floating through the walls of my weird little prison.

At first I thought it was just my imagination. Memories of my existence echoing through my disembodied mind as I made the transition from life to death. Except this doesn't seem like any transition I ever heard about. And the things Sara says to me and the soft, cooing inflection in her voice aren't memories. She never spoke to me like this when we were together. Okay, maybe once or twice in bed when we were role-playing. But now it's as though she's talking to someone much younger. I might be wrong, but it's how I'd imagine she would speak to a child.

Something about this seems kind of creepy.

The thing is, Sara's voice seems to resonate all around me. It's as though I can feel her through this barrier, through this durable membrane of a prison. I can almost imagine I hear her heart beating. And I'm enveloped in a comforting warmth. It's as though I'm incubating.

I feel like I should know what's going on but I can't seem to grasp it. It's there just beyond my reach. An awareness. An understanding. A realization that will put my current circumstances into context.

The floating in water.

The cocoonlike prison.

The radiant warmth.

The sound of Sara's voice and the vibration of her heartbeat.

I'm not sure if it's the moment when I kick out again and get another response from Sara or when I reach down between my legs and realize my seven inches of manhood have shrunk to the size of a single shelled peanut, but my epiphany arrives like the voice of Jerry.

This most definitely isn't how I saw things playing out. And it's kind of weird when you think about it. But at least I won't have to worry about that restraining order. And this sure beats the hell out of being dead.

I'm not sure how far along I am. By the size of my peanut I'm guessing around three or four months, so I've got some time to start preparing for my postfetal future. Of course, once I get out of here, I won't be fully formed and ready to go like I was when Jerry created me. So I'll have to deal with the frustrations and limitations of human physiology. But I always was a quick learner and I always prided myself on my memory.

Still, it would be nice if I had something to write on in case I have any ideas. It's kind of hard to keep a journal when you're surrounded by amniotic fluid. And somehow I don't think a digital recorder is going to make it through the vaginal canal.

That's not something I'm looking forward to. The whole birth thing. All the placental blood and bodily fluids. All the screaming and the squeezing. And honestly, how the hell am I supposed to fit through that narrow opening? Hell, I barely fit when I was on the business end of this whole thing. Of course, that was when I was bigger than a peanut.

Still, I'm looking forward to getting out of here. Problem is, once I'm born, most of my memories will be expunged. The whole Law of Reincarnation corollary. I never thought it would apply to me, so I didn't pay much attention in class. Go figure. I suppose I can hope to bring some suppressed memories with me, but regardless of whether or not I remember her, I'm looking forward to seeing Sara again. I'm looking forward to her face and her smile, her scent and her laugh, her love and her affection.

I'm also looking forward to the opportunity to continue what I started.

I can teach humans how to live better lives. How to make better decisions. How to create more beneficial futures. I can teach them how to eschew their consumer addictions. How to stop depending on the external world to define them. How to find happiness that doesn't come in a dime bag from Macy's or an eight ball from Toys R Us.

All without having to worry about reprisals from Jerry. True, there's the whole crucifixion thing, but I'm hoping I can figure a way out of that.

I wonder if anyone will bring me frankincense and myrrh.

I wonder if I'll be able to turn water into wine.

I wonder if Sloth and Gluttony will make good disciples.

The thing about me is that I'm the next Messiah.

Photo by Leslie Laurence

S. G. Browne is the author of *Breathers*. He graduated from the University of the Pacific in Stockton, California, and worked for several years in Hollywood. He currently lives in San Francisco. Visit his Web site at www.sgbrowne.com.